IN THE CASE OF
BABY
GIRL V.

A Novel

NED W. SCHULTZ

Printed in the United States of America.

Cover Painting: Derek W. Schultz

Published by Archtop Press.
archtoppress@gmail.com

First Printing, 2020

ISBN-13: 978-0-9966946-5-0
ISBN-10: 0-9966946-5-X

To my mother, Jane Murphy Schultz

"...it was written I should be loyal to the nightmare of my choice."

Joseph Conrad, *Heart of Darkness*

Chapter One

WELL ABOVE THE STEEL-AND-GLASS lecture hall and the shaggy eucalyptus trees surrounding it, a juvenile hawk rises on a fountain of October air. Its wings stretch to dark fingertips that test the warm currents. Gliding in a broad circle, it releases three shrill cries. Sun beams pass through the hawk's rusty tail feathers, igniting them and sending intense color toward the earth.

There, undergraduates dot a campus walkway. A solitary young woman moves against a minor stream of students exiting the hall. Her boot jeans and boatneck pullover draw fleeting glances from girls hurrying by in yoga pants, sweatshirts and flip-flops. This year, for the first time, she calls herself Suzanne. A brushstroke of sunlight touches her hair, darkened to brick red from childhood shades of copper and honey. Overhead, the hawk repeats its cry and dives, carving an abrupt shadow across the young woman's path.

Suzanne pulls at the building's heavy door by herself. As she enters, daylight shifts from bright and polished to dim. Two stories below, on the stage of the classroom, a professor checks her laptop connection to an overhead projector. Filling the screen like the calm blue sea, a slide reminds students that this is PSY 256: Lifespan Developmental Psychology. An over-amplified guitar melody erupts from the room's speakers. Stooping to lower the volume, the professor looks up with a smile and bobs her head to the tune.

Suzanne drops her eyes. As she studies the steep incline of the rows, she draws back against a swell of dizziness. Concrete stairways lead down to the stage, dividing the hall into three thick slices. She starts for the right stairs, changes her mind and takes the ones to the left. There is no hand rail. With each step she pushes against the fear she might tip forward and crash all the way to the stage. Four rows down she steps sideways to a seat by the aisle. One beat of reconsideration passes through her mind. Then she sits. She can see the professor well, but the distance from the stage will keep her anonymous. Suzanne closes her eyes. I'm not here, this is not happening.

Slapping footsteps and a gust of murmuring voices bring her back as students swarm the lecture hall. Rows fill; laptops snap to life. Suzanne unfolds the printed copy of the syllabus and smooths it on her lap. Three girls juggling backpacks and neon-colored tumblers offer brisk smiles and slide by Suzanne. One raises an eyebrow, suggesting Suzanne nabbed her favorite seat. Suzanne keeps her attention on the syllabus and checks the date. The topic for the day: Attachment Processes and Adoption. The guest speaker, announced in outsized type: Dr. Daniel Tunbridge. Even unspoken, his title and name cause her to shift in her seat.

Uninvited memories tumble through her mind like shells caught in surf. The judge speaking in monotone, eyes fixed on paperwork. Her mother rising and shoving a chair so hard it falls over, thrusting her face at the judge, yelling, "No! No! You cannot destroy a natural family!" Her father blank-faced in shock, half-standing. Her mother's emphatic demand: "That baby belongs with us!" A bailiff pinning her mother's twisting arms from behind. "No! No! No!" Her mother's eyes burning black, a trembling finger aimed at the judge. "You will rot in hell!" Her father paralyzed, looking to Suzanne for answers. Suzanne's muffled cry, escaping from a deep stone well, "Make her stop! Make her stop!"

Suzanne forces her eyes closed against the chaotic fragments of memory. Using both hands, she sweeps her hair back from her temples. For a sweet moment everything vanishes. She wants to cup her palms over her ears to block the din of the lecture hall and the unsettling music. Not here, not now, not me. This is not happening. Beneath her feet, Suzanne detects the building shuddering as the planet strains against an uncertain curve, hurtling like a stone on a taut string.

...

Dan Tunbridge jumps into his car, dropping the wrapped stems of Stargazer lilies on the passenger seat atop a pink bakery box from the Madonna Inn. Cakeman on the job. The lilies are his personal gift for the afternoon receptionist at the mental health clinic. His cake budget – the amount his colleagues at the clinic agreed to contribute once he persuaded them of the value of celebrating each other's birthdays – won't stretch to flowers. Dan remembers Dorothea raving about a hotel in Las Vegas where she went to see her idol, Gladys Knight. She was stunned to find the vivid pink blooms in her room and came close to fainting at their fragrance. Dan's pleased the flower stand had some, but the extra stop has him running late.

Someone may grumble that he's overspent on the flowers. Dan shrugs that off. Most of them are happy with his cake initiative, especially that he volunteers to be the cake procurer. He's also admired for a willingness to speak frankly to the unpopular administrator of the county health agency. Twice Dan's pushed for information and explained that problems at the jail with inmate health are having negative effects on the public's view of their work at the clinic. Where others fret and address him as "Director Kneff," Dan calls him, "Jim." Though Kneff brushed aside his comments with a disdainful tone, Dan earned accolades from his peers for speaking up. They like him even better as Cakeman.

He clicks off the rapid chatter on the radio, which is only stirring his nerves about this morning's presentation at the university. The quiet grants him a moment of peace while he waits at a traffic light. Dan stretches to check his face in the rearview mirror. Dr. Tunbridge, I presume? The title still trips him up. He's needled once in a while by that imposter feeling his mentors assured him would slip away in time. Dan felt proud to enter a field he admired and find a position in such an appealing stretch of the California coast. But the world holds skeptical views about his profession. No matter how you say you're a psychologist, people give an initial startle, like you've caught them dressing. When they recover, there's often a moment when they'll scan your face. For what? Dark intent? Shamanistic powers? The unit's guidelines suggest titles and last names, but he prefers to introduce himself as Dan Tunbridge and let them ask about his position. With the special needs kids and families, he goes by Dr. Dan. That would bring open snickers from the college students. Only a decade out of undergraduate courses himself, he's had to learn to draw professional lines that titles alone won't. In a college town with enough bars to guarantee rowdy twenty-first birthday crawls, mistakes can be made.

Fortunately, by the late twenties the pulsating churn of the bars loses its appeal. That thought brings Brynn front and center to his mind – her appealing squint and wry smile and, before he can stop himself, her satin inner thighs. He wrestles with a tiny frown. This is not a good place for her to be. So, back to Malmö she goes, to the cafe in the cobblestone square at Lille Torg and her dreams of solo European travel and adventure. Happy wandering, Brynn. No time for hangdog expressions. Dan blows a stream of air through his nostrils, trying to chase away the tinted skies of a long summer night in Sweden.

As the red light lingers, the faces of his imagined audience rise up before him, swirling. Dan drums his fingers on the top of the steering wheel: thump-thump-thump. The second time he does it, he hears the chant, *Go Big Green!* and he's all the way across the country, back on the ice at Thompson Arena, on defense for Dartmouth. Okay, I can face these guys. The light changes and he accelerates through the intersection.

He tells himself to shake off his misgivings about the talk. It should be a no-brainer. A couple of hours away from the clinic and credit for community service to boot. A favor to the course's instructor – a neighbor who treats him as family – and a favor he's done before. When Margaret Becker first invited him, she asked him to give her class an overview of how the courts rely on psychological evaluations in adoption. The case of Baby Girl V. – still a clear echo for him – fit well. He used it to illustrate the court's prioritization of a child's needs over other concerns. Today's talk will be his third visit in the four years since his court-appointed evaluation of Baby Girl V.

After the initial talks Dan asked Margaret for tips on how he might improve his presentation. Now he feels confident enough about the outline of his talk that he hasn't altered it or rehearsed, other than making sure his notes and slides are in order. But a question about repeating his performance chafes him. Isn't the truth always more complicated than any one telling of a story can show? How many angles do you need to consider to provide a fair overview? An echo of memory hits, the voice of a coach exhorting him between periods. You get one chance. You never get to replay the game. Dan looks off toward the coastal hills.

Checking his watch, he comes to a halt at a crosswalk before campus. Two older elementary school girls walking their bikes pause to assess his intent. Dan gives a friendly wave, yielding to them. As they pass he returns their smiles, happy to see kids being careful. Buddy system too, he thinks.

At the hulking campus garage a security guard in a starched white shirt greets him. When Dan tells the guard he's there as a guest speaker and gives his name, the man consults a printed list. "Dr. Tunbridge," he says, his voice affirming Dan's appointment. He hands the psychologist a parking permit to hang on the rearview mirror and points him toward a space on the third level. Dan thanks the man and pulls forward. Glancing in his side mirror, he spots the guard tracking him and has to shake off irritation at the guard's lingering gaze.

Rivulets of students move around him toward classrooms and the massive recreation center as he works his way across campus. Dan

4

considers a memory of all-nighters with teammates, drinking beer, getting high, firing lines from Monty Python at each other, and arguing over the surreal and paranoid episodes of *The Prisoner*. An old doubt returns, tempting him to wonder if going to law school in conjunction with his degree in psychology might have been possible if he'd tried harder. Or if he'd played a little less hockey.

At the lower entrance to the lecture hall, his short, heavy-set neighbor greets him like a proud aunt. His career fascinates her. She likes Dan's influence on her son. Once in a while she brings over containers of chili or garden soup. There might be an obscenely rich chocolate pie for him tonight.

"Morning, Dan," she calls in a sparrow's trill.

He bends to accept her embrace, yielding to her warmth and a hint of sympathy her hug delivers. Margaret Becker has noticed that Brynn is away. Dan appreciates that she hasn't pressed him for more than his casual assurance that Brynn's enjoying herself and he's fine.

"You found the Silo again. Parking was okay?"

"Yes, very smooth. I don't remember them saving a space for me last time."

"I'm glad they had your spot. It's been such a nightmare. People parking wherever they saw an opening." She studies his face. "You're not nervous, are you?"

"Yes, actually. Can I cancel?" He hopes a joke will hide his uncertainty about repeating the talk.

"No! Not a chance." She points to his college tie. "That shade of green looks good on you."

Dan pictures his mother's face and remembers how pleased she was about his initial talk at the university. "Dress Dartmouth proud," she told him.

"And I like your cologne," Margaret says with a grin.

Dan blinks and sniffs at his jacket. He lets out a suppressed laugh.

"Stargazer lilies. I bought some for our receptionist – for her birthday. They are strong, huh?"

Margaret says, "Very snazzy, Dan. Isn't she lucky?"

He starts to shake his head to dissuade Margaret from imagining any romantic possibilities for him. Before he can say anything she shifts.

"Listen, thanks so much for doing this again. The students love hearing about Baby Girl V. I mean it, they mention your talk in the evaluations. Do what you always do, and it'll be great."

Dan nods. "Fingers crossed."

"You'll do fine without luck." She offers a smile, then turns serious.

"Dan, I wanted to say…I don't want Lucas to pester you. I told him you're busy and he can't be hanging out with you all the time. He loves that car and…well, he's a little lonely too. I don't know. Raising a son…"

"Margaret, it's not a problem. We're buddies. He's a good guy."

Lucas is fifteen and a little too obsessed with magic tricks and Elon Musk's hyperloop. But a great kid, and they share an interest in Dan's Miata. Lucas made him promise never to sell it to anyone but him. Dan's taught him how to change the oil. He's taken Lucas driving once – to an empty parking lot in the evening on the promise he wouldn't let his mother in on their secret. Lucas shifted like a pro with minimal instruction and beamed like they were riding the hyperloop itself. Dan figures he'll be helping with the driver's license in another year. He's not as sure what to do about the magic tricks.

"Well, he can be a pest."

"Nope, not to me," Dan says.

Margaret checks his eyes long enough for Dan to give her an unblinking, affirmative nod.

"Okay, if you're sure," she says as she turns to usher him through the door.

•••

Inside the building, Dan recalls the peculiar architecture of the lecture hall. He and the instructor stand on a semi-circular stage at the lowest level of the building. Students flow through doors two stories above them, stepping down steep aisles to their seats. Twenty-some rows rise toward the upper story, making room for over two hundred students. From his lower vantage point the descent appears treacherous, but the students handle it as nimbly as mountain goats.

Despite its size the hall's design provides an intimate view of most of the seats from the stage. But Dan struggles against a feeling of claustrophobia. On an open rink, he could maneuver. Here there is no protective glass separating him from their bodies. Far more sober than sports fans, the seated students form an oversized jury. He can't let himself acknowledge the vast number of faces gathering in the hall – it would destroy his resolve. The instructor shuffles across the stage to ask a technician for a lapel microphone. She returns, and they sit together.

Leaning toward him, she whispers, "It's like being in the Coliseum, isn't it? I like to think I'm the emperor, but I don't tell them that." She pulls back to see if Dan likes her joke. Then she leans closer. "I guess that makes you Spartacus."

He's surprised by the gladiator's name. A college memory: an opposing goalie who tried to rally his teammates by yelling, "Gladiators!" It rarely worked that way for Dan. He liked knowing the ice, anticipating positions, out-skating and trying to outsmart opponents. For him, hockey was a game of laser-quick, subtle moves.

Dan declines her compliment with a hesitant smile and a shake of his head. "Not sure I'm the gladiator type." His heart rate jumps a beat and he tells himself to relax.

She stands. "I better check the overhead projector. Don't worry, they're a thumbs up group."

Dan pivots to a last-minute rehearsal of his notes on the contested adoption of Baby Girl V. He flexes a small deck of notecards. With the essential facts of the case etched in his mind, the cards only serve to occupy his hands. Murmured conversations echo in the hall, surging and receding in waves. Student faces examine him with a range of expressions from sleepy to hyperkinetic. Though these students haven't heard him speak before, he hopes the hour will be like his previous talks.

In some respects, the case of Baby Girl V. is a textbook example of how the court handles adoptions. He has legal passages, statistics and graphs to illustrate how often adoptions are disputed and how they are resolved. Dan's also selected the case for its complexities and haunting questions that remain unresolved for him. He wants the students to discern the subtleties and the subjective elements of the case.

Surveying the audience, he calls up a deferential smile, breathing evenly to keep himself composed. Comrades! He's in their house, not his. He buries the one vulnerability he does not want the students to notice: a fear that the forces at work in the case of Baby Girl V. pre-determined what was to happen with the adoption. A fear that his role had been scripted to validate a preset outcome.

To place the undergraduates in the midst of case, he frames the story as a conversation with a solitary listener. He scans the audience for a lone pair of eyes to assume the role of the teenage mother in the case of Baby Girl V. The sound in the hall swells and recedes again, slowing time. He pictures himself circling the net, warming up. Those heightened moments before bodies fly. That vital point in time when everything lies wide open – and nothing matters but his eyes on the puck.

The instructor moves through her announcements and prepares to introduce him. The rustling in the room quiets. He straightens and prepares to stand. Margaret Becker jokes about her mixed feelings at having a clinical psychologist as a neighbor, laughing with an unintended snort. Here and there students chuckle. He hears his summons: Dr. Daniel Tunbridge. Before the applause welcoming him fades he is in place at the podium, greeting the undergraduates. He sets his blades on the ice.

...

Dan runs through his degrees, his job responsibilities and the role psychologists play in court-appointed evaluations. Trying to intrigue the students he displays a few statistics about adoptions on the overhead. Then he jumps to the particulars of the case of Baby Girl V.

"Picture yourself as you were a few years ago. A junior in high school, not close enough to graduation to be packing for college but dreaming of it." He paints a scenario for an end-of-school party, the essential fact being that his listener is seriously drunk or high, for the first time, and in a sexually charged atmosphere.

"Maybe it's alcohol. Or ecstasy. Maybe something worse – something you don't know you've taken. It leads to a blur of faces, dancing, bodies moving as they want to do. Somehow, and you aren't clear the next morning or even today how it occurs, you have intercourse. You're not certain who it was. For weeks you pray for a safe escape. You delay testing yourself until you can't stand another sleepless night. Across the summer you hide each sign of what's happened, hoping it will magically disappear. But before school starts in September they learn you are pregnant."

He emphasizes the ominous realization that too many weeks have slipped by to do anything but proceed toward a birth. He notes the shame and anxiety of beginning the year pregnant – without support from the phantom father.

"But you're not alone. A guy from your church youth group becomes attracted to you over the summer. I'll call him, Steve. Let's call you, Marie."

Upon revelation of the pregnancy Steve is adamant: he loves Marie, but he is not the father and he's not ready to be one. At a checkup Marie's family doctor, in response to her desperate questions, retrieves a dozen manila folders from his files. These contain names, descriptions, and photographs of infertile couples who are seeking private placements. The doctor's wife is a lawyer and an independent adoption agent.

"Suddenly you face a choice. You can let events unspool as they will and accept the thread of life the fates have spun. Or you can choose to make a decision – an attempt to discover your own path. Think of the glimmer of hope. You're offered a chance to select a family, to know your baby will be given better care than you can provide, and at the same time rescue yourself from the worst quagmire of your life. Do you think you might consider that option?"

Dan imagines one of the students yelling, "No!" and jumbling the events encompassing him. One voice alters the story. But he doubts anyone will rise to protest.

To the relief of her mortified parents, Marie agrees to relinquish parental rights and the child is born: a baby girl. The adoptive parents, selected by Marie, arrive at the hospital on the day of birth. By her choice – made in panic as the last minutes evaporate – they do not meet. Marie sees the baby for fleeting moments. The adoptive parents and Baby Girl V., as the court calls her, return to their home in a nearby town. Marie resumes her life and her relationship with Steve, who casts himself as Marie's protector.

In covering the aftermath of the birth and adoption of Baby Girl V., Dan injects some ambiguity. No psychologist or judge could gauge the young mother's precise state of mind during this interval. He reports that Marie's parents relent in their negative views, yearning for their missing grandchild. Marie remains haunted by vagueness in the words not only of her doctor, but also of the lawyer who arranged the adoption and the social worker who interviewed her. She speaks of Steve's change in attitude. Ashamed that he rejected the child, he is prepared to marry Marie, enter the Navy and raise Baby Girl V. as his own daughter.

"The law gives you one month to petition for a revocation of your consent. Your circumstances have changed in dramatic ways. It appears realistic for you to provide your baby with a life you thought impossible."

Scanning the audience, Dan pauses. "Everyone around you now wants this child. How do you weigh your options? The days are counting down for a decision. How do you make the right personal choice in that whirlwind? Someone finds the paperwork for revoking consent. On the last possible day you sign the form and your parents rush off to deliver it to the court."

The litany of facts echoes in the hall and Dan waits for it to fade. He reveals that Marie's petition for the return of Baby Girl V. is denied. The paperwork has not been dated correctly, so the time limit is considered exceeded. Over the chaotic next weeks, the family rallies to protest the decision. Interviews and paperwork requirements turn weeks into months. The court's social worker misses an appointment, creating further delays. Finally, a court hearing is set to consider Marie's appeal. In less than two hours before the judge, the lawyer for the adoptive couple argues their stable home is best, and that Baby Girl V. has known no other human faces. Marie's disheveled lawyer, who has shown little curiosity about her life, argues that parenthood should never be decided on a technicality. He offers the platitude that a biological mother is preferred when she is capable of rearing her child.

And Marie can. Her parents volunteer to provide for the baby. A high school program for student mothers is located. Marie will marry following graduation. She wants to be a mother now. The judge makes a disapproving face at each lawyer's presentation. With briefs filed, he requests impartial information on the child's welfare and an evaluation of her attachment to the adoptive parents. More time passes as the court seeks a psychologist to conduct the evaluation of Baby Girl V.

The students jot notes as Dan uses an overhead slide to detail the normal stages of attachment formation. By the time his evaluation is arranged, the infant is close to six months old. He describes his observations of Baby Girl V.'s behavior when separated briefly and then reunited with her adoptive parents. He compares those to normal bonding patterns.

"Here's what I wrote in my report: As a typical six-month old, Baby Girl V. had not yet formed a full-blown, exclusive attachment to her adoptive parents, but she was, without question, in the midst of that attachment process.

"The truth is we don't understand attachment fully. You can't do the research that would pin down the moment when infants and parents bond. Who's going to separate babies from their parents at birth or two months or six months, then see if the attachment still forms naturally?"

A small wave of nervous laughter descends from the seats.

"It has to be somewhat subjective. We watch for key behaviors – or the absence of them. Does the infant show distress? Joy? Is she nonchalant about a separation or a reunion? You're trying to observe something that is happening real-time between two human beings, something almost mystical. Ever been around two friends who might be attracted? There's something about the way they look at each other, how they move closer and then farther apart, then closer again. You can tell. Something about the way they engage."

A stronger ripple runs through the hall at his use of 'engage.'

"I remember one moment in particular with Baby Girl V. and her adoptive father. It was subtle and quick, but definite. She was sitting up, balancing herself with her arms out. His arms were out too. They made eye contact. She leaned toward him and he opened his arms. And then they fell toward each other without a word. Attachment is the mysterious force that lets a moment like that happen."

As his words roll through the hall, Dan is gripped by an unexpected memory. He checks the waiting audience.

"It's funny. I'm remembering something from one of my high school classes. I think it might be related to attachment, but to be honest this is the first time I've thought of it since high school."

He turns to the instructor. "Mind if I tell a little anecdote?"

"Sure, why not?" she says with a half-wary glance.

He gives an unassuming shrug as the students wait, some trading whispers. He clears his throat.

"We had this teacher who was kind of dramatic. Hair clipped in a flattop, like a Marine. This was ninth grade science. He put a lot of energy into his teaching and he knew how to impress ninth graders. Gas balloons igniting, foaming liquids, stuff like that."

The instructor shifts in her seat behind him. The college students go quiet. Young eyes track him.

"He was teaching us about gravity, which he claimed was the weakest force in the universe. An invisible attraction between two bodies. But the weakest force, he kept saying. Without any warning he jumped up on the laboratory table at the front of the room and held up a clay pot. Waiting just long enough for us to wonder if he would do it, he let the pot drop to the linoleum floor. Of course, it shattered. I'm not sure if it was the noise or the flying pieces or the fact that he destroyed it without blinking that thrilled us.

"Here's the point. He said that even though gravity was the weakest force, it exerts itself on space and time. He told us – and I still remember how he whispered it like it was a delicious, grown-up secret

– that when there is a disruption of space and time, two physical bodies will always fall toward one another."

Dan pauses to check their faces.

"That's the mystery of attachment. Two bodies that, for some invisible reason, fall toward one another. When I did my observation, I saw multiple signs of Baby Girl V.'s developing attachment with her adoptive parents. But I have to admit, that little falling together stuck in my mind."

He returns to his notes. The students break eye contact with him to jot words and phrases. He describes his report to the court and recounts his recommendation that the chances of disruption to the attachment and resultant distress were significant enough to suggest Baby Girl V. not face a change in custody. Then he reveals the decision of the judge – an ex-district attorney known for a complexion that grew fiery at any hint of disrespect in his courtroom. Describing the biological mother as a teenager "acting more on whim than sound, mature considerations," the judge rejected the petition for return of Baby Girl V. and moved to finalize the adoption.

As he steps aside from the podium and prepares to conclude his talk, Dan's right foot catches. He steadies himself and checks to see if anyone has noticed his misstep.

He wants the students to grasp that the story could be told a few different ways, each with an ending that addresses a unique facet of the dilemma he perceives, each tugging listeners toward different conclusions. What if he made the biological mother sound completely unselfish? Should the pressures on her be emphasized to the point that her decision to offer the child for adoption is obviously made under duress? Could he have her plead before the court that she made one mistake with the best interests of her child in mind, a mistake she now wants to correct? Should the adoptive parents stand in indignation and document the unwavering love they've provided Baby Girl V. from her first hours of life? Would it matter if they glare or scoff at their adolescent opponent?

For a split second he wants to experiment with the story, adding a confounding detail. But he yields to the record of the case. Winners in the eyes of the law, the adoptive couple is left understanding that some people want their daughter. The biological mother, who has done no harm to her infant, faces the reality that her choice eliminated any legal rights to the child to whom she gave birth.

"You can examine a case like this from different perspectives, and you should," he tells the students. "I'm not going to claim Baby Girl V.'s situation was handled perfectly. I can't stand here and tell you she is fine without her biological mother – or her biological father for that matter. Adoption is a noble act, but also a complex experience for the people involved. Sometimes the repercussions play out over many years. I do feel confident that relevant psychological input played a role in how the judge decided the case. This child was placed with loving parents – a voluntary placement – and she was developing a normal attachment bond with them. But you can see that every adoption of a young child might be different. I hope I've raised as many questions for you as I've answered."

...

Respectful applause marks the end of his talk. Dan acknowledges the class with a tight smile and squints, dodging the glare of the lights. He's saved time for students to come forward with questions. Several climb down the stairs to ask about details in the case or inquire about internship opportunities. Grateful for the interest of the students, Dan nods and compliments their thinking. That no one challenges his recommendation in the case or disagrees with the judge's ruling leaves him uneasy.

Despite his attempt to cast each listener as Marie, one student says, "People need to think about these things before they start having sex." He doesn't disagree, but crosses his arms, alarmed at how early in life a heart can grow cold. "Sometimes life pulls you in very unforeseen directions," he replies.

A well-dressed young woman, whose striking ox-blood hair falls below her shoulders like tassels on an antique lampshade, waits for her classmates to leave so she can speak with him in private. This is also a situation Dan has come to expect.

He resets himself and examines her. Is she a year or two older than the others or matured by some responsibilities? His gut and experience tell him a roommate or friend is pregnant and in need of advice about adoption. It may be something more dire. She's the steady ally trying to assist with difficult choices. He recognizes her desire to help from the women he studied with in graduate school. One day she may be a therapist or an advocate for abused children, anorexic teens, or homeless mothers.

Dan meets her earnest gaze, which considers him from a face dense with freckles. Until her words register he does not comprehend that this is the moment he envisioned once, but never quite believed would occur. She reaches with an unfaltering hand, her eyes fixed, and says, "I'm Suzanne Verdin."

Chapter Two

EARLY ARRIVALS FOR THE NEXT CLASS force them to exit the lecture hall. Dan looks about for a place where they might talk. Margaret Becker thanks him and signals she'll stop over this evening. He tries to keep his focus on her while twisting toward the young woman. He's anxious she might walk away. Suzanne Verdin. The shocking syllables cut through him again. The weight of her spoken name presses against his chest. He asks if she has time to chat. She nods. Dan turns back to the psychology instructor, acknowledging her thanks and calling that he'll see her later.

Outside the lecture hall he and Suzanne locate a low retaining wall near the building's entrance. They sit angled toward each other with their knees almost touching. Jasmine bushes, without blossoms, brush their shoulders.

Everything about his presentation falls away. He's been knocked from a dream he believed to be realistic only to fall into a sharply-focused moment that feels imaginary. Staring at the young woman's profile, Dan marvels at her presence. He holds no doubts she's the birth mother of Baby Girl V. An electric vibration jolts his heart; his cheeks burn. Deep breath, he commands himself. Psychologist mode.

They wait for students to drift away. She holds a shoulder bag on her lap. Dan says, "There've been times in the last four years when I wondered if we might cross paths someday. I didn't expect it today. I hope it wasn't uncomfortable for you."

Suzanne shakes her head. "I wondered that too. It's a little weird. Surreal." She adds, "You're younger than I expected. Or thought."

Dan manages a minor laugh. "I get that a lot. No gray beard."

She stares at him without expression. He blinks and clears his throat.

"I was a little over a year out of my post-doc at the time of your case. We did a fair number of attachment evaluations at the clinic where I trained. Yours was my first one here."

When she doesn't respond, Dan adds, "I'm 29." He scans her face, trying to sense what she might be feeling.

After an interval of unsure silence, Suzanne says, "I appreciate how you tried to make them see what it was like for me. I was surprised at how much you knew."

Dan braces himself against a mass of bewildering emotion. At the same time, he tries to guess at her intentions. But as she looks away, he can only study her profile. For a moment he gets lost examining her mosaic of freckles. He can't think of another face he's known that was so freckled. He debates whether her copper flecks and speckles are exceptional or simply uncommon. Was she ever teased about them? They seem ready to come alive, like an illusion capable of reconfiguring itself. Their tint blends like camouflage with her rusted hair, and emphasizes her keen eyes and unshowy lips. Suzanne Verdin is not typical of women he's known. She's not as animated or as immediate as Brynn. But he finds her appealing in an effortless, self-possessed way. She's a thinker – a reader. Bright, he guesses. If not solitary, then private or quiet. A stickler about health and nutrition. She's not an angry person – she lacks that bodily tension that twists itself from irritation to frustration to outburst. He's intrigued by a faraway look that emerges like mist rising on water. Alert that she may be noticing his gathering of first impressions, Dan averts his eyes. He takes another moment to experience the astonishment that she is sitting beside him. He works to form the words in his mind: the biological mother of Baby Girl V.

Her hands grip the retaining wall where they sit. His sense is that she wants him to speak.

"May I call you Suzanne?"

Her slight delay in responding alarms him. She says, "Yes."

"How has your life been…since the adoption?"

Suzanne appears taken aback by his words or the tone of his voice. "I'm okay. I'm good."

He smiles, trying to project warmth.

"Suzanne, I'm a little chagrined I used your case without your permission. If I trivialized any aspect of it, I apologize. You heard that I changed some parts. I didn't know much about you or the specifics of what happened. Some parts I guessed at – to keep it from being, well, from being your story exactly. I've always kept it anonymous."

She nods her head, keeping her eyes on the path before them. A sparrow hops in the sunlight, pecking at tidbits. "I appreciate that. It's strange to hear yourself described as a case. But that's kind of how it feels to me now."

After a moment he says, "Some people might be very angry having gone through everything you did."

Suzanne Verdin tilts her head, weighing his words.

"Do you think anger like that could last this long? I don't believe anyone could live with anger like that. There are lots of other feelings besides anger."

Dan blinks at the clinical tone in her voice.

To his tentative questions, she indicates she is studying biology with a focus on genetics. He smiles at his error: he didn't see the scientist in her. For some reason he linked her to his own field. Suzanne says she'll finish in June and look for a graduate program in genetic counseling or something similar. Ah, he thinks, recovering a small measure of pride. Before that, however, she would like to travel.

Dan winces and shifts his weight, then nods, trying to suppress thoughts of Brynn and instead convey enthusiasm for Suzanne's wish. He scolds himself for being overly agreeable, and for the discomfort it covers. Then he bristles at having any reaction. Travel is a lot of things other than your girlfriend moving to Sweden. He shifts back to psychologist mode.

"Do you have a list of places you'd like to see?"

She considers his question, crossing a leg away from him. "I would love to visit New Zealand. I haven't seen much of the U.S., either." She re-establishes eye contact. "A lot of places, I guess."

At first he's surprised she didn't marry the high school boyfriend, but quickly understands that of course she didn't. He runs a few rough calculations. Baby Girl V. – Emma, he reminds himself – would be four years old. She will turn five this next year – in March, he remembers. Suzanne must be 22 or 23. Two fine lines at her eyes impart a touch of maturity – or is it tenderness? Younger women cast glances and toss their hair with more risk. Suzanne's head and hair shift the way leaves drift and turn on a stream. She communicates in precise gestures. Her replies feel less guarded than he expects. Her face remains shield-like. She speaks in a voice that strikes him as candid, but shy of friendly. Dan considers their conversation not quite melancholy and not light – an exchange between two people who've failed to keep in touch for reasons neither understands. He uses his voice to tiptoe forward, like a shadow proceeding him down a dimly-lit hallway. When he hears himself interviewing her like she's a client at the mental health clinic, he stops. He asks if he can tell her about the day he delivered his evaluation to the court and the lawyers.

Suzanne nods without speaking.

"I walked around the block the courthouse is on, dropping off copies with the court clerk and then the two attorneys. When I finished my circuit I came to the bar where the lawyers all gather. I remember thinking two things: I wanted to get a drink, and I wanted to write a letter to you explaining my recommendation. I didn't do either.

"It couldn't have been as hard for me as it was for you. I want you to know that it was far from an easy, routine thing. I wondered about you. I thought you made a selfless decision to allow your daughter to be adopted. I assumed you had conflicted feelings. It wasn't my role to contact you, but I worried how it all felt for you."

She says, "I've thought about some of what you told the class. A lot of it, I guess. I read your report many times. Hearing you say it helped."

He nods, accepting her at her word. He begins to sense the time she needs between thoughts. A moment of quiet. One beat longer than he takes.

"Is the story about the teacher dropping the pot true?"

He draws back, amused. "It is. I'm not sure why I remembered that. But yes, he dropped it."

Again, the extended pause. "I wonder who had to clean it up?"

Her comment is aimed toward a vague point across the campus. Dan keeps silent and studies her profile. He can't discern what caused her to approach him. It concerns him that she harbors a concealed request. He rules out impulse. In all likelihood she knew he'd be talking to the class. How long has she been anticipating or preparing for his appearance? Did she consider skipping class that day? Had she ever considered contacting him before? Nothing on the mask of her face addresses his questions or reveals her intent.

"Have you been in touch with anyone about the adoption?"

She shakes her head. "I was curious to see you in person. Everyone else I had seen. You were just a name on a report."

Sensing she might want to question his evaluation, he says, "I want to be honest and tell you that I would recommend the same thing again. Under the same circumstances."

Suzanne Verdin turns and meets his eyes. "Yes." She takes another pause, her emotions behind a circumspect expression. "I don't think they were ever going to let a teenage mother get her baby back like that."

Dan swallows.

"My life would be a lot more complicated now if I had a daughter." She looks off. "People say it's better things worked out this way. I hear that sometimes. I guess I think it as often as anyone else."

"You've never seen your daughter."

"No. Not after her birth. I saw her face. Her eyes and her lips."

"You haven't had any information about her?"

Suzanne says no.

She explains that for months after the hearing she desperately wanted to see her again. A glimpse might have been enough. Something to reassure her the little girl was safe. Something to block the jarring, fragmented night terrors. Once she began to search for the adoptive parents' last name to see where they lived, but stopped herself.

"I might be able to find them or contact them. It might be better not to see her with her adoptive family. I'm sure they wouldn't want it, after the court case. Not that it's bad. I think they surely love her very much. It's better for me. I keep my imagination alive that way."

Suzanne quiets and he waits.

"She may want to find me someday. On her birthday I drive by the hospital. I can't think of her all the time. Have you ever wanted to disappear? Vanish into the world somewhere? I used to think about that. Another life where the past was – gone. It's silly, but I used to imagine it. What if I could vanish and appear in an entirely new life? A sheep farm in New Zealand. Paris. Would I like that? It sounds crazy, but if you think about it, it might be something a person could do.

"But I can't, because she wouldn't be able to find me. I have to leave bread crumbs. It's like a fairy tale – a real one. Fairy tales are dark. You probably know that. People suffer a lot. Sometimes it's their fault. Often they're innocent or they don't grasp what's happening. Whatever her family tells her, she may not understand it all. If I leave a trail of crumbs she'll be able to find me – if she ever wants to."

He opens his mouth to ask a question but catches himself.

Abruptly, Suzanne says, "I need to check on Annie Fisher."

Dan tilts his head.

"My dog," she answers.

"Ah. Annie Fisher?"

Suzanne smiles to herself.

He says, "It's kind of fun that she has two names."

"She's named after Anna Fisher. Do you know who that is?"

"No, I don't think so."

"She was an astronaut. The first mother to go into space."

Dan tracks Suzanne's eyes.

"She – I was kind of intrigued by her when I read her story. I mean, to go into space and be orbiting the Earth, looking down. With your daughter down there. It's a little like what people think heaven might be, seeing the world like that. Her daughter was a baby when she went into space. It kind of amazed me. I didn't think anything was wrong with it. I thought she was…brave.

"People smile, like it's a strange name for a dog. I guess it is, but it fit her. Annie Fisher. Some names feel natural that way."

He waits for a moment. "Is she brave? Annie Fisher?"

"She is, yes."

He nods. Suzanne drifts into private thought. Overhead the sharp cry of the red-tailed hawk punctuates their conversation. She stands, and he joins her.

Before they part Dan retrieves a card from his wallet and invites Suzanne to contact him at his office if she ever cares to.

"If you have any questions – or anything you want to say to me, it would be fine. You can call this number. I'd be happy to talk – to listen. It wouldn't be – there'd be no fee."

She accepts his card. Gazing at him, she begins to form a thought.

"My parents…"

He alerts to her words.

Suzanne says, "Never mind. It's nothing."

When she takes an anxious glance away, Dan prepares to say goodbye.

"Annie Fisher?"

"Yes," Suzanne says with a partial grin.

"I'm sure it was difficult to introduce yourself," he says, offering his hand. "That took a lot of courage. I really appreciate that you did."

She accepts his handshake. Once more she considers an uncertain horizon. Then she turns to his face and says, "Have you ever thought of a way that it could have been fair for everyone?"

Daniel Tunbridge startles at the very question that lies at the center of his thoughts about Baby Girl V. He ransacks his mind for the words a psychologist should use. He wants to tell her that the judge in the case asked him a similar question and that he's struggled with it ever since. The concept of justice torments him. Not because of anything he regrets. The handling of Baby Girl V's case was reasonable. Rational. Based on sound clinical observation. And the judge's decision rested on a lot more than his report. It was not unfair. But was it fair and just? Suzanne is not asking him for a legal opinion. He wants to tell her he trips every time he thinks about the words. When he locks on Suzanne Verdin's hazel eyes, all he can say is, "No. I'm afraid I never have."

...

The late afternoon heat in her apartment presses against Suzanne's face, no matter which way she turns. She raises the front window, but with the curtains closed – and to keep neighbors from prying they must be – little air enters. October heat like this rattles people. Wild fires burn in the mountains to the north of Big Sur and in coastal hills to the south. Everyone searches the skies, wondering when the season's rains will begin. One day a blood-red cloud from a fire two hundred miles away stains the sky and menaces the sun. In the morning cars at the ranch sit speckled with ash.

Her apartment lies in a weather-worn two-story wooden building with four units side by side, joined by a common entrance balcony. Used in the past by ranch workers, the apartments rent to a mix of locals. Suzanne is friendly with the divorced older woman who works at the DMV and the young couple next door who do something with yoga and social media. Jeff at the far end is a problem. If she leaves her doorway open with only the screen door to block him, he will wander over with a joint or his battered guitar. She's learned he can spot a bottle of wine on the kitchen counter all the way from the front porch. She's tired of putting him off. She doesn't want him in the apartment. Good thing Annie Fisher safeguards their territory. Suzanne prefers to keep her interactions with the others to the stairs or the carports under their apartments. So, the front door stays closed, and the window curtains drawn, despite the loss of a breeze. Baked air from the uninsulated flat roof presses down like waves of oven heat.

Suzanne paces, frantic over the thoughts and feelings she's unleashed. It all feels too big. Dr. Daniel Tunbridge was no more than a name from that tormented year. Wasn't she over that? Now his face, his voice, his mannerisms grow, spreading like dark wine spilled on a lace tablecloth. Why did you introduce yourself? What did it prove? She's no stronger, no wiser, no more sure of anything. She remembers her breathing. Draw deep, hold on a seven count, exhale on an eight

21

count. Again. Again. It's enough to stop the pacing. Her cheeks tingle and her chest loosens. But the thought of the zippered black file folder sends a ripple of shame creeping through her body. Suzanne closes her eyes and banishes the image.

When she opens her eyes, they dart to the sofa cushion. She steps to the sofa and grabs the cushion, as if the folder may have been taken. As if Jeff may have jimmied her lock and slipped in to invade her refrigerator or peek in her dresser drawers. What if he sat on the couch, waiting for her with some lie about finding the door open? What if he felt the zippered folder, opened it and spread the pages across the coffee table? "You stalking this guy?" he'd say with a loopy grin. He'd throw out some movie reference – a spurned, wild-eyed woman stealing a family's dog or springing out of a bedroom closet.

The folder lies where she left it. She pulls it out and grips it with two hands, turning her body to survey the apartment. The heat swirls around her and rises like a dust devil. In the kitchen, on the cooler linoleum, Annie Fisher cocks her head.

Suzanne goes to the kitchen table and sits, pushing through another curl of shame. She unzips the folder and retrieves the collection of papers. Their thickness feels right. They haven't been touched. She checks the front door before laying out the papers on the table. Her shoulder bag lies half-spilled nearby. She finds his card and places it on the pile. The embossed seal on the card and his name in boldface pull her back to court. She locates the official documents, slides those to one side and places the card atop his report.

The other papers are printouts – web pages she's collected. A listing of personnel from County Behavioral Health. Dr. Daniel Tunbridge, staff psychologist. Neither his listing nor the other names include photographs. A second page with the mental health clinic's location, hours and procedures for appointments. A web page from UCLA, dated six years before, mentioning Daniel Tunbridge, Ph.D., pediatric neuropsychology intern, in the description of a newly dedicated hospital play space for children. From the University of Denver, a page listing doctoral degrees awarded, including Daniel Tunbridge, candidate in child clinical psychology. Five different pages from Dartmouth College. Daniel S. Tunbridge, bachelor's in psychology, Phi Beta Kappa. Dan Tunbridge, Dartmouth Hockey. Big Green Sports: Late Push Fails as Season Ends at Cornell. Rookie Power Play Goal Beats Harvard. Season statistics: Tunbridge, D. Elected to Dartmouth

Student Assembly: Daniel Tunbridge, sophomore. Hometown: Walpole, New Hampshire.

Suzanne has found five social media profiles, none of which is right. Another search yields a local on-line article from two years earlier about the Central Coast Craft Beer Festival. It includes a photo with a group of friends, one identified as Dan Tunbridge, of Cayucos. Until this morning Suzanne thought the guy in the photo was too young, as if the Dr. Tunbridge who wrote the court report was his uncle or father. Now she examines the face for details. He smiles to his friends, raising a glass, one arm around the bare shoulder of a shorter woman with zigzag, outdoorsy hair. Brynn Byerly, the caption reads.

Suzanne pushes her chair back and stands. She sweeps the web page printouts together and turns them face down. Even in the zipped folder they can't stay in the apartment. Until today they were no more than late-night web searches. Now that she has seen him – faced him – spoken with him – the printouts seem more like evidence than curiosity. They can't go in the trash either. Jeff pokes around there. She saw him standing a little too close to her bin one evening when his pot dealer – a bald, vampire-like guy with skinny tattooed forearms – rolled up in a cloud of dust on a whiskey-colored Harley. Suzanne gathers the pages and folds them in half. She has to get out of the apartment. She can hardly breathe in the still heat.

"Annie, should we go to the beach? You want to go to the beach?"

The dog shifts her head at each mention of the beach. Then she snaps to her feet, tail wagging.

Suzanne kicks her shoes toward the bedroom and slips her toes into sandals. She grabs her shoulder bag and stuffs the folded papers inside. Turning, she surveys the apartment for anything she's forgotten. The problematic folder lies on the kitchen table. She places the court documents inside, zips it and replaces it on the table. In an afterthought she picks it up and buries it under the sofa cushion. She decides to leave the kitchen window open, then walks to the living room window. If she closes it the apartment will be roasting when she returns. Suzanne nudges the window so the security pin can slide into place. This leaves it open a few inches. She yanks the curtains together.

Before she starts the car, her phone chirps and she sees a missed call from her mother, no voicemail. If she doesn't text something soon there will be a barrage of messages. Suzanne types, "at beach w/dog" and hits send. Her mother will be annoyed, but it will buy time.

Suzanne heads north on Highway 1, avoiding a look at the men's prison and passing the community college. Hollister Peak rises, a majestic, ruined shell of a volcano, with a verdant blanket of shrubs and grasses spilling down its flanks. Suzanne wrestles with conflicted emotions at how long the mountain has remained standing after its final anguished eruption. It's beautiful and sad – a fractured survivor with a history that can only be imagined. Not at all like its husky, chiseled sibling, Morro Rock. That plug of compacted stone stands angry and defiant, its dormant energy barely contained. Yet the harbor it guards serve as a refuge for her. As the road turns toward Morro Bay, Suzanne draws a breath of the cooler offshore air. She's thinking of the broad strand north of the massive rock. In that moment she remembers the papers in her bag. She drifts to the right and takes the exit for Morro Bay Boulevard. At the Valero she pulls into a space away from the pumps and parks. Taking the folded papers from her bag, she flips through them. In the back seat, Annie Fisher pants and presses her nose to the window. Suzanne glances back.

"Here you go." She presses a button to roll down the window. The dog pokes her head out, sniffing the air.

Suzanne starts to tear the folded pages, but they resist. She opens the papers and tries tearing from the side. This time she succeeds. She takes each half and tears again. Then she crumples the torn pieces together and squeezes them into a wad of paper. Checking her rearview and side mirrors, Suzanne opens the car door and hurries to a trash can. She pushes the hinged lid and stuffs the wad deep into the cavern of refuse. Without looking around, she turns and walks back to the car. When she climbs into her seat, Annie Fisher gives a whimper.

"I know, I know. I promised the beach." She starts the car and raises the back window. "Watch your nose, Annie."

Before pulling back on the main street, Suzanne glances at her rearview mirror. The trash can stands alone. A tall, elderly woman pumping gas watches. Suzanne reaches for her sunglasses and slips them on. She exits the gas station, crosses the overpass and loops onto the ramp for Highway 1 North.

On the road again, she uses her breathing trick to calm her heart rate. It works, and the pleasant sensation of moving in the car begins to overtake her. The visual landscape sweeps past as in a movie, the car's tires humming the score for her. She aims high on the road and drifts into semi-hypnosis – fixed on her target and hyperaware of all around her. The curious brew of sensations migrates like warm blood to her feet, her fingers and her cheeks. Like a lazy morning with coffee. Like one tiny tab of lorazepam – ten minutes later – the gentle floating. Suzanne reaches to her bag and digs to check that the small plastic bottle remains stowed and ready. She replaces her hand on the steering wheel and lets the road pull her into the cool, swirly late afternoon.

Missing their favorite turnoff nearby the towering rock dome, Suzanne shrugs at her error and decides to head for the wilder strand of beach beyond Morro Bay. It will be less crowded, she guesses, with one or two fewer faces to reproach her for letting Annie Fisher run off leash. She signals a left turn and finds a spot to park along the frontage road. The terrier dances an anticipatory jig at familiar smells.

Suzanne carries an old knee sock stuffed with a tennis ball that Annie Fisher loves. She tosses the sock toward the ocean and the dog bounds after it. Suzanne breaks into a run, trying to catch up and outdistance the receding image of her apartment, the papers, Dr. Daniel Tunbridge.

Now the misty ocean air engulfs Suzanne, rinsing away the afternoon heat and invigorating her. This, too, is as good as the little pills. Much better. She closes her eyes and listens to the waves slapping the beach. If she could live at the beach, like this, everything would feel right. A tent in the dunes. A campfire. Why wouldn't it work? Surely there are people living like that somewhere in the world. Nothing on the horizon but sand and ocean. She smiles at the silliness of her daydream, but as she turns to take in the expanse of the beach, she asks herself, Why not?

Suzanne wrestles the sock ball away from the playful growling of her dog and sends it as far as she can across a beach sculpted by the tide. For a moment the folder of papers is banished from her mind. It comes back as fast as the sock ball. Did she throw them away? She did. She did. Annie Fisher begs her to toss the toy again. Suzanne follows her tracks. The pace of her steps becomes more regular; she is marching to a sing-song beat. Dan-iel Tun-bridge, Dan-iel Tun-bridge. After a few repetitions, she breaks from the dog's trail and steps closer to the water. She takes in a full breath. The foaming aftermath of a small breaker approaches her feet, returning to the sea before touching her sandals.

She replays their conversation outside the lecture hall. Images swirl, as in a dream. It's her dream, and she sees and hears it all. She didn't say anything that would hint at her printed pages. Did she show something on her face? Did her eyes say she knew more? Can psychologists see hints of thoughts or the glances and expressions that hide thoughts? Of course, they can. Anyone can. Did he? She doesn't think so. He kept blinking – the shock of meeting her would not wear off. When he studied her face, he was trying to decide things about her, not decipher her. That's a different look. He was remembering what he knew of her and trying to fit it to what he saw in front of him. He stared at her freckles. He didn't dislike them. He could have been formal in his assessment of her. She saw his shy glance and its definite suppression. He was a man, a guy. Not the formless name and title he had been. Not the puppet-like figure on the stage. From her seat she imagined reaching, lifting him and placing him on a shelf of memory. Not now. Now he's germinated into a living being. Eyes that scan with some uncertainty. Brown eyes, with flecks of midnight. A subdued voice, not unlike her brother's. Something concealed in his heart – an ember? She hadn't anticipated his becoming a person. The cache of printed pages appears before her face as a flurry of seagull wings. She dashes across the sand, leaving the papers spinning in the air.

Annie Fisher sniffs at washed up kelp that attracts small clouds of black gnats. "Annie! Annie-girl, come on!" Suzanne calls. "Hey, bring the sock! Get your sock." When the dog obeys and returns, Suzanne rubs her head and ears. "What a good girl you are!" She launches the sock ball again and Annie Fisher races up the beach.

Why didn't he say her name? They both know she was named Emma. No one knows her birth name – no one. In his presentation he only said, "Baby Girl V." Afterward he said, "your daughter." Was he testing her? Was he protecting the little girl or her family? Suzanne knew beforehand he might be suspicious or alarmed about her approach. It was a surprise not to sense more skepticism from him. She prepared for him to tell her in unequivocal terms that it wasn't appropriate to approach him. If it wasn't skepticism, what was the inner state she'd seen on his face? Pity? No, not that. He defended himself. He didn't apologize, at least for what he recommended. It wasn't sadness. She tries mimicking his face – something about the way he crinkled his eyes. A pang of sorrow erupts in her chest and she catches her breath. No, not here, not now. Not here. Disappear.

An older couple stops to pet Annie Fisher. As Suzanne approaches, the woman calls with a smile. "Is she a wired-haired? We had one years ago. They're so smart."

"Yes, she's a mix," Suzanne replies. "And yes, she's a smart one."

Annie Fisher wags her tail and offers the sock ball to the man.

"Oh, you want to play! Ok, let's play. Ready? Ready?"

He launches the sock ball up the beach and laughs.

Suzanne says, "You've made a friend now. She'll play that game forever."

"What a sweet baby!" the woman replies.

Suzanne blinks. The woman catches the change in her expression.

Suzanne says, "Thank you," but has already turned away from the couple. She trots after the dog.

Another ten minutes and Suzanne arrives at the point where the beach turns north and becomes cluttered with driftwood. Annie Fisher is finished with the sock ball for the afternoon. She leads the way, content to paw at the sand.

Suzanne locates a mound at the edge of the dunes and sits, facing the ocean. The sun drops to the upper boundary of the fog bank lying offshore. The air cools her face. She attempts to review the list of tasks that need to be done in the next few days. Instead she sees the zippered black folder on her kitchen table. Did she take all the printouts from it? Not the court documents or his report. She saved those, along with his card. She zippered those in the folder? What if one of the printed pages slipped onto the kitchen floor? Did she check for that?

The sun disappears in the fog bank and Suzanne shudders at the sudden drop in temperature. Had she stood and turned the other way when he finished his talk – had she walked up the stairs and exited the way she came – he would still be the doll figure, safe at an arm's distance. She could have settled for what he offered; there would not have to be more between them. The name of Dr. Daniel Tunbridge would fade and maybe, just maybe, the torn pieces of adolescent Suzy's story could be taped together and set aside, the story of Suzanne begun. She pictures the card with his phone number, then averts her eyes from it. The plan was to stare, to scrutinize his face, to listen for a note that might ring satisfactorily. To pluck the tiny stone from the heel of her shoe. Why did she walk down those stairs? Now he grows before her like an unpredictable genie from a dented lamp untouched for years. Now there is a man. She sees that it cannot yet be over.

Suzanne stands with the ocean to her back and for an anxious second fails to locate Annie Fisher. Momentarily the dog emerges from a scattering of driftwood twenty yards ahead. Suzanne takes one more deep breath of the chilly air drifting onshore. Painted in twilight hues, the beach stretches unpopulated for several more miles to the north. In the far distance she finds the vacation cottages and beachfront properties of Cayucos. Beyond them, evening lights glow on the sentinel pier. Cayucos. Dan Tunbridge, of Cayucos.

...

He wakes in bed, alone. Pressing his phone, he deciphers the time as 4:32 a.m. Dan can't recall a dream or anything else that's caused him to stir. He tells himself to sleep for two more hours, then get up and run. But he's not sure he can drift away from the abstract images arising in his mind. Justice. Fairness. He reminds himself to call his mother in the morning. She'll want to hear about the talk at the university. He wants to hear her speak about justice and fairness. In previous conversations she's expressed clear opinions on the topic. Justice and fairness. Fairness and justice. Mocking his attempt to corral them, the two unrestrained words bounce around his bedroom, where no hint of morning light yet appears.

The ocean rolls and tumbles, a runaway chorus of kettle drums. Most nights he finds that soothing and great for sleep. Dan turns to his left side and punches his pillow, trying to get the contour right for his neck. He closes his eyes and concentrates on letting his leg muscles relax. Tiny pricks of light dance on the movie screen of his eyelids. They assemble into a sea of freckles and reveal a pair of amber-green eyes. Suzanne Verdin. His mouth forms the words, Baby Girl V. In a scene that flashes and dissolves into an afterimage, Dan Tunbridge sees a young girl with red hair sitting at a table in a preschool, shaping clay. She looks up and offers an assured smile, as if they have known each other a long time, as if to say, "Here I am."

Chapter Three

MAC WATCHES THE CASHIER LOOKING FOR his hardware discount card listing in the computer.

"Verdin?"

"Yes. Mac."

"I've got an Andrew."

"That's it," he replies, crinkling his eyes. "Andrew. Mac. It's a bit of a story."

He waits for, "Big Mac!" It would not be the first, second or third time someone connected his height with his nickname. The only puzzling part is why they act surprised when the association pops into their minds. People are odd that way. A little too eager to go with trends or fads. Not their fault, it's the culture we live in, he reminds himself. Without fast food and jingles and all that advertising, a Mac would be a Mac. Or one of those computers. A tall guy named Mac? In America that's a Big Mac to nine out of ten people. Maybe in other parts of the world, too, he thinks, suppressing the urge to shake his head.

Transaction completed, Mac heads toward his truck. He's got plenty of time to get the light switch replaced this afternoon. Finally, a little free time to take care of things at the house. Maggie will be pleased, though there might well be a comment about how long his errands took. Either way, Mac's happy to be getting it done. This is why you work for yourself, he reminds himself. He'd make more money with one of the local companies, but he likes the handyman life much better. Everybody loves an easygoing handyman, even the cranky folks.

He's about to turn the key when he spies a blue Honda Fit passing on the road outside the parking lot. Though he misses the driver's face, it's got to be Suzy. Maggie's trained him to keep an eye out for their daughter and the easily-recognized car. He catches the Seahawks sticker on the rear window. Her car for sure. Why she never scraped that off baffles him. He should have done it for her. It's definitely her car. Annie Fisher in the back seat, like usual.

Mac's surprised to find his daughter driving in the south county. He's seen her there a few times. Generally she steers clear of their territory. They keep an unspoken truce. Not one that his wife accepts, but Mac does his best to keep things from spinning out of control. Suzy's got her classes at the university and that's kind of foreign territory for them. San Luis Obispo is where they cross paths most often. Mac understands that Suzy thinks they take every chance to peek at her life. Maybe it's not untrue. He does his best to steer Maggie away from San Luis, to create a little space for Suzy. Maggie acquiesces and stamps the deal with a scowling face. She refuses to give up Thursday night's Farmer's Market, where the tables of fruits and vegetables serve as backdrop for barbecue, street performers and the throng of tourists and locals. Mac and his wife get tri-tip sandwiches and take their time walking the crowded blocks first one way, then back, then always one last time. He's seen Maggie watching for a hint of their daughter, but he doesn't protest. He keeps her moving, pointing out grapes or nectarines that look tasty, stopping to watch young girls from a dance club strike poses in mystifying precision. Mac's noticed Suzy at a distance more than once. They make furtive eye contact, then turn quickly to other sights. Over time his daughter has come to skip the Thursday ritual, or arrive only at the end of the evening, when knots of college students begin their invasion of the bars.

Mac weighs his problem. If he goes home without any further information, Maggie will see something in his eyes or hear a tone hinting at his sighting of their daughter. "Where was she going, Andrew? What was she doing? You didn't follow her?" If he says he doesn't know or he was too busy to follow her, it will be hell to pay. There's not much choice. So, he turns the engine over and exits the parking lot, accelerating to the speed limit but nothing more. His daughter is a quarter mile down the road, more if he's lucky. He slows enough that a white SUV waiting at a stop sign pulls onto the road ahead of him. Yes, I did follow her. She was alone – I already told you that, Maggie. I'm not sure where she was heading – maybe over toward Pismo. The outlets? Could be. Well, no, I didn't see her turn that way. She was pretty far ahead of me. No, I couldn't, because that's when the Amtrak came through, down at the end of Grand in Grover Beach.

He double-checks his watch because Maggie will ask him what time it was when he saw Suzy, and somehow she'll know the afternoon train schedule. Mac keeps both hands on the steering wheel and decides to take his time. No need to rush. He's feeling lucky. The day's too fine to get twisted up in dramatics. He has no trouble imagining the lights and crossing arms at Grand Avenue that will keep him safe from the on-coming train and all that lies beyond.

...

On Thursday evening Dan gets a text from TJ, his colleague from mental health, asking him to call her about the wedding. TJ is marrying her girlfriend, Deb, on Saturday. Everyone's looking forward to the "two-bride extravaganza." The women could be twins: both feature surf-bleached shoulder-length hair and athletic profiles from a shared love of hiking. Each bought a showy white gown, a poorly-kept surprise to one another. Two fathers will walk them down the aisle. Dan isn't quite sure what to expect – it's his first gay wedding. There will be a few other people from the mental health center. TJ's mentioned he'll be seated with some of Deb's fellow deputies from the sheriff's department. He figures he'll stay to applaud the first dance, then slip away. The wedding is on the beach at Pismo and Dan offered his help in setting up. He's guessing something along that line has cropped up.

"You are still coming, right?" TJ sounds anxious.

"Of course! Wouldn't miss it. Bridezilla vs. Bridezilla – who could resist?"

"Oh god. Tell me about it," she laughs.

"What's up? Can I help with something?"

"Well, yes, I hope. I remember you told us you weren't using your plus one. Is that – are you still planning on coming alone? Because it would be fine if that changed and you wanted to bring someone."

TJ's heard plenty about Brynn's move. He guesses she's being polite.

"No, I'm solo. Don't tell me you've got a cousin."

"I don't. Deb does. And she's straight and she's a knockout. Don't be close-minded. But that's not what this is about. You remember Pat – the EMT? Well, Patty is freaking out. She and Lawrence are feuding about his cat. I don't know what it is, and between you and me I couldn't care less. But she's a mess about the wedding."

Dan shifts on his feet, trying to make sense of the call. Pat Kealani works for one of the ambulance services and is a friend of TJ and Deb's. He's seen her at the mental health center many times and at happy hour a couple of times. She's always come across as easygoing. He is pretty sure she's a lesbian. Lawrence Coleman is his and TJ's colleague, a licensed clinical social worker. He's heard about Lawrence's spoiled Persian Longhair, enough to imagine some cat-related complication.

"They're involved with each other?" Dan says.

"No, no, god no. Well, they're totally co-dependent, if that counts. They're like a sister and brother who can't let go of anything from the past. I mean, they're kind of best friends too. Lawrence is completely gay, and Pat is, well, no – it would be like sleeping with her brother.

"No, they're feuding, and Patty won't go with him. And she doesn't want to go alone, for some reason. I can't talk her into it. She doesn't mind sitting at the same table as him. Nice of her, huh? She just needs a little buffer."

"Aha."

"I know. I don't want to impose, but is there any way you could pick her up and bring her? This is not a date, of course. You don't have to hang out with her. Trust me, there'll be plenty of other lesbians there. She just needs a little distance from Lawrence."

"I don't mind sitting with her," Dan offers. "But, I don't know – I'm not sure she'll want to go with me."

"Well, actually she does."

"You guys talked about it?"

TJ waits for him to catch up.

Dan laughs. "Okay, so this is set to go."

"She asked. Don't tell her I told you, but she likes you, Dan. There's nothing freaky. She thinks you're cool – her word. And she was a soccer player. You guys could talk about sports."

He laughs again. "What time did you tell her I'd pick her up?"

TJ lets out a big laugh. "Thanks. You're good. I promise, she's not going to cling. You don't even have to take her home. There's a singles thing afterward and Deb's friends are going to pull her into that. I promise. A ride to the wedding, that's all. For some reason she can't come alone. An EMT, can you imagine?"

"Let me guess, you have her number for me."

TJ rattles off the number.

He says, "Text me that, okay?"

"Done. You're a sweetheart, Dan. I will totally introduce you to Deb's cousin." She pauses. "I mean, if you want to. No pressure."

"Let me get back to you on that one. I'll have my hands full for a little while."

"Okay, I gotta run. You're the best, Dan. I'm so glad you're going to be there. It's going to be fun."

"Can't wait, TJ. I'll give Patty a call."

"Praise the lord! Ok, bye."

Dan puts his phone back in his pocket and reorients himself to Saturday and the wedding. Pat lives somewhere in San Luis, so he can catch her on the way in from the beach. If his memory is correct, she played soccer for Ohio State. Probably never played Dartmouth, but who knows? They'll be able to commiserate about working for the county, the insanity of the local real estate market, and their fortune in moving away from blizzards. The phone buzzes a text notification. Pat's number. Dan shakes his head. Not quite what he expected for the wedding, but the prospect puts a smile on his face.

...

When he pulls to the curb at the house on Branch Street, Pat Kealani is waiting at the front door. She comes down the steps with a little wave. By the time Dan's out of his car, she's already to the passenger door.

"Hey, Pat," he calls across the convertible roof. "You look sharp!" Dan barely gets his compliment out through his surprise. Pat sports a white, three-piece suit, a pink hibiscus print tie, white shoes and a white fedora. She could be a jockey headed to the winner's party after the Kentucky Derby. Or a groom, he laughs to himself.

"It's not too much?" Pat says, with a smile.

He likes her confidence. "No, it's perfect."

"This is great," Pat says as she climbs into her bucket seat. "I didn't know you had a Miata. Is it a '93, '94?"

"Yes. 1994." He takes an extra-long look at her face. "I'm the second owner. Bought it from a guy who loved it to death but owned two newer ones. It broke his heart to sell it."

"They're neat little racers. Do you ever take it up to Laguna Seca?"

"No, I haven't."

"They hold rallies up there every so often. Good place to see what they can do."

Dan asks how she knows about racing, and Pat offers a detailed story that takes them half way to Pismo Beach. He finds an opening to ask about Ohio State and they talk college sports for a few minutes. Then they're near the hotel, scanning for a parking spot.

As they walk to the building together, Pat says, "Thanks for picking me up. I'm not usually that big a baby."

Dan smiles at her joke. He gestures to their suits. "Hey, I think we make a good-looking pair." She gives him a twisted smile. "We look like Arnold Schwarzenegger and Danny DeVito in that Twins movie, whatever it was." He laughs again.

Pat stops and turns to face him. "Before I miss my chance, I wanted to tell you that I heard about your girlfriend. It's not any of my business, but people gossip. People gossip a lot. Anyway, I was sorry to hear that. That's not why I asked TJ about this. I was upset with Lawrence. I shouldn't have bothered her about that. Now I'm glad I did. It feels safer coming with you. So, thanks."

He wants to look away, but can't. Her sympathy hits him as unexpected and generous. He grimaces at how little he understands what it's like to be gay and single. He hadn't thought twice about going to the wedding alone – what's a wedding without lonely hearts? Dan doesn't sense pity in her eyes or words. He can see that Pat holds some concern about him. The thought that he's an "ex" – that others might categorize him that way – confuses him. It's true, of course. But he fights the feeling. He doesn't want to succumb to it. Not today. Not at a wedding.

"Thanks, Pat. That's kind of you to say. I'm glad we came together. I'm happy to get to know you better. Even if you called me Schwarzenegger."

They head to the lobby, where a mix of celebrants surges, welcoming them.

•••

Maggie stays silent through two spoonfuls of chili. She puts her utensil down and selects a square of cornbread, which she slices and proceeds to butter. When both halves wear a thin coating, she rests her knife.

"You don't take it seriously."

Mac looks up from his dinner. History whispers not to speak.

"What if Suzy knows where she is, Andrew? What if she has some arrangement that we don't know about?"

"Maggie…"

"No! You don't know. Maybe she knows where she goes to preschool or some park she plays in. She would not tell us. You know that."

Mac pictures his daughter's blue car slipping away in the distance and fights a twinge of guilt for not trying harder to follow her.

"Maggie, she was running errands."

"Well, you wouldn't know that, would you? You could have known, Andrew. If you came home and told me, 'Oh, I saw Suzy's car at Trader Joe's or I saw Suzy heading into the outlets.' You would have known. But no."

He sighs at the truth of her words. The familiar ache of not knowing returns. Why he can sometimes let it go, while his wife cannot, puzzles Mac. Something about motherhood, he supposes. Though it presents difficulties, he admires his wife for her persistence.

"God is going to amaze us someday, Maggie. I believe that. He will take care of this."

She closes her eyes, blinks wide open and takes a bite of cornbread. For a minute silence hovers over the couple.

Mac notes tears damming in his wife's eyes. He strains to send a consoling smile, trying to lift away her pain.

"Well, Mr. God is obviously too busy for my prayers. Or he's got Alzheimer's and he's forgotten this family! I'm sorry, but we are a family. We're a natural family. We're natural, Andrew – we're exactly the way God made us. And that little girl needs to know her grandparents," Maggie says. "It breaks my heart."

...

The ceremony on the sands at Pismo unfurls in spectacular fashion. Sun splashes the beach; the Pacific swells and glows – an opulent, painted backdrop. A fair breeze fills the bridal gowns like spinnakers. Each is attended by bridesmaids in hues of lavender and aquamarine. With the fathers of the brides seated, there isn't a male on stage, which gives the entire scene the glamour of a Disney princess fantasy. TJ and Deb are having a grand time, blowing kisses to their guests and the cameras of strolling tourists who've stumbled upon the wedding. Dan sits next to Pat, soaking up the joy and laughter. She bites her lip. Blessings, kisses and cheers bring the ceremony to a close. Music erupts, topped by a happy ovation of waves foaming ashore. The barefoot brides link arms and lead their attendants, families and guests back up from the beach, to the amplified chorus of a rapturous Brandi Carlile song. Pointing to each other, laughing, ecstatic, they sing, "It's true, it's true, I was made for you!"

Inside the hotel guests sprint to the bar and amble among the tables, scanning name cards. Pat slips away, leaving Dan adrift, scanning the reception. Turning around, he finds Pat near the table with the wedding cake. Lawrence speaks to her with emphatic gestures. For a second Dan wonders if his commitment requires him to move closer. No one has had enough to drink for real fireworks to begin. Pat and Lawrence face each other, bodies close. Lawrence lifts his hand and in the lightest possible way touches Pat's floral tie. She breaks into a smile. She says something complimentary about his hair. A moment later they shift to a full body hug.

Dan glances at the bar, deciding he's earned a Pacifico. Two bridesmaids cruise by, one casting an over-the-shoulder grin. He asks himself what he'll do if Deb's knockout cousin materializes.

Later, after toasts and seafood skewers and growing calls for the DJ to start up the music, Dan is talking with Matt, one of Deb's fellow sheriff's deputies. From time to time they cross paths at the mental health center. Once they were both on the panel at an elementary school's PTA meeting. Matt is a Sharks fan; they talk a little hockey. But the Angels are still chasing the playoffs, and Matt's worked up about their situation. Two other deputies sit next to Matt, each a little more muscular and further along with his drinking than the rest of the table. A fourth deputy, Jorge, and his wife round out the table, creating some professional-personal confusion for the men. The two inebriated deputies – one crewcut, one in a Hawaiian shirt decorated in wind-blown palm trees – barely contain their needling of Jorge for coming with his wife. She gets up for the second time to go talk with other people.

"I thought we were on patrol today, dude," one complains.

"Hey, not my choice. She's in a book group with Deb," Jorge says.

Matt cocks his head toward the brides. "Crazy how much they look like each other. Twinsies."

Dan considers saying something about attraction. The deputy in the bulging shirt jumps in.

"Law of nature, bro. Couples always look like each other. People and their dogs, too. Married couples are worse – longer they're together the more they end up looking like each other. Ain't that right, Jorge? Know what I mean?"

Jorge shifts in his seat and parries the jab. "Hey, that's how come I got such a beautiful face." He pats his cheeks and flashes a bright white smile, drawing laughter.

"You're a real beauty, that's for sure," the deputy says, reaching for his beer and taking a hard swig.

"Hey, maybe that's your problem, bro. That's why you're still single. They haven't made a woman yet who's ugly enough to match you." He chuckles wildly at his comeback.

This gets a snort from Matt and the crewcut deputy. The guy in the Hawaiian shirt takes a long finishing swig and looks off toward the dance floor.

The crewcut deputy attempts to divert the conversation. "Dude, explain it to me," he says to his buddy, who's twisting his neck, trying to crack a joint. "I thought one of them was supposed to be a little more mannish. They both look hot. What is that? I'd screw either one of them."

It works. The muscular deputy breaks into a wheezy, cartoon animal laugh.

"You'd screw Deb?" Matt says, like the guy has said he'd steal his mother's car.

Dan catches Matt's eye. Matt shifts in his seat, shrugging at what might be a familiar routine.

"Hey, a little respect," Jorge says. "She's the bride. Or one of them is."

More snorts of laughter. The two deputy buddies launch into a snickering game of pointing out the bridesmaids and giving thumbs up or thumbs down. "Do her. Do her. Princess Fiona? Might do her," the sloppier one says.

"All yours, Shrek," the buddy grunts.

Dan gives Matt a half-grin saying this is your problem, and gets up from the table. A little fresh air will help. As he walks away he passes a middle-aged woman who might be an aunt to one of the brides. She raises her eyebrows and shimmies by him, saluting with her drink and a sporty grin, all geared up for dancing. He smiles back and fakes a dance move to cruise away from her, hoping not to be rude. Her hair is dyed a showy red. The unnatural color causes him to frown for a reason he can't quite pinpoint. He scolds himself for being critical.

On the back deck of the hotel he leans over a rail and takes in the ocean. Music from the dance floor kicks up, along with whooping. Dan grins at the celebrating, then lets his mind drift away from the wedding. The rhythm of the ocean's song helps. He detects some restless energy and understands it stems from thoughts of Baby Girl V.

and Suzanne Verdin. For a few nights he's played with the seed of an idea that only serves to keep him tossing and turning in bed. He needs to gather more information and he needs to think.

That can't happen here, so he suppresses the nagging thought and attempts to stay connected to the mood of the moment. It's impossible to be at a wedding and not think about Brynn. He stops trying to force her away. She appears for a second, and the feeling's sweet. The wedding would make her laugh and glow with tender appreciation of the happy couple. She'd signal him to join her on the dance floor – and if he didn't yield to the pull of her voice, she'd dance alone.

Beyond the deck another wave crests. Dan reaches into his pocket for his phone. Without thinking too much about why he's doing it, he pulls up his key contacts. Calculating the time of day as a bit after six back in New Hampshire, he presses the icon to call his mother.

After the second ring, he hears, "Daniel?"

"Hey, Mom."

"You caught me on the porch. I'm rocking like an old lady."

He smiles. "Got the cat on your lap?"

"Oh, yes. We're keeping each other warm. They say it might drop down to 36 tonight. That's a little too cold for October. The little ones have Halloween coming up."

Dan flashes on the tree-lined streets of Walpole, dry leaves scattering before a whistling wind. Halloween was the best time of the year for him as a kid. Walpole featured irresistible small-town enthusiasm, where despite costumes, you recognized everyone. That and old New England spookiness in its grasping tree limbs and watchful gables.

"How's the house, Mom? Everything steady there?" On his last visit, in June, he painted shutters and cleared sumac at the rear of the property. Summers satisfied him, too. Floating in sun-warmed waters at Sunapee. Crisp air dropping down from Canada to clear away humidity. After rain, polychromatic sunsets.

"Everything's smart, dear. Same as usual."

"You'll need to wrap the spigots this month, Mom."

"Yes, yes. Kenny dropped by two days ago and we talked about winterizing. He offered to help, but I told him I was on it."

Dan laughs to himself, surprised he didn't anticipate the name coming up. "Kenny" is his mother's neighbor – her famous neighbor, she's quick to emphasize – the documentary filmmaker, Ken Burns. No director anywhere has a bigger fan. Dan appreciates that a caring family keeps an eye on her. He's thanked Burns and traded phone numbers with him. Dan enjoys feigning confusion when his mother brings up her association with the celebrity.

"Kenny?"

"Yes! Kenny. He said I should call him that. We're friendly, you know. He loves our blueberries. People are neighborly here. They care about you."

That's her signal for a throw-down on California vs. New Hampshire. Or New England, as she's likely to include Vermont's mountains, Maine's coast, the Red Sox and anything else in the region that will serve her brief. She is unabashed in wanting him closer to home, though she's never once asked him to return. The facts, to her mind, make the choice obvious.

Dan gazes at the far horizon of the Pacific. If the world is as round as they say, this point of origin might launch him to any spot on the globe. That thought reminds him he's facing away from his mother. He swings around to see the easterly view cluttered with hotel balconies and a warren of hillside homes. Her voice, distinct and melodic, flows through him like the song of a familiar brook.

"I miss you, Mom."

She waits for a moment. "Oh, Daniel. How are you doing?"

"Well, I'm at a lesbian wedding, which is kind of fun."

"They simply call them weddings now, dear."

"Yes, well. This one has two lesbians. I thought you'd appreciate that."

"I do, I do."

"Good one."

"Oh! Ha! Very witty. I didn't hear myself."

"I'm staring at the ocean, Mom. I'm breathing it."

"That's wonderful, Daniel. I'm sure it must be appealing. Very surfy out there. We have one too, you know. Did you take someone to the wedding?"

"I did," he says, drawing out his words to bait her. "She's Hawaiian."

"Stop that. Go on, tell me."

"A friend, Mom. A mutual friend of the brides. We know each other from work." Just to prolong their game, he adds, "She wore a white, three-piece suit."

"Fashion always changes, Daniel. There are no rules anymore. Is she nice?"

"Yes, she's nice. She's an EMT. She's a lesbian, Mom. Or she might use a different term. I'm not sure. Just a friendly person. No possibilities, Mom."

"You're to ask about the pronouns."

"Pronouns?"

"She might have pronoun preferences."

"Aha. Well, she's not my date, Mom. She's a friend."

"You're too fussy, Daniel."

"Mom, a lesbian? That's kooky."

"I don't mean that. I mean you don't put yourself out there enough. You can't simply be friends with everyone or hang out, whatever they do in California. Young women want to be asked out. You need to make an effort."

"Says the world's greatest loner."

"I earned my solitude. I have books to read. Don't shrink from life, Daniel."

He winces. "I know."

"I'm afraid everything you love is at a distance."

He lets her words settle. "Don't exaggerate, Mom. I need some time."

"No, Daniel. Don't use slipshod thinking. Life doesn't work that way. Your father was 38 years old. You don't always get more time. That's callous to say, but it's indisputable."

Her mention of his father sends Dan into a cloudy whirlpool. A man he knows only from photographs and his mother's stories. A state game warden, struck and killed by a pickup on an icy road as he assisted another driver who'd collided with a moose. Dead three months before the birth of his son.

She gives him a moment. "You have his instincts and his willpower. And his hair."

"Thanks, Mom."

"In other news, I saw a bird yesterday evening that I've never seen before. It had a beautiful rusty-orange belly, black wings with dabs of white, and a black mask. I looked it up. It was a Black-headed Grosbeak. We don't get those here. It's one of yours, Daniel. Western. Do you know it?"

"I may. I'll keep an eye out."

"Keep a list. You might enjoy that. You've got all those shore birds. And the California Quail. That's such a charming bird, Daniel. I will give California that."

"Mom, do you remember Baby Girl V.? I gave that talk again this week."

"Yes, of course. Good for you. How did it go?"

"It went well. It was – I'm always surprised how talking about it leaves me unsettled." He doesn't want to mention Suzanne Verdin. He hasn't been able to pinpoint his thoughts on the young woman whose enigmatic gaze keeps invading his quieter moments.

"You have a teacher's sense for things that matter."

"I don't know about that, Mom. Too many questions about fairness and justice."

"Well, those are major questions. People should think more about them."

"How do you know with certainty? How can you be sure?"

"I don't think you can be sure. You can be thorough. You can be careful. You must be. Fairness is the easier one."

"How so?"

"The law is one of humanity's finest creations, Daniel. There's a lot of accumulated wisdom in it. When you apply it with care, it is usually fitting."

"Usually."

"Yes, usually. We're humans."

"And justice?"

"That's more complex. Justice is an ideal. Fairness is the way you play the game. You know right away. At least you should. Justice may be a longer story. And it's a more demanding one."

Dan refreshes his image of her on the porch in the Shaker rocker. Her animated hands, as familiar to him as his own. The understated elegant cut of her silvery hair. Her nut-brown eyes, the color of his. For so long she remained a mystery to him – a woman with a phantom husband, raising a boy by herself. A relentless tutor and zealous sports mom. A person whose simple pleasures lay in books, in a rambling garden of bee balm, lemon thyme, and blueberries, and in the circus of cardinals, jays, waxwings, and warblers she welcomed there. At some age he began to discern a different image, reflected in the faces of the locals. Later he learned her title and the significance of her profession.

But she was never one to talk about the week's cases, choosing to leave her robe and its complications sequestered in her chambers at the courthouse.

Dan turns back to the ocean. From afar, his mother's voice washes through him.

"I like what Gandhi wrote," she says. "The court of the conscience supersedes all others. I suppose justice requires that of us."

Chapter Four

HE DIALS FOREST ELVES PRESCHOOL, HOPING for luck. After yet another sleep-disrupted night, he's got to address the question tearing at him like the raptor sent to torment Prometheus.

"Vicky, hi, it's Dan Tunbridge from Behavioral Services."

She greets him in high spirits, saying "Ay" several times to signal friendliness. Vicky, the chummy, 40-ish director of the school, wears her irrepressible West Country accent like a small Union Jack tucked in her cap. She says "Dr." with a ripping "r" – sinisterly enough that he might be in danger of being sent to walk the plank. Then, in a reprieve, she adds a delighted exclamation point after his surname. The second time he visited the school, she knocked him off guard, crowing, "Alright, my luvver!" as her greeting. When he heard a "Yes, luv" and a "There you are, luvver" used with others, he decided she wasn't teasing him. She's urged him to visit Cornwall and her hometown on the coast, Padstow. "You'll do it one day?" How could he say no to such a merry pirate?

Dan doesn't have an appointment to visit the school, but he should. He's overdue for an observation of Manny Galvez, the four-year old from his case list. Manny is being watched for early signs of autism, a referral from a local pediatrician. Dan asked the staff to track a series of behaviors and emotional reactions that might help him with the boy and his parents. Vicky's been an enthusiastic collaborator. She'll have "proper notes" from her staff for him to check.

"Vicky, my afternoon's open and I wondered if I could come down to observe Manny. If it's not a good day for you guys, no problem. I thought if he's there today…"

Vicky assures him it would be fine. Manny is there, typically until 6:00. Dan prefers not to see his parents until their next conference. If he gets to the preschool by 4:00, he can be out in an hour with his monthly update. They talk for a minute or so about Manny's progress, which is noteworthy in Vicky's view. She's dubious about the pediatrician's concerns. He thanks her for keeping notes and expresses how much that helps him.

Emma Robinson's name pushes to the front of his mind. He remembers her adoptive parents chose not to give her a middle name. The mother wanted it kept simple. At the time of his attachment evaluation of Baby Girl V. they already called her Emmy. Dan spotted the little girl at Forest Elves a year ago on his first visit to observe Manny. Seeing her name on a roster electrified him. Something about the little girl's eyes remained familiar, despite the maturation of her face from infancy to early childhood. He's seen her several times since – pointing to words in a book, shaping clay, racing to climb the tree in the play yard. He's tempted to ask Vicky whether the girl is still enrolled and whether she is there today. But what would be his reason? Any question would pique Vicky's curiosity. He drops the idea, hoping his luck continues to hold.

Vicky is fine with his timetable. "See ya dreckly," she sings.

Dan packs up at 3:15 and heads to his car. He considers putting down the top. It's warm enough. The long drive down from the clinic in San Luis to the southern edge of the county will leave him wind-blown. Better idea for the return. He pictures himself flying under a sky of clouds.

When he enters the parking lot at the preschool, young children are running between an oversized sandbox and an oak offering generous shade at the back of the play yard. He doesn't spot Manny or the young red-headed girl who's visited him in dreams three times this week. Grabbing a folder of notes, he navigates a wobbly gate, making sure not to pull the hinge loose, and walks to the director's office.

Inside Vicky wears a welcoming smile. This time, instead of a Cornish greeting, she offers her hand. Dan smiles in return, wondering if someone's complained about her native expressions. It feels too formal for him.

"Dan. Please, it's Dan," he says when she calls him by his title.

She pats a file folder on top of the counter, wanting him to see she's prepared the staff notes on their interactions with Manny.

He thanks her and says he'll look them over after he watches Manny. He wants to observe without any expectations.

"Well, he's at the clay table," Vicky says. "Least I think so."

"How are your kids? One's in first and one's in – third, is it?"

Vicky appreciates his inquiry and gives him a rundown. "Champion speller, she is. He likes kicking things, so we've got him in football year-round. Soccer, I should say." Her grinding "r" leaves him picturing kids in pirate costumes chasing each other's long, bouncing shots at the net.

"How about you? Any plans for Europe?"

Dan is surprised she's remembered his trip. Their trip. Brynn's half-trip and his round-trip. Vicky expressed disappointment they hadn't passed through London, as it would have been "easy as pie" to take a train out to Cornwall.

"Nope, nothing for now," he replies, checking her eyes, then glancing at the floor.

She smiles, taking care not to say more.

When he looks up, he says, "May is great for that area, am I remembering that correctly? Maybe I'll take some time and go exploring on my own next spring."

"Oh, that would be just right. You'd be a happy feller there. You let me know and I'll connect you with some folks. Best cider you'll ever taste, too."

He smiles, struck by the way some women grasp the shape of things with so little effort. He wonders if Vicky grew up with a younger brother. For a moment he wishes he wasn't an only child.

"I better peek in on Manny," he says, excusing himself.

Kids wander in and out of the playroom, some hurrying to use the bathroom. Manny stays focused on the clay. He's rolling long noodles and dangling them from his finger, like stretchy worms. Some of the children stare at Dan as they walk by. He can't find Emma Robinson; none of the young girls resembles her. He makes notes, hoping Manny will tire of the clay and head out to the busier playground. He starts to form a plan in case Manny stays in place.

Luck swings his way again. One of the teachers comes to Manny and asks if he's finished with the clay. "There's lots to see outside today, Manny," she says. Dan nods to himself – this is one of the suggestions he's offered to help encourage Manny to try a variety of activities. The teacher glances at him and says, "That would work?" They haven't been introduced, but she recognizes him as Manny's psychologist. "Yes, no problem," Dan assures her.

He stands and stretches, giving Manny and the teacher some time to make their way outside without him overlooking. A collection of bird drawings pinned to the bulletin board catches his eye. Dan surveys the names and finds "Emmy" on a wide-winged bird filled in with vivid shades of pink, lavender and gold.

When he gets outside he scans the play yard. Manny and the teacher head to a swing. Running ahead of her peers, a little girl with striking red hair races toward the sandbox and bunny hops in.

Dan stays close to the fence protecting the children from the parking lot. He remains standing, knees wobbly, as if he's forgotten to eat lunch. Manny squeals in delight on the swing. Dan makes a mental note, then shifts to the young girl who's been occupying his mind since his talk at the university and his encounter with Suzanne Verdin.

As she spin-turns in the sand, getting ready to run back to the towering oak tree, Emma pauses to study him. He's taken aback at how the sun highlights her hair exactly as it did the day he sat talking with Suzanne. What is their hair color? It has too much sheen to call it rust-red. Is it auburn or mahogany? He conjures Suzanne approaching him in the lecture hall. Brick red? Red ochre? The color is a pigment rich in iron oxides, pushed from deep in the earth. Arizona canyons. Tuscan hillsides. Terra-cotta absorbed and transformed, somehow, at a genetic level. An ancient color on such a young face. That is the red-brown shade Suzanne and her daughter share. He sees no hint of maternal freckles. The little girl's glance lingers just as in his fractured dreams: "Here I am."

Twenty minutes pass as he tries to keep his focus on Manny, not Emma. Dan pulls out his notepad and forces himself to write descriptive phrases for Manny's behavior. Twice Manny initiates contact with another child; Dan underlines "initiates." Breaking from his note-taking, he discovers Emma perched on a low branch at the oak tree. She watches him, then wiggles sideways a little further out.

He replays his memories of the Robinsons. The father's features return more clearly than the mother's. She held back during his observations, taking care not to seem dominating. They were about his age – a year or two younger, in fact. She was applying to a marine biology graduate program at UC Santa Barbara. Dan has checked some online records. Their address is still in the southern part of the county, where it is easier to make that commute. If he saw them by chance, would they recognize him? Would they want him to acknowledge their shared history? He wonders which of them drops off Emma and who picks her up. Would they stop by the preschool unannounced?

At 4:40 Dan decides to check the staff notes. Vicky insists that he sit at her desk. She opens the file folder with the staff's observations. For a few minutes he busies himself copying key moments from their daily notes. Manny greets the chickens in the yard. At snack, Manny offers a carrot to a classmate. Manny insists on completing the same puzzle three times in a row. Dan sorts through several pages until his eyes wander to Vicky's desktop. A folder marked "School Photographs" sits at the corner of her desk. He closes the observation notes.

"Are these current photos of the kids?" Vicky is filing paperwork on the other side of the room.

"Yes, we did those last week. The photographer took them out at the Mother Tree. The kids look so cute. Take a peek."

Dan opens the folder and finds a dozen or so pages of photos, each with two children's portraits. Under each photo, a hand-written name and birthdate. Manny's picture is on the third page. The photographer's caught him with an excited smile. Flipping two more pages, he sees the little girl's photograph at the top of the page. "Emmy Robinson, 3-7-13." The seven holds that ornamental British slash through it in Vicky's handwriting. The birthdate catches him. It's exactly as he's remembered – March 7th. One day after his father's death in that shadowy prehistoric year. Dan closes the folder, the flickering visage of the girl in his dreams captured in a school portrait.

"Manny looks happy," he says to Vicky. "What a champ."

She brags about him for a minute, eager to convince the psychologist that her pupil is not a problem. "Such a sweet-art," she tells him in her sailor's lilt.

"We'll cover it all at the next parent conference," Dan says. "This will be a huge help. And thanks for the last-minute accommodation today. I appreciate the flexibility."

He heads to his car, taking one last over-the-shoulder glance at the kids on the playground. He closes the loose gate with too much force and has to wiggle the top hinge back in place. At his car, he decides to put the top down and drive home along Highway 1 to catch the sea breeze. Dan pulls off his tie, starts up the Miata and pulls away from the preschool.

At Shell Beach he turns down to the oceanfront to change his shirt and enjoy the waves for a few minutes. The visit to the preschool leaves him in a swirl. He considers the thrill of seeing Emma Robinson in person. When he thinks of Emma, Suzanne Verdin's face appears – and vice versa. Too many scenarios and possibilities rush through his mind. He decides he'll head into San Luis for Farmer's Market, get a bite to eat, and drift in the crowd for a while. Things will get clearer if he gives it a little time.

Behind the seat he's got a Portland Sea Dogs baseball jersey from the guys back in Maine. It's a joke for them. Lemair and Stevens, his teammates at Dartmouth, both ended up on the Maine coast after school. Dante Stevens works at the Allagash brewery. Kevin Lemair gave up a chance at med school to work with his dad on the Portland ferries. Though none of them are huge baseball fans, the Sea Dogs are the Red Sox AA farm team. The three friends spent a memorable night together at a game when Dan visited in June. He wears the jersey with pride, though on the West Coast people only know the Portland north of them. He's shipped his buddies shirts from the San Luis Blues, the local summer college team. In the photo they sent him, Kev and Dante mug like the Blues Brothers, Jake and Elwood, the inspiration for the team's mascot – a baseball tricked out in fedora and shades. Dan changes into the jersey and takes time for a long draw of ocean air.

...

By the time he parks and makes his way over to Higuera Street and Farmer's Market, most of the shoppers have bagged their produce and slipped away. Tourists, parents of college students, and local families with strollers amble up and down the street. Though Dan might see a familiar face or two at the market, it would be unusual for him to run into many people he knows. Brynn would encounter a friend in the first block. She liked Farmer's and sometimes met girlfriends there before rendezvousing with him for the evening. She and the girlfriends tended to hang out at Amsterdam Fine Coffee because, she told him, the coffee actually was damn fine coffee, as advertised. He felt unsure about the cafe's hipster appeal, enough that he'd never been inside. It was Brynn's place before their life as a couple – something kept it hers in his mind.

At one of the food stands he orders a burrito bowl with carnitas and chooses a place along the curb to sit. In a nearby intersection, blocked off for pedestrians, a juggler tosses bowling pins in exaggerated arcs, feigning loss of control and threatening to bonk the delighted kids who crouch in front of him. People surge by in a natural cadence, as if someone's choreographed the steps and dodges that keep it all working.

Children secured in strollers lock eyes with Dan – he's almost the only thing at their level. He's fascinated by how long they hold his gaze. Once, and then again, he offers a little wave. Another time, he flashes his eyebrows in surprise, trying to elicit a grin. Their chubby faces – little moons crossing his plane of orbit – remain unperturbed, satisfied to observe him. What is he, other than a stranger? They watch so carefully. Are they searching their memories for a clue that he might be known to them? Would they trust him if he came closer – or would some deep uncertainty trigger a protest? Again, he sees Baby Girl V.'s clear eyes and the cheery young girl at the preschool. A rumbling at the back of his mind intrudes. He breaks his gaze with the babies to dispel the stampeding goblins of his night anxieties.

After a while Dan rejoins the crowd in its wandering. Music emanates from the lower end of Higuera. A young couple sings in minor-key harmony, he on a shiny resonator guitar, she in a fringed vest. Dan stays off to one side, trying to appreciate their song. The guys cooking outside McClintocks bark and whoop every time they flip their racks of half chickens and beef ribs. Smoke from the open barbecue wagon swirls around the street, stinging Dan's eyes. He blinks, looks across the street and finds Amsterdam Fine Coffee.

Moving toward the entrance gets him out of the smoke's reach. The yelling of the barbecue mongers does not abate. He studies the coffee shop and considers going in. He's got his hand-sized sketchbook in his back pocket. The Book of Chairs. After a one-time Saturday drawing class at the community college, Dan picked up the pocket-sized notebook, determined to develop his drawing ability. In the class he spent the better part of an hour trying to decipher the geometry of Van Gogh's chair – without the pipe. The breakthrough came when the instructor revealed the trick of which legs to start with. He's got three versions of Van Gogh's chair as the inaugural pages of The Book of Chairs. Back in Walpole he drew his mother's Shaker rocker, as well as a kitchen ladder-rail chair and one of the Adirondack chairs out back. Since then, a few more, though he hasn't been consistent. He's not sure why he's drawn to chairs, though he can find a trace of personality in each. His swiveling, ergonomic office chair confused him and ended up resembling a robot. Once in a while he's sketched in coffee shops, as they often have appealing chairs. What catches his eye at Amsterdam is that the chairs are a deliberate mixture of styles. When he spies beer taps behind the counter, he walks in and orders a Negra Modelo.

Two sips into his beer, he selects a chair across the room and begins to focus. The high-back Windsor's slats taper to mere spindles at the top and bottom, causing them to appear to float. The chair's arms bend playfully, while the legs hold a slight flare. Dan is surprised he's selected it because he's observing it from behind. This is the first time he's tried to draw a chair from that perspective. The chilled beer knocks away the cobwebs in his mind. He zeroes in on the lines and angles before him.

Fortunately, no one sits in the chair. The afternoon shifts into evening as the after-work coffee drinkers disperse. A few students, heads in their laptops, sit at the edges of the room. As he draws the finishing curves of the chair's broad head rest, soft piano notes arrive from the other side of the coffee shop. From where he sits Dan cannot see the person playing. A chalkboard announces, "Music at 7." Someone's drawn a small red flower in the bottom corner of the slate.

A stream of notes permeates the room and rises toward the ceiling, where table lamps hang upside down – artful decorations, yet fully functional. Daylight is fading, and the lamps offer an agreeable amber glow. The slow and careful pace of the instrumental being played fascinates Dan. The notes, three at a time and syncopated, pull at him. Unexpected pauses interrupt the melody, then it continues on its way. It's in a major key, sounding sweet and child-like, yet it expresses some weightier, concealed feeling.

The music eddies around Dan, sweeping him out of the cafe. He pictures Brynn stretched out on the bone white sand at Malmö, then cuts to his solo runs toward Morro Rock. He fights a swell of emotion. The notes pour over a waterfall. A moment of hope emerges as three quiet chords rise. Then the quaking melody repeats.

He sits back in his chair, placing his drawing pen in the open spine of the sketchbook, trying to keep it steady. He admits some sadness or disorientation over Brynn's decision. It's been painful – he hasn't hidden from that. But it hasn't left him depressed. Overall, life glides on in routines that keep him grounded and moments that hint at new horizons. They decided to take a break. Sure, that's the safe road to a break-up. Dan doesn't hold any illusions about that. To each of their credit it wasn't an awful parting. They exchanged a few emails, then stopped. The change is good for Brynn – necessary – he's got no doubt about that. You can't know what's down the road. The extraordinary piano melody brings his entire post-Brynn self into question. For the first time he wonders if he is mourning. The word surprises him. How many times has he seen clients mourning a loss? How many times has he gently tried to raise the topic with them? How often has he drawn on the concept to explain puzzling behaviors? And yet, a heart-breaking, tender refrain by itself pierces his shield.

Dan shakes off the momentary jolt. He wants to see who is playing the piece. He stands and walks slowly around the coffee bar, aiming toward an alcove off the main room. A few feet from the alcove he stops in his tracks. A young woman sits at a portable digital keyboard.

Her hands press the last gentle notes of the song. The shocking hue of her hair – a rich blend of brown and red – sends an alarming shiver through his body.

When the melody ends, a whisper of applause comes from a corner of the room. Suzanne Verdin turns her head to the left, offering a quiet "Thank you." She glances up at the shadowy man standing nearby and makes eye contact. For a second, time locks itself; the planet skips a beat in its rotation. Suzanne stands abruptly, knocking the keyboard forward. She looks at him again, her face blanching, then erupting in a sudden blush. Before he can say a word, before he can steady himself against the alcove wall, Suzanne rushes off to the kitchen at the back of the coffee shop.

...

Back at his table, Dan places the heels of his hands on the surface and centers his attention on what is happening. The day spins out of control. He wants to get up and leave. In the moment after Suzanne stood and hurried off, Dan looked around, acutely self-conscious. Not a soul noticed their encounter. He stared at the glowing buttons on the keyboard, convincing himself that what he'd seen was real.

Dan considers walking back toward the kitchen to see if she's upset. If he leaves, what does that suggest? The whole situation puzzles him. He replays his walk down the street, his bowl of food, the smoke and the sharp calls of the food barkers. How did he get here? What spooky force pulled him to this moment? He thinks back to his visit at the preschool, to young Emma's face. How could the timing be such? For the next minute all he can do is to sit and blink, haunted by the notes of the song she played.

Suzanne emerges from the kitchen. Dan takes a breath as she approaches. She walks to his table and pauses. He considers standing, but doesn't trust himself to be steady on his feet. He waits for her, but can't stop from saying, "Hi."

"I'm sorry about back there," she says, tilting her head toward the alcove.

"No, no, I'm sorry I surprised you. I didn't..."

"I didn't expect to see anyone. Anyone I know."

He lets out a small embarrassed laugh. "Me either. I was just having a beer..."

"You didn't know it was me?"

"Not until I walked over. The music, it was beautiful. I was swept away by it." He catches himself and says, "Here. Would you like to sit? Do you have a minute?"

"I work here," Suzanne tells him.

"Oh, oh. Right. I don't mean to interrupt." He reaches for his pen and closes his sketchbook, aware of being the outsider. "I should be taking off."

"No, it's okay. I shouldn't have run off. Bad habit."

Something in her face prompts Dan to ask her again to join him. She sits in the chair opposite his.

"How long have you worked here?" He watches her take a deep breath and a long exhale through her nostrils. She's practiced her breathing but doesn't want it to be noticed.

"Since sophomore year. About two years. Sometimes it feels like a second home." She adds, "I haven't seen you here before."

Something clicks in Dan's mind and he downshifts into psychologist mode. He pictures Brynn laughing with her girlfriends. Could Suzanne have met her? He falls into a kaleidoscopic tunnel seeing Brynn's face, Suzanne's and little Emma's, repeated in geometric patterns. What the hell? Do these odd connections have something to do with Brynn? It doesn't feel right to ask Suzanne about Brynn. He sits back in his chair and scrutinizes her face. Her incredible mask of freckles. The eyes – hints of an owl. For a moment the confluence of the day's events alarms him. Then another switch throws itself and he takes a sharp breath. Jesus, man. She's the one who's freaked out. You look like a creepy stalker.

"You know, I came in for a beer. The smoke outside, and the noise. I haven't been in here before." He indicates his sketchbook. "I was drawing a chair."

She glances at his sketchbook before examining his face.

"I had no idea you worked here, Suzanne. Or that you were going to play. Honest. I'm sorry if it feels odd. I'm a little thrown off by that myself."

She gazes at him with such focus that he has to resist an urge to stand and leave. What's peculiar is that her stare doesn't intimidate him. It's like she's trying to read his face. Then he laughs to himself. It's therapist face. She's doing what he does with clients. A calm, attentive gaze. Patience. Acceptance. Permission to open. That's it – she's been in therapy. Of course. The breathing too. She's also caught a detail of something behind his shield. He can't dismiss the thought that she might know about Brynn. He double-checks his memory for a time he was here with Brynn. Some afternoon he met her? A hug or a kiss? He comes up empty. He's sure he's never seen the shop's murals and quirky decor from the interior.

"You were drawing a chair?"

Her question puts him at ease. He nods and lets out a quick laugh at the eccentricity of his admission.

"The Book of Chairs." He pushes the sketchbook forward. Suzanne waits a half note beat, then reaches and turns it around, opening to the first page.

"I'm not even a rookie," he explains. He points to the first drawing. "I took a one-time class and got fascinated with Van Gogh's chair."

Suzanne turns to the second and third pages, pausing to assess the progress in his images. She flips forward to his most recent drawing, the coffee shop's armchair from behind. She studies it for a moment, then looks over her left shoulder, finding the subject. When she turns back to his sketch, she says, "Not bad. I recognized it."

Dan reaches across the table and flips a few pages with his index finger. "This is the one I'm happiest with. A rocker at my mother's house."

Suzanne examines the sketch. She reads his caption aloud. "Shaker Shawl Back Rocker, Walpole."

"Walpole, New Hampshire. Tiny little place, you know, New England quaint. I grew up there."

She hesitates, then says, "I can't picture my mother in a rocker. Way too much nervous energy." She steals a glance out the shop's front window and makes a semi-exasperated face to Dan.

"I remember your parents' involvement in your case. I didn't meet them, but the background notes – I had the impression they held a lot of strong feelings."

Suzanne takes a more obvious breath. "Yes, very strong. They're still that way. They got involved in some grandparents' rights groups afterward. My mom's way out there. It's ridiculous because they have no legal rights. They never did. They think of it like custody after a divorce. No one could convince them the laws on adoption are different. They're a little alternative – kind of skeptical about the system. Some of it is religious. A mix of Old Testament stuff and nature beliefs. My mother was actually in some kind of hippie group when she was a kid. Like a commune? Or a group of families. Something like that. It was up in Big Sur. It all fell apart when she was 9 or 10. I think she loved it there. She doesn't like modern society. Way too worldly for her. She works in a thrift shop, which is perfect – she'd live in the past if she had her way. My father isn't quite as extreme. They're different than most people."

"They're around here?"

Suzanne glances toward the front windows and laughs to herself. "Yes. They may be out there tonight."

"At Farmer's Market?"

"They say they like the produce, but really they like keeping an eye on me. You wouldn't believe how often I run into them, out of nowhere. It's a little spooky. If they knew anything about technology I'd wonder if they were tracking me. They live down in the south county. In San Luis we have a truce. They stay away from this block. Sometimes they wear their grandparent buttons. My mother had these oversized buttons made: Ask Me About Grandparents' Rights. She makes my dad wear one too. People stop and talk to them about it. Who knows what they say? I'm sure people run the other way once they get wound up."

Suzanne twists her mouth and gives a little shrug.

"Small town," Dan says. "It must feel a little crowded at times."

"They do keep track of me. Mostly my mom. I remember when I was little, whenever I would try to do something she'd put her hand on my shoulder – sometimes both hands. Even if we were out walking – you know, around other people. She thought she was helping me or encouraging me or supporting me. My brother and sister were smart enough to move away, so I get all their attention now. That and…"

He waits before saying, "Do they bring up the adoption to you?"

"Not any more. I won't listen. Everything's been said. We're kind of at a draw on it all."

He notes a slight waver in Suzanne's voice. He remembers that when they spoke after his presentation she began to say something about her parents before breaking off. He resists the urge to probe, shifting in his chair.

"I have a mother who keeps a close watch on things too."

She smiles. "Is she in this county?"

He shrugs to acknowledge her point. "Well, no. She has clairvoyance or something. Maternal omniscience. I haven't considered whether she might be tracking me."

Suzanne says, "Your father too?"

He presses his lips. "He's not alive. He died a little before my birth. He was a game warden and was killed in an accident."

"Oh, I'm sorry."

"Thanks. It's a strange feeling to know of him – his existence – and not know him. He's a ghost, in a way. A good ghost."

Right away Dan sees his slip. The reaction on her face shows him she's drawn her own parallel. She, the childless mother. They tumble into an awkward thicket and Dan can't find a path out.

Suzanne says, "I understand about good ghosts. It's strange how much an unseen person…their spirit or their essence…is that the word? The fact of their existence and how much it can affect you."

Her words force him to measure the loss of his father in a different light. He understands the sorrow of wanting to feel the presence of a person who's gone forever. Now he senses the shock of a loss when that person is not gone. Her loss. He swallows.

Suzanne tilts her head and says, "My father's a handyman. And a minister in a fairly obscure church. He and my mother might be the only members."

Dan smiles at her remark.

"I'm not sure the church is real. He baptized us in a hot spring up in Big Sur when we were kids. They still have a trailer up there. Are there religions that allow that?"

"I'm pretty sure there are. Good fit for Big Sur."

She shrugs, then turns serious. "My mother blames you for the judge's decision. They're both suspicious of psychology and counseling. It's all mind control, in their way of thinking."

Dan checks her eyes. "You don't seem to look at it that way – counseling."

Suzanne agrees. "I like to think I'm truly different from them. I hope I am. I'm a bit of a dreamer like my father." She glances around. "I should probably get back to the kitchen."

"Of course. I should be on my way too."

They stand, facing each other on opposite sides of the small table. She checks the logo on his shirt and cocks her head.

"Portland Sea Dogs. They're not connected to the Seahawks?"

"No, that's Seattle."

"Oh, right. And this is baseball?"

"Yes. A minor league team back East. Some college buddies live there. The other Portland."

"Maine."

Her reply pleases him.

In a soft voice, Suzanne says, "Thanks for letting me see your chairs."

Dan returns a self-conscious smile, embarrassed by the intimate tone of her comment. "It was good talking again. And I really enjoyed the piece you played. I'm sorry I startled you. I was startled myself."

"It's okay," she says.

"What was that called? Is it something you composed?"

Her face lights up. "No, no. It's by someone called Goldmund. I don't think that's his real name. It's a piece I love. It's called, 'Threnody.'"

He blinks twice, activated by a hint of anguish in her voice. "I'll look for it. It was beautiful. A little haunting, but appealing. I see why you like it so much."

Suzanne scans his face, again with a composed gaze. He hasn't seen her take the settling breath this time. Her sea of freckles swells and recedes. He detects a faint warmth to her cheeks. Or is it light reflected from her hair?

She says, "It means 'lament.'"

Chapter Five

"OH MY GOD!" MAGGIE JUMPS BACK from the garden row, tripping on her Mexican sandals. She panics at how close she's come to stepping on the snake. It coils back in an angry posture, hissing. Dark splotchy diamonds ripple down the length of its body.

"Andrew!"

She takes a few backward steps, turning to check that her escape path is clear. She runs toward the kitchen door. Inside, Maggie plants her feet to steady herself. "Oh my god. Oh my god!" She reaches to the cabinet above the refrigerator. The revolver lies on its side.

Maggie seizes the gun and grips it with two hands. She knows how to shoot. She's made her husband teach her. From childhood she's held an outsized fear of snakes. The unnatural smoothness of their scales and their squirming, legless locomotion revolts her. She checks the shells in the cylinder. The gun holds snake shot for this moment.

The stubby barrel of the gun gives Maggie pause. But she recalls the gun's powerful crack. Andrew assured her it would be fine for snakes or rats. She's fired at targets and cans up on Westhauser Ridge at the trailer. If she's four or five feet away – about as long as her shadow in the early morning – she can hit her mark.

Maggie heads back outside, moving with great care toward the sprawling zucchini vines that shelter the snake.

"Andrew! Andrew!"

She takes tentative steps into the garden row and rediscovers the waiting reptile. Using two hands, she aims the revolver at the center of its head. It coils again, writhing and spitting its tongue.

"Hey, hey, what's going on?" comes the voice from behind her.

"It's a rattlesnake, Andrew. There!"

"Okay, Maggie. Step back. Here." He reaches along her forearm and guides her backward. He doesn't want the gun to go off and he doesn't want her to turn. "Let me take that."

The snake hisses again and Maggie grunts in disgust. She releases the handgun to her husband.

"Shoot it, Andrew. Just shoot it!"

"Hold on."

Mac inches forward, towering over the snake. He leans closer to study the snake's patterns and colors.

"Shoot it and get back, Andrew. Don't let it bite you!"

"I got it, Maggie. Here, let's step back." Keeping the gun pointed in the direction of the snake, he puts his free arm around his wife's shoulder. They take several steps backward. At the edge of the garden, Mac says, "Stay here."

He pockets the gun and picks up a pointed tip shovel with a long wooden handle and moves toward the snake.

She says, "Andrew!" as if he's disobeyed her.

"I don't think that's a rattler, Maggie."

He gets close enough to poke at the snake. It coils again, then begins to slither across the garden row.

"Look, Maggie. That's a gopher snake. See how the head's rounded? Look how slender this guy is. Rattlers are fat. See the tail? No rattles. That's a gopher snake. I don't think we'll come across a rattler here. Up on the ridge, maybe. More likely up there."

"It's hissing!" she says.

"Well, you kind of scared him. He's more scared of you, believe me."

"I can't tell the difference. I don't want to see any snakes. Stop poking it, you'll make it mad."

Mac whacks the ground and wiggles some vines, sending the snake away. He surveys the rows of the garden, feeling content that he's solved the problem. Before he can turn back to Maggie something catches his eye. Halfway down the row of zucchini plants movement stirs a mound of dirt. He focuses. Again, the ground trembles.

Mac takes three slow and deliberate steps, placing his work boots like cat's paws. He raises the shovel with two hands, its blade and tip pointed inward and down. When the dirt shifts for the third time he drives the blade into the ground, yanks it out and thrusts it twice more. When he sees no further movement, he flips the shovel blade and digs in again, this time turning over a heavy clod of soil. He swings the shovel load toward Maggie, for her inspection. Streamlets of dark soil trickle off, revealing the mangled body of a gopher.

Maggie issues a sickened, "Ugh!" at the sight of the gopher's inert head and its yellowed pair of teeth. "Andrew, get it away!"

Mac grins, testing the weight of his kill by bobbing the shovel up and down. "There's the hombre who's been tormenting us." He beams at his triumph, eager for Maggie's approval.

"Ugh, no," she says, holding up her left hand.

"Okay, he's gone." Mac turns and walks toward the compost pile.

Returning, he pulls the revolver from his pocket. "Were you really going to shoot this thing?" He examines the gun, pleased to find it loaded and ready, as he left it.

"Yes! Didn't you hear me calling you? Where were you?"

"I heard you. I was half under the truck."

Maggie mutters something.

"Wear your mud boots in the garden," he says, nodding to her exposed feet. "It'll feel better if that old guy surprises you again."

"No snakes. I don't care if they eat the gophers."

Mac shrugs. He heads to the house to return the revolver to the kitchen cabinet. He reminds himself not to forget it next time they drive up to the trailer. Stopping for a glass of water at the sink, he considers the afternoon. It's no more than a fifty-fifty proposition that the woman from Cambria with the rotted porch rails will call back. She hesitated, probably over his inability to give her a firm estimate without seeing the damage. Mac decides not to fret about it. He finishes his drink and alerts to a familiar sound outside. When he looks out, Maggie is folded on a plastic chair, weeping into her hands.

"Hey, what's going on? Maggie? It's over. The snake's gone."

"It's not the snake," she growls. "I'm upset!"

Mac closes his mouth.

"I don't understand why she doesn't try to get some custody. Visitation! She should have some type of visitation. It's not right, Andrew! It's not right for that baby."

Mac sighs. "I know."

"No!" she says, yanking her hand away from his.

"That's not something we can control, Maggie. We've been through all that. Suzy won't do it."

Maggie throws him a bitter stare.

He says, "That's not to say she won't try someday. People's hearts change over time. God takes his time – we can't rush that."

"Oh!" Maggie says, sputtering, unable to articulate more.

"It won't always be like this," he says.

"Oh, and why not? That baby might not be baptized, Andrew. What about that? Is that what Mr. Tyrant God wants? I don't think so!"

"Maggie…"

"What would be wrong with a day of visitation? She's her mother, Andrew. We're her grandparents! Grandparents have rights. It's natural. One day a month. We could go to a park for a picnic. How would that hurt her? Why are people so selfish? You can't own children – they aren't yours to own!"

"That could happen someday, Maggie. It can happen. That might be exactly what God has in mind. Maybe when she's a little older. She'll want to meet us someday. She'll be curious. We can help her get baptized. All of that can happen, Maggie."

"Suzy won't try. She's weak."

Mac grimaces. He wants to speak, but censors himself.

"She doesn't care. She's selfish. We spoiled her, Andrew. I did. I fed her whenever she cried. I got up every night! I don't know how it happened, but she's so full of herself. The mirrors! Remember how she would spend half the afternoon looking at herself in the mirrors. Making faces and braiding her hair. Why? How did she get that vain? She only cares about herself! We didn't teach her that."

"Maggie, you're working yourself up."

"No, I'm not. This is the rotten truth. We spoiled her. She only cares about her hair and school and whatever it is she wants to do. She has a baby! How can she ignore that she's the mother of a baby?"

"She's growing up, Maggie. Things might change."

"Don't tell me!" his wife shouts. "Don't tell me, God!" She jabs her index finger at the sky, ignoring her husband. "Don't you tell me to be patient! Don't tell me to wait! You're a tyrant! Why? Why! Why!"

•••

Dan stops back at the clinic to stow some files before heading home. A challenging afternoon of meetings with distressed and bitter parents leaves him drained. People concerned the schools aren't doing enough to accommodate their children's needs. Desperate for an ally and convinced a battle is the only way to win. He sighs at the pain and fatigue creasing their faces, wishing he could offer some relief. A cold beer at home beckons.

TJ calls a greeting as Dan walks by. He brakes and pops his head in her doorway.

"I took a call for you earlier," she says. "I covered while the staff had their meeting. She might have been a client? She asked for you by name. Younger – college student? She didn't want to leave a message or her name. Something was on her mind."

He twists his mouth.

"She had an interesting way of pausing between thoughts. Long pauses."

Dan says, "Aha. Yes, I think I know who that is."

TJ tilts her head slightly. "She sounded okay. I didn't detect a crisis. You know, she didn't sound high or anything like that."

"A little dreamy?"

"That could be it."

He affirms her observation with a nod.

"She didn't leave a number. I told her early afternoons might be the best time to catch you."

"That's great, TJ. Thanks for the head's up." To show he's not off balance, he adds, "How's married life?"

She gives him a thumbs up and grins. "Recommended."

"I'll file that away in case I ever, you know, become a lesbian."

"Hey, no feeling sorry for yourself."

He tips his head in a bow, accepting her reprimand. In an abrupt shift, his mind steers to another thought.

"TJ, do you have pronoun preferences?"

"Yes. She/her." Her smile holds a mix of surprise and pleasure. "Thanks for asking that, Dan."

"My mother the judge," he replies.

TJ raises her eyebrows, saying mama knows best.

Dan shrugs as he heads to his office. Stepping inside, he closes the door with two hands to avoid a noise that might reveal frustration or worse. He drops into his chair and spins like a roulette wheel. His discontent hangs in the room. This is the call from Suzanne he's been hoping for. He bites his lip. Maybe she calls back tomorrow. That he's missed the opportunity to ask if they can meet again bothers him. The vexing part is that she didn't leave a number, so he's back to waiting.

But the day's almost over. He doesn't want to drive home and try to forget about it again. Sitting up to the computer, he implements his backup plan and fires off an email to Margaret Becker, the psychology

61

instructor. He could stop by her house after dinner and ask in person, but he's feeling too impatient for that.

Dan bends the truth, telling Margaret he promised some information to a student and misplaced the email address. Would she be able to send it? "Her name was Suzanne Verdin. I think her email might be sverdin, but I wanted to confirm it." Then he adds, "Thanks, Margaret." Dan reads his email twice and sends it with a hard click.

When it occurs to him that he's going to have to head home and forget about it for a little while, despite the backup plan, he shakes his head. Crappy day, he thinks – no way around it.

The email notifying sound whoops before he can stand up.

"Dan, I don't have a Suzanne Verdin. But she's in the campus directory. smverdin. cheers – M."

He writes back immediately. "Thanks a bunch. She's not enrolled in your class?" Whoosh.

The response flies back in a moment. "Nope. Someone's roommate or girlfriend? I get that sometimes."

He types, "Must be," and thanks her again.

Dan stands up at his desk and says, "What the fuck, Suzanne? What the actual fuck is going on?" The goblins of the night rise up laughing.

...

She paces back and forth between her couch, where she tells herself to sit down and put her feet up, and the kitchen table, where she has a tablet and pen. Nancy is cooking and whistling next door, thank god. Creepy Jeff has already knocked on her door once, raving about a Netflix series with children who've gone missing in a cave system that holds time-travel portals. She digs her nails into her palms to keep from screaming at him. He accepts her lie about homework, and adds, "I'll check back later!"

The yellow tablet holds the list of crimes she must confess to Daniel Tunbridge – Dr. Daniel Tunbridge. Nothing sounds right – his title, his last name or his first name. She doesn't know what to call him. It doesn't matter. She has to clear everything away. She wants to shrink him. The call to his office was a disaster. She sounded like a lost sheep.

She has to get it on paper. So, she shifts back to "I" statements and reminds herself she can control those. I looked you up on the web. I know you went to school in Denver and at UCLA. I found your graduation at Dartmouth. Phi Beta Kappa. I know you played ice hockey for Dartmouth. You scored a goal that beat Harvard. You were in something called the student assembly. I knew you came from Walpole before you told me. I'm not in the psychology class. I saw your talk listed on another student's syllabus and wanted to see your face. I wanted to hear your ideas about adoption. I wanted you to see my face. I knew you liked beer before you came to Amsterdam.

Suzanne squeezes her eyes tight and swallows.

I know you have a friend named Brynn.

I haven't told you any lies.

I'm sorry.

I won't bother you again.

I'm not here. Invisible. Invisible.

•••

It's late when Suzanne rouses from the nap she hasn't realized she's taken. Annie Fisher curls next to her on the couch. Her laptop has beeped. Now the phone quivers on her coffee table. An email. The header reads, "Dan Tunbridge." She's shocked to the point that all she can think to do is turn the phone over. On the laptop the same name pops out at the top of her emails. She snaps it closed.

When she's collected herself, she sits at the kitchen table, her list beside the laptop. A mug of lemon honey water rests to the left of the laptop, radiating warmth. This is not the way she wants to do it, but this is the way it will be done.

Suzanne expects something long and complicated. His analysis of her. A recommendation that she get help. A warning to the court, to her parents, to anyone who might know her. She finds something else.

"Hi Suzanne – I got your email from the campus directory. I'm wondering if we could talk again. It would help me. I've got a couple of things on my mind. I'd be more than happy to listen to anything on your mind. It feels like we've got slightly crossed signals? If you're open, give me a call on my cell – evenings or weekends are fine. If you prefer, let me know your number and I'll call. Nothing weird, I promise." He ends with, "Dan Tunbridge" and his number.

Suzanne closes her eyes for a moment and calibrates her breathing. She checks the time on her laptop: 9:17 p.m. She takes a sip of lemon water from her mug. Her cheeks flush at the risk but she pushes ahead with her impulse. Picking up her phone, she taps out the numbers.

After the third ring, a voice says, "Hi, it's Dan."

"Hi. This is Suzanne Verdin."

"Hi, Suzanne."

She hears a surprised breath.

"Thanks for calling. I wasn't expecting that. I mean, tonight."

She grimaces at his words. "It's not too late? I meant to leave my number when I called your office. I got a little flustered."

"No problem. Somehow it worked."

She waits.

"I hope you don't mind that I tracked down your email, Suzanne. I wasn't sure what else made sense. I thought about leaving a note at Amsterdam, but that seemed a little too…"

"Yes, it's fine," Suzanne says. "I was going to call tomorrow." She worries he might hear that as a mild rebuke or a complaint. "This is better," she adds. "I won't have to think about it all night."

He takes another breath and says, "It feels like we've been talking around some things, but not talking directly? I'm not trying to be a therapist here. And I'm not trying to be overly friendly or personal. I promise. I'm just unsure about what you might be thinking. I felt a little unresolved about our conversation about the adoption. Your question about fairness. It feels like we should talk about that."

"Yes," she answers right away. "I need to say some things. I need to apologize for some things."

"We keep startling each other," he says.

She says, "Yes. I – I don't…Sorry. I'm a little nervous."

"Me too. I get it."

Her words spill out. "We could go to lunch." Silence reigns long enough that she squeezes her eyes as tight as fists.

"Lunch would be perfect," he says after the excruciating pause. "That's excellent. The phone feels awkward. So much better in person."

"Yes. In person is tricky for me, but I do a little better. I don't like holding the phone. I'm not sure why."

He says, "I get that. It's a weird device."

They begin to explore possibilities for lunch. He asks if she likes fish tacos. She does. He mentions a small place near the beach at San Simeon. She's surprised at the distance, but warms to the idea right away. They decide on Saturday afternoon. He asks if she'd prefer to drive. She likes that he's given her a choice. He says, "I do have a convertible." She laughs and says she does not. He wonders about

Annie Fisher. Suzanne says she'll be fine at her apartment, then adds, "It would be okay if I brought her?"

"I'm sure we'd fit," Dan says. "As long as she doesn't mind the wind."

"Oh, she wouldn't mind," Suzanne replies.

When they settle on the details, Suzanne explains that she might need to bring some notes. She has some things to tell him and doesn't want to forget anything.

"Sure," he laughs. "I'll be winging it, so bring whatever you need."

"Well, I might not need them. No, I will."

The phone call is winding down when he says, "Suzanne, can I ask one thing now? I need to clear up one thing that's been rattling in my mind. It's not a problem or anything. Just a question."

She hears herself taking a long pause – too long. "Okay."

"About the psychology class," he says. "When I thought about getting your email address, I asked Margaret Becker for it. She checked and told me you weren't enrolled in her course."

"Yes, that. That's one from my list."

"You are going to the university?"

"Yes, yes. The class – I happened to see a syllabus for the psychology class. Someone left it in the library. When I found it and saw your name, I was amazed. It felt like a clue had been left for me. Not really, of course. It felt strange to find it like that."

"So, you just came that day. For my talk."

"Yes. I was worried she'd ask who I was. But the class is huge."

"Okay, well it helps to know that. I thought it was surprising you were in the class, but not impossible. When Margaret didn't recognize your name – I didn't know what to make of that."

"I'm sorry. I should have said something that day."

"No, no. I get that. I think I let my imagination run away from me. Not my imagination. I was a little perplexed."

"It probably seemed weird."

"I hadn't considered that you weren't enrolled. Nothing weird. Like I said, we've had a funny string of moments where we startle each other."

He thanks her for calling and checks a last time about the plan for Saturday. After he says goodnight the phone goes silent.

Suzanne surveys her apartment. Annie Fisher snoozes on the couch. The lamplight's warmth surrounds her; the room stands quiet and calm. Suzanne yawns and visualizes herself falling into bed. Before Jeff can return she hurries to the living room lamp and clicks it off.

...

The drive up Highway 1 to San Simeon extends like a never-ending glide on ice. The incongruous October heat and the sun-lit stretches of the Pacific shoreline don't interfere with that sensation. Dan wishes the California coast got cold enough for ice in winter. As a kid he often wondered what it would be like to skate long distance. The frozen stretch of the Connecticut River where he and his childhood friends raced and challenged each other to cut perfect circles was less than a quarter mile long. He settles for an imaginary ribbon of ice. Though the top is down, he's got the windows up, protecting Suzanne and himself from the wind and noise. Annie Fisher watches from the rear half seat. Dan tilts and leans secretly as the car edges through the curves, holding itself tight to the road.

"Have you ever skated?" he says to Suzanne. Her hair, pulled back in a loose knot. Her freckles radiant in the sunshine.

"On ice?"

He signals yes. "This reminds me of the feeling."

She takes a moment to watch the road flowing toward them, then recites a line: "*I wish I had a river I could skate away on...*"

An image enters his mind: the skating woman, crow-like in black cape and beret. "Joni Mitchell?"

She smiles.

"You sing, don't you?"

"No!" she laughs. "Not in public."

"Not at Amsterdam?"

The car floats through another curve.

"Well, not often."

"Were you planning to sing last week?"

She tilts her head.

"I'm really sorry if I threw you off. I apologize for that."

"No, no. Speaking of apologies..." Suzanne reaches into the leather cross body bag at her feet for a folded sheet of paper. "I promised myself I would do this before lunch."

He glances her way, before returning his eyes to the road.

"I need to tell you these things. Sorry, I have a list."

"Sure," he replies.

"These are things I need to apologize for."

He shrugs, trying to tell her there's no need.

"I haven't been upfront about everything. I want to clear the air."

Dan swallows and tugs at the top button on his denim shirt. He's not yet ready to reveal the thoughts he's been debating for days.

"First is that I pretended to be a student in that class."

He nods, referencing their conversation on the phone. "That was some high-level trickery, that was."

"It wasn't honest."

"I didn't think it was dishonest. You wouldn't have had to tell me your name. I didn't have any mental image of you."

"That's the second thing. I wanted you to face me. I mean, to see my face. I wanted to see your reaction."

"Not unfair."

"I didn't consider how you would feel. I didn't weigh it."

He agrees, trying again to minimize the concern. "May I ask what you saw in my reaction?"

She takes her time considering his question. When he checks her face, he spies a tiny, suppressed smile. She says, "That you're an inquisitive person?"

"Aha." He looks back to the road, intrigued by her choice of a word that could be a compliment or a mild criticism.

Suzanne clears her throat. "My third apology…I looked up stuff about you on the internet."

Dan says, "Huh," and shifts in his seat.

"Mostly educational things. Your degrees and your schools."

"I think I mentioned them in my talk."

"Not all the details. Not Dartmouth. I knew you were Phi Beta Kappa. And in the Student Assembly."

"The Student Assembly?" He laughs. "That's on the internet? Really?" He takes a longer look at her.

"I knew you were from Walpole before you told me."

"Hmm. Did you trace me back to England?"

She cocks her head slightly.

"Tunbridge is a place name. South of London. Someone told me it means a causeway with a toll." When he sees she's puzzled by his remark, he adds, "What else does the internet have to say?"

"Ice hockey."

He nods. Okay, not unexpected.

"Rookie Power Play Goal Beats Harvard."

Dan blinks. "You did a little digging."

"There was a lot about hockey. You're in a lot of articles."

"That was so long ago. Hockey's big back there, that's for sure."

"Do you still play it?"

"Yes. Well, not recently. I still have the equipment, but rinks are few and far between out here. I do skate when I'm back East."

She returns to her list. Dan shifts again, racing through memories. An unconstructed biography – a flurry of faces and moments. What other odd bits from his past might she have found?

"Did you come across a Janet Tunbridge in Walpole?"

Suzanne hesitates, then replies with a slightly defensive "no" that comes close to being a question.

He says, "My mother. She's a district court judge for Cheshire County. She's well-known, but not well-known because of me."

Suzanne appreciates his joke. He sees her trying to incorporate 'son of a judge' into her mosaic of him.

"She did a decent job of not being a judge at home."

Suzanne says, "I'm guessing you were a well-behaved kid."

"I was a dumb kid more than a few times. But yeah, I suppose I was all right. I carried a real concern about not disappointing her."

Suzanne nods.

"She worked hard to be both parents to me. I saw that at an early age. I saw what other kids had."

"Being a disappointment is about the worst thing you can be."

Dan says, "Well, that will eat you up if you go there. If you're making a good faith effort at being a decent human being, you shouldn't worry about disappointing anyone."

Her lips go tight. "There's one more thing." She locks on her paper, gripping it with two hands. "I found a picture of you at a beer festival."

"Ah, yes. The craft beer festival. Avila?"

She stays silent.

"Brynn," he says.

"I'm sorry. I wasn't trying to find out about your private life. I did check for your name on Facebook. I was trying to find your picture."

"No, I don't mind. Huh, I almost forgot that photo. It was in the paper. I guess everything's on the web too. Some buddies of mine were in it, Dante and Kevin. Teammates. I mentioned them."

"Yes – your shirt?"

"Yes."

He sees that she's letting him slip away from talking about Brynn. For a second he wonders if Suzanne might be attracted to him. He convinces himself otherwise. She watches him but doesn't gaze. Her eyes don't dart to and from his face. Her smile is unforced and when she laughs she doesn't lean toward him. Her hands and fingers move like a pianist's, not in the freeform, riskier language of flirting. She doesn't flip her hair or sweep it back with an impetuous stroke.

Dan checks his own feelings, not for the first time. He likes her – there's no denying she's bright and appealing. She's more anxious – more dissociative – than women he's known. He guesses she's not in a relationship. Her bond with her dog seems dominant. She's too young for him, even though he acknowledges her appeal. Brynn was so straightforward – so frank and open. He wonders why Suzanne's diffidence or self-protectiveness intrigues him. Is it that she's something of an unresolved case for him? Is there some other hidden pull?

Not discussing Brynn doesn't seem right given what he has in mind. He doesn't want her wondering about his interest or second-guessing his intentions. If his offer is going to work – if he can keep it from spiraling into a disaster – she has to know that his aim is direct. His relationship with Brynn can't remain a background cloud.

A sudden realization causes him to drift too close to the double yellow lane divider in the next curve. The coffee shop.

"Did you ever meet Brynn? At Amsterdam?"

Suzanne draws a sharp breath.

Wow, he thinks. What the hell have I missed? For a moment he questions everything about Suzanne Verdin and how they've met.

Her cheeks flush and she answers, "No."

"You never saw her at Amsterdam? Suzanne, please tell me if you've met her before." Her immediate look of alarm warns him to pause.

"Sorry, that came out stronger than I meant. Brynn loved Amsterdam. She used to meet her girlfriends there. It's a small town, but I'm a little thrown off that you might have met her."

Suzanne drops her eyes from the road ahead to the paper in her lap. "No, I don't think so. Only her picture in that article."

For a reason he can't explain Dan remembers a despondent college student he encountered during a weekend on-call shift the winter before. Distressed about her courses, her brother's drug abuse, and the fifteen pounds she'd gained at the university. Her poetry, the one spark that kept her talking and open to the future. The flow of poems she sent for weeks afterward and their increasingly angry verses over the lack of response from her "lost knight." The team meeting that left Dan doubting his ability to manage a complex client. The group's suggestion that an older female therapist pick up the case.

But it's not like that with Suzanne, he reasons, trying to smooth his anxieties. You're on edge. Why so touchy about Brynn?

Brynn and Suzanne at the coffee shop. Farmer's Market. The same bars and restaurants everyone hit. Such a small town for the mass of young adults the university attracted. He begins to calculate the number of times he and Suzanne may have passed each other without knowing. Her place at the ranch – he drove by it twice a day. What would an impassive satellite record reveal of their paths as they went about their daily lives?

Dan recalls a childhood trip to the Museum of Science in Boston. Before his incredulous eyes, a massive brass orrery revealing the planets in their orbits. The mysterious, coordinated gears choreographing a dance – a fine-tuned prediction of each sphere's passage and each crossing of a partner's plane. He was amazed by the known celestial patterns – the machine could be run forward and backward for thousands of years.

Farmer's Market. Boo Boo Records for new vinyl. A Genius Bar appointment at the Apple Store. Trader Joe's. The beach at Pismo or Avila, North Morro or Cayucos on any of a hundred sunny days. Lunch over the creek at Novo. Beers at Firestone or SLO Brew or Mother's. Dancing at Luna Red. So many young people tumbling through space with him – with Brynn and him. How many times had Suzanne's and his orbits missed intersecting by minutes or seconds? Had he ever seen her out of the corner of his eye? A polite smile between drivers at a light? A lingering glance of curiosity?

He wrangles his phone out of his pocket and scrolls to the contact for Brynn. Careful not to hit the call button, he taps on her picture icon. The full photo appears, and he offers the phone to Suzanne.

"She looks different now. She changed her hair since the beer fest."

Suzanne takes her time studying Brynn's picture. Dan wants to scrutinize her face, but he's got to concentrate on the road. Suzanne turns to him and says, "Does she have an attractive Black friend?"

"Yes! Short, stylish hair? Big laugh? Amity. Her name's Amity."

"Yes, I have seen them." With a nod to his phone, Suzanne adds, "She's beautiful too."

Dan lets his mind decelerate to a reasonable pace as he sighs. He fends off a feeling of astonishment at how suddenly things shift with her. He remembers opponents who would skate right at him, faking a move more than once, refusing to pass, trying to get him to commit – holding out for a sudden alteration in the geometry. Suzanne doesn't try any of that. She seems spontaneous, or at least unpremeditated. And yet she's knocked him off balance more times than he can count. Hidden gusts at her back sneak around and smack against his legs before he can detect them.

So, he lays it out as they close in on San Simeon. He starts by telling Suzanne that Brynn's living in Sweden. He says they're calling it a break. In his mind the romantic relationship may have run its course.

"Maybe not," he says. "But I think so. It makes more sense to look at it that way." He gives Suzanne a brief rundown on how they met and how their two years together felt. "We had a lot of fun together." Immediately he's embarrassed by his word choice. "She's a lively person – you know, fun to be with."

Suzanne stays silent, keeping whatever questions she holds to herself.

"It was good, but she needed to explore the world – to test herself. The dream of the twenties." Dan glances with a friendly squint, acknowledging Suzanne's wish to see New Zealand. "I didn't want to be the guy who derails that."

When he pauses she says, "I bet people would notice you guys."

"I don't know. I wonder what they would have seen." He's drawn back into his reverie of orbits crossing – celestial bodies arcing in synchrony or straining from each other's pull.

"We'd have these deep conversations when we drove up the coast. Good conversations. Something about being out on the road seemed to do that." He offers a smile.

When they arrive at Hearst Beach and the San Simeon Pier he takes the quick turn from Highway 1. Shortly after he angles into the parking lot of the outdoor restaurant. Customers fill fewer than a third of the picnic tables. A tempting aroma of barbecued fish greets them. Dan sets the parking brake and cuts the engine.

"The truth is I'm not over her. It might be one of those deals where your heart's a little slow in catching up with reality? So, I'm taking some time off to let everything sync up. I don't know about you. The dating world is about the last place I want to be. I don't even know if people date anymore."

Suzanne says, "It helps to have a dog."

He laughs. When he reaches back to rub Annie Fisher's head, the dog hesitates, sniffing at his hand.

"What I'm also trying to say – not very well – is that I'd like you to feel sure that I'm not hoping for us to get involved. You're a bright and appealing person – intriguing to me, to be honest. But I'm not looking for anything. I'm kind of assuming you get all the attention you want from the college guys."

Suzanne opens her mouth in protest.

"Well," he continues, "You may be keeping them at arm's length. It's none of my business. I don't know how to describe what you and I are to each other. Something keeps bumping us together. Not bumping. More like our orbits keep crossing. It feels natural, but unexpected. Everything feels okay to me. It feels friendly. A little unusual, I guess."

Suzanne lets his words hang in the air. Then she tells him, "One summer I took the train to Denver to see my sister. There was an Indian woman sitting across from me, in a beautiful teal sari. I'd never talked with someone who grew up in another country and left it all behind. The surprising part was how I opened up completely to her. I told her everything about my life – the hard parts, too. She was a total stranger, but I shared more with her than anyone else in my life." She hesitates before finishing. "That's a little how this feels."

Trying to keep his smile restrained, understated, Dan says, "Thanks." He takes an extra moment to check her eyes.

Chapter Six

THEIR ORDERS ARRIVE – HERS, A SALAD with moist chunks of crab and his, fish tacos. The server returns, offering a water dish and a biscuit for Annie Fisher. Suzanne sits under the half circle of shade from a red and white umbrella. The sun warms Dan's back. They compliment each other's food. Each waits for the other to start.

After a few bites, Dan says, "It's crossed my mind a few times that your case – your daughter's adoption – stayed with me because I was raised by a single mother."

Suzanne pauses her eating to consider what he means.

"Do you mean a single mother or your biological mother?"

"Yes, I can't separate those. That's the knot for me."

"Single mothers get very little respect."

He agrees. "I'm not sure how she did it all. If I hadn't experienced it, I'd think it would be impossible."

"Especially if the single mother is a teenager?"

He answers with a reluctant nod.

She turns back to her food. He takes it as a signal to wait.

When Suzanne finishes another bite she says, "And yet, she was your biological mother, so it felt natural."

"Another part of the knot."

She tilts her head.

"Do you think I was not fit because I was single and too young? Or do you think I could have become a good mother because I was her biological mother?"

"That wasn't my role to say."

Suzanne turns away in irritation.

"Sorry. I don't mean to duck your question."

Dan waits, then tries again.

"You may have been too young or too alone – whatever that means. Honestly, I can't say. You might have become a fine mother. You might

73

have grown into it. I was asked about your daughter's attachment. That's a narrower question."

He starts to say more, but stops himself.

"I was too young. I like to believe I would have become a good mother. I don't know if any of it is natural – from pregnancy or birth. Maybe a genetic bond or something like that. In my heart it feels like it would have been natural."

The word 'natural' echoes between them. They return to quiet eating.

In another minute Dan replaces his taco on the plate. He stops the anticipatory jiggling of his left leg. He looks at Suzanne, checking his resolve and the dark risk he has spent days weighing.

There is a future with everything he's worked for burned down to ash. How ludicrous to consider it. Only a madman would point down a path like that, pretending it might be a viable way forward. He guards against a deep cold wave of fear crawling through his body. A future wiped clean of his work with children. An ex-communication. A self-created wasteland, with little but broken guideposts and sun-blasted bones from the crusades of fools gone before him.

Could he reinvent himself somewhere else? Does he have the courage to stare into that abyss? All of it bet on trusting a young woman he barely knows. And yet, with no risk it wouldn't feel important. Dan twists his mouth at his state. He cannot answer his own questions. The forward momentum calls.

"Suzanne, I have to ask this. You don't need to answer – today or ever. It might be best forgotten. For my own peace of mind I need to ask it."

Her fork and hand pause in midair.

"I'm wondering if you would want to see Emmy – if you could."

The name elicits an eye blink.

He says, "Emma Robinson. They call her Emmy."

She puts down her utensil and cocks her head.

"I used to want that a lot. I don't have the panicky dreams anymore, where she's lost and I can't find her. She doesn't feel lost to me. I like to think she's safe."

She picks at her salad before continuing.

"It might help to know that – to see that she's healthy and happy. If it came down to seeing her face to face, I don't know what I would do."

After a pause she says, "I don't think there's any way she would recognize me. It wouldn't be for her. Not yet anyway."

"Would that matter?"

She brushes her hair behind her ear. "No." She glances at his eyes. "I'm a little afraid of how I'd react."

Dan presses his lips closed. Suzanne takes a bite of salad without saying more. Doubt screams at him; a crash of angry surf knocks at his legs and chest. She's retreated into a far-off gaze, leaving him vulnerable, his question lingering.

She lets the silence hang in the air. As he picks up his taco to take another bite, she says, "Why do you want to know?"

He swallows, then takes aim, not at all confident about his vision or his goal.

Dan reveals that Emmy attends a preschool where he consults. He hasn't had any contact with her parents, but he's seen the little girl several times over the past year. Something about her stayed with him from his observation of her as an infant. He's checked the class roster for her last name and confirmed her identity by her birthdate.

"She has your hair color. Almost exactly."

Suzanne blinks.

He lays out as objectively as he can that he's willing to help her visit the school on the pretext she is an intern under his supervision, needing to observe a client. He describes Manny and the behaviors of his they track. He tells her that if she wants to spend an hour at the center, he will arrange it without the staff knowing who she is.

"It's possible her mother or father might show up. We can minimize the chances of that by picking the right time of day. It's a risk. It can only be a one-time visit, an hour. You'd have to understand that."

Suzanne puts her fork down. She scrutinizes his face as he takes a sip of ice water. Dan swallows hard, feeling like he has suggested something far seedier.

Her eyes narrow; the wall of freckles fortifies itself.

"Is this something you feel you have to do for me?"

"No. I don't feel obligated, if that's what you mean. I'm making a choice."

"Do you think I'm broken?" Her voice becomes heated.

"Not at all, Suzanne. This is not therapy."

She looks off for a moment, then snaps back before he can look down.

"I'm not responsible for helping you feel better about what happened. About your report. It's not fair to use me for that."

Dan shifts his body.

"I'm not offering this out of guilt or second thoughts. I've considered that – a lot. I told you before I would make the same recommendation again. That's the grown-up truth of it."

The adversarial tone of his voice startles him. He takes a breath and twists in his seat.

"This isn't about undoing the past. I was a part of those events, like you were a part of them. I tried to use my training for Emma's well-being. I actually think adoption is a noble choice. I hope you don't feel guilty. You did a courageous thing. But it's not a simple story that ties up in a neat package."

She's stopped eating and her face hardens. He reaches for the glass of water, his fingertips slipping as he grasps it.

Suzanne leans toward him and speaks in a vehement whisper.

"What if someone found out? What would happen then? You say they might show up? What would you expect me to do if they found me there? People get arrested for things like that! I would never forgive you if I had to go back to court. Tell me one reason why I should ever trust you."

He winces but holds eye contact with her.

"There are more reasons than I can list why I shouldn't offer information about Emma to you. Not only am I bending the standards of ethical conduct for psychologists, but if anyone found out I'd be finished working for mental health. You don't have to trust me at all. I'm unprotected on this."

"Then why?" she says, her eyes still fierce.

"I'm not sure I know why – not the exact reason."

With a forefinger Dan traces the grain of the tabletop. "For once things do not fit together. Most of the time I try to be a team player. That's what I did in your case. I thought I was helping to make sure a process took place the way it should. I'm questioning whether that served you well. Or Emma."

He draws in a long breath.

"It's complicated. The outcome made sense if you are trying to be hard-nosed and practical about it. I'm sorry if that sounds harsh."

76

"It's not harsh. That's the reality. I made choices. I wasn't a hapless victim."

"You made a significant sacrifice for your daughter, even though you weren't sure. I admire your choice. I admire the adoptive parents. I met them, and they struck me as good people – genuinely caring. I admire that you still wanted to raise your daughter.

"I have a few questions I would have asked the judge. What I'd like to know is whether he had already made up his mind. I don't like thinking I got called in to validate a generalization about teenage mothers."

Suzanne says, "You don't think it was fate? Maybe it was a story that was meant to be a certain way. I haven't found that we get to control everything in life. Things happen, and we have to find a way to live with them. We don't always get choices. Sometimes we have to work with other people's choices. Do you always expect a happy ending?"

Dan looks her in the eye.

"No. But I don't like thinking that any story I'm in has already been written."

"What if it has?" she says. "I don't mean every word. But some things might be inevitable – more than we know or want to believe. What if there are forces at work we don't understand? If you draw two lines off into the distance and they aren't perfectly parallel – if they tilt slightly toward each other – isn't it a sure thing they will cross at some point – somewhere, somehow? Even though it's all unknown?"

Dan considers her words. She watches the bay, beyond the trees and picnic tables at the edge of the beach. He follows her gaze.

"Suzanne, we don't know each other well. I'm going on gut instinct. I don't mind the future being unknown. That feels raw and very real to me. I want to believe that your choices in this situation matter. And there's also this. I know my biological mother. She's mattered to me."

Suzanne holds still, biting her lip.

He stammers. "You have to decide what happens next. I don't have any right to influence you and I don't know what you need. I needed to offer this. In the scheme of things, you're owed a chance to see that Emma is healthy and doing well. If we still lived in small villages she would have been raised by a family down the road and you would have had some type of presence in her life. You might have created an arrangement like that.

"If I felt it wouldn't raise suspicions, I'd go to her parents and ask them to write you a letter about her. Maybe it should be up to you to make contact. It's true there is something in me that is not at peace. I needed to say this and show you I'm willing to have faith in you – to take that risk. If that's all there is to it, I can shut up and go away.

"Am I sure this is the right thing to do? No. I think it can be done with care – respectfully – without trampling on anybody else's rights and without hurting anyone. I'm offering it, but I'll be the first to admit it's not my call."

Suzanne says, "What does Judge Tunbridge say?"

Dan raises his eyebrows, impressed by her unexpected question.

"When I did the evaluation, I asked for her advice on what the court might be expecting. Language that would be helpful or unhelpful, some things like that. I wanted to know what a judge weighs. I sent her a copy of my report after I finished it. She had an interest in the judge's ruling."

Her chin rises, signaling that she understands his mother agreed with the judge.

"Most of what we've talked about revolves around the question of fairness and justice. The balancing of the scales is the way my mother puts it. The difference between societal standards of justice and conscience.

"When your mother's a judge, trust me, you hear about right and wrong. In fact, you may end up thinking a little too much about your conscience. That can tangle you up. The heart does not always weigh the same things the conscience does. Mine doesn't."

Suzanne's eyes scan his face, not watching with patience or acceptance or understanding, but taking rapid measurements and checking calculations against some undisclosed reference. His opening question hangs in the air.

He breaks from her assessment of him to take a drink of water. No matter what she might say, his offer knocks them off magnetic north. Dan begins to feel Suzanne pulling, like a centrifugal force, drawing him from an anchor point he's tried to stake in the ground. She remains before him, but he notes an accelerating energy.

It's one thing to understand you are taking a risk – to tell yourself that. It's another to find it rising about you like a water spout. A cacophony of horns and drums bursts over the scene: wind and shore break to any of the restaurant's customers but him. He understands there's nothing more for him to say. From any angle this is a wild card shot. And yet.

Dan reaches for his taco and takes a last bite.

When he looks again, Suzanne's face undergoes a transformation – scrubbed by fiery sunlight sweeping across it. Her eyes narrow and her brow sets itself. The army of freckles assembles like a Roman phalanx. She resumes eating, slow bites that accelerate with a vigor that frightens him.

For an extraordinarily long period the only sounds between them are his muffled swallows and the piercing of her fork into crisp lettuce and cold white crab meat.

Breaking the silence, without returning his look, she says in a firm voice, "Then I accept."

•••

In the middle of the morning on the following Thursday, Dr. Dan Tunbridge stands with Vicky, the director of the preschool, introducing Suzanne Verdin as "Marie." He's asked ahead of time for the names of the children who will be there on Thursdays so that his intern can observe and record Manny's social contacts. Emmy's is among the names. Vicky runs through what to expect over the next hour and waves a hand toward the room, signaling her welcome.

"I'll get her started," Dan says.

They've already reviewed the diagrams she will use to track Manny's interactions. Suzanne holds the clipboard at an angle to her waist, assuming a professional posture. He points to a central circle with Manny's name and repeats something he's told her about lines to draw.

It's pretense and she ignores his comments. Her eyes scan the classroom, stopping to note each face. Emma Robinson is not there.

When Suzanne turns to his face, he says, "Wherever he goes is fine. He'll probably go outside at some point."

She glances out the window toward the yard and checks his face again. He tips his head, confirming that the little girl is there.

Suzanne walks to a child's chair in a corner of the room and sits. She begins to watch the playing children.

"I think I'd better go," he says.

"Yes," she replies in a flat tone, as if he is already miles away.

"You'll give me a call this evening?"

"Yes."

79

He resists an urge to say more, wondering how he will survive the uncertainty of the wait. She makes eye contact and says, "Goodbye," her voice striking like a single chime marking an unknown half hour in the night. Then she turns her head back to the children.

Dan walks down the hall toward the entrance, trying to hush the squeak of his shoes on the linoleum. Near the play yard gate, he thanks Vicky again.

"Your intern's all set in there?"

"She is. You probably didn't need me to come down, but I wanted to answer any questions."

"All hunky-dory for me," Vicky says. "I have to point Emmy out to her. That little girl's got the precise color of her hair! Did you notice?"

Dan clenches at the rocky punch to his gut. He fights to hold his expression.

"Huh. No, I didn't." They watch the little girl together. Then he finds a diversion. "Is she what they call a ginger?"

"Oh, she's a ginger. Royal hair. Elizabeth the first. The virgin queen."

He nods and makes a sudden shift. "Marie is a little self-conscious about her hair. Or her freckles. A lot of childhood teasing, I think."

"Ay, the redhead's curse," Vicky says, considering his message. "Thanks. I'll keep that to myself. She'll see the resemblance, I'm sure."

Dan keeps his sigh of relief cloaked. He shakes Vicky's hand and promises to be in touch about Manny.

When he gets to his car door, he lets out a silent scream. Collapsing into his seat, he blanches at his stupidity. How could he not have anticipated that? Vicky must know Emma is adopted. Wouldn't she know? Is there any chance the parents have kept that private? He checks the rearview mirror to see if anyone is watching. Goddamn. He considers texting a warning to Suzanne. No. She's already on edge and there are enough unknowns at work that he can't risk how she might react.

There's nothing more for him to do. He starts up his car. Backing out, he aims for the road and accelerates. An unintended spray of stones kicks out from the back tires. He curses again.

•••

When the little girl comes marching into the play room like a drum major, Suzanne gasps. Her felt name tag says, "Emmy." She offers Suzanne an impish smile as she passes by.

Suzanne buries her eyes in the diagrams on her clipboard, choking on an upswell of shame. Not here, not here, she chants, forgetting to breathe. This is not happening. She drills the clipboard papers with her eyes, refusing to look elsewhere. Breathe, Suzanne, breathe. Count and breathe.

Daring to look up again, she finds the children and teachers moving about the room in practiced and comfortable patterns. But it's all slow motion. The chaotic pounding is in her head, not in the room. Not here, she tries again. Not. Here. She lets her breathing slow. The tilting room establishes its equilibrium. The wave of nausea retreats.

Manny sits alone flipping pages of a picture book forward and back, forward and back. No other children interact with him. Twice he's looked at her as if she is a teacher. She remembers the psychologist's suggestion that she not interact. Instead, he said she could try turning toward other activities in the room. His thought was that Manny might follow her line of sight and become interested in others. Strengthening social initiative is one of the goals for Manny. They want him to be included, but to learn to join in on his own.

Each time that Manny catches her eye, she tries the redirection technique. But her smile fails, like she's trying to fool her dog. She glances back to find Manny holding her eye contact. She understands why he sits there waiting. Smiles and redirection will not sway him.

Emmy seats herself on the carpeted floor, next to a boy and a girl who are assembling wooden train tracks. She picks up a ramped piece – half of a bridge – and snaps it onto the section of track the little boy works on.

"My train is red," he says. "I'm going to Morro Bay."

Emmy tilts her head to one side and the other, saying, "I know where Morro Bay is. With a big rock!"

A teacher and several children return from the bathroom. The teacher calls to no one in particular, saying, "Who's ready to go to the Mother Tree?" She catches Suzanne's eyes and stops to bend toward Manny. "Manny, would you like to go out to the Mother Tree?"

Before Manny can answer several children surround the teacher, chanting, "I am!" They take her hands and pull toward the door leading to the playground. Emmy stands and spins in place. She begins to follow the group, but when she comes closer to Suzanne, she slows and walks up to her.

Suzanne freezes, unable to break eye contact with the little girl. She studies the face before her, fighting against a confusing sense of dread.

She's a beautiful girl. Suzanne startles at the length of her eyelashes. She traces the contours of her pink lips, stumbling into a deep cave of memory. If she touched them, she would know. One touch of her ears or fingers.

The little girl's hair color is so familiar. Not from anguished memories of labor and delivery – that hair was damp and matted. The hair before her summons Suzanne's grade school photos, distorting them into an uncanny three-dimensional avatar – a visitor peering from a magic mirror. Suzanne turns her head a few degrees; the visage she watches does not reciprocate. The face before her glows like a creamy, porcelain vase, wiped clean of any blemishes. Like a desperate wish from her own childhood – a yearning to be freckle-free like the other girls.

"You have freckles!" the ghostly face announces.

Before Suzanne can think what to reply, Emmy points her finger and presses against Suzanne's cheek. "One, two, three!" She flashes an exaggerated smile and says, "Goodbye!" With a spin turn on squeaky sneakers, she races to join the children going outside.

Suzanne stands in panic as the room lurches in a dreadful roll. She draws two quick breaths and scans the room. Where is Annie Fisher? Where did she leave her? As Suzanne fights an acute warning from her bladder, the teacher who recruited the children to go outside comes back to the room.

"Come on, Manny, we're all going outside! Jump up, dude."

She turns to Suzanne and says, "You can observe him outside, right?"

Suzanne suppresses a frown. "Is there a restroom?"

The teacher says, "Sure," and points. "Just beyond Vicky's desk."

Suzanne thanks her and hurries that way.

When she emerges from the restroom, her face is washed, her cheeks cooled. She has tied her hair back the way she would for an interview. She holds the clipboard and marks the chart: Teacher takes Manny outside.

In the yard Suzanne chooses a seat at a picnic table where she can see all the children. Some race; some attempt cartwheels. Manny walks to the sandbox and perches himself on a corner seat. He bends and draws lines with a finger, using his feet to erase the marks. Twice. Four times. Seven times.

Emmy walks to the sandbox at one point. Suzanne makes a note: Manny accepts stick from Emmy. In the next half hour Suzanne draws more lines between Manny's name and the names of playmates, adding information for each interaction. She sees Emmy climb to the first branch of the oak at the back of the yard. She swings. She swings and sings. She beats two boys in a foot race. She squats to capture a bug, carrying it on a blade of grass to show her teacher.

She does not approach Suzanne again. The more Suzanne watches the scene, the more she pictures herself in a long, echoing cylinder, removed from the figures playing at the bright end of her visual tunnel. They spin and laugh and walk hand in hand, figures on a magic screen. Suzanne floats, the lorazepam blossoming through her bloodstream, reaching her fingertips and her toes.

When a car pulls into the preschool's parking lot, she's jolted back to the play yard. She reaches into her bag to find her sunglasses. Her watch says she's been there under an hour. Suzanne turns enough to track the woman who's arrived. She's older – a grandmother, Suzanne decides – and she's carrying a bright blue lunch bag. She hurries toward the cubbies outside the main door and hangs the bag there. With a wave toward the teachers in the yard, she returns to her car and drives off.

Suzanne tells herself to leave. She clicks her pen closed and hurries to the office. Vicky sits at her desk.

"I think I have enough documented on Manny," she says, indicating the papers on her clipboard. "Thank you for letting me observe."

"Are you sure?" Vicky says. "You're welcome to stay during lunch."

"I need to get back for a class."

Vicky smiles and nods. "What did you think of our kids?"

Suzanne catches Vicky studying her.

"Manny's very sweet," she answers. Vicky's amiable stare hangs in the air between them. "I liked them all. They're…beautiful."

Vicky tilts her head. "Are you well, luv?"

A shiver grabs at her shoulders. Suzanne turns her head toward the door, then looks back at Vicky.

"I'm a little…my tummy's a little upset."

"Let me get you some water," Vicky says, standing.

"Oh, I have a bottle in my car, thank you. I'll be all right."

"Okay…"

Suzanne offers her hand. "Thank you again. I appreciate your time."

"Tell that gorgeous Dr. Tunbridge hello for me," Vicky whispers with a glint in her eye.

Suzanne blushes, trying to decide if the woman is teasing or testing her. "Oh…I will. Bye."

In her car Suzanne unscrews the water bottle and takes a large gulp. She replaces the cap and tosses the bottle to the passenger seat. She turns on the ignition, checks all around and flees from the preschool like an alarmed bird.

...

"It says 'Chester draws', Andrew. Chester draws! Who would ever spell it that way? It's a dresser – a chest of drawers! Oh my god, the American educational system is a disaster. Chester draws!"

With a little wag of her head, Maggie celebrates her discovery of a free item of furniture on Craigslist, despite its ludicrous description. It'll be perfect for chalk paint, she tells herself. Technically it's for clothes. Chester's drawers, she jokes to herself.

She'll paint the dresser and use it in the dining room for linens. Sea Wind or Afternoon Sky would be perfect, she decides, comparing the powdery shades in her mind. She's called, and the woman promises to hold it for two hours. Oh my god, how will I keep from laughing if she says 'Chester draws', Maggie thinks. Try to be nice.

She clears out the back of the '91 Country Squire that Andrew rescued from a wrecking yard. College kids snicker, but what do they know about being practical. And yes, she locks the steering wheel with that red club gizmo because there are people at Walmart who would take a car like this. She likes all the windows. They let her see in every direction. How many times has she spotted Suzy walking the dog or getting gas because she had that view on the world? Maggie admires the roominess of the station wagon too. Try putting a chest of drawers in your mini-SUV, she crows. Maggie bangs the tailgate closed and yells to her husband that she's leaving.

Rather than risking that the woman's directions to her ranch might be as scrambled as her identification of furniture style, Maggie simply jotted down her address. Mac said they should call it up on the Google Maps.

"Look, there's only one road down there," Maggie said when they found the exit from Highway 101. "How could I get lost?" Mac insisted on printing out the map.

Maggie reminds herself that she doesn't have the Almighty Google on her phone – her screen won't show pictures. Do people need pictures on their phones? Is that where we are? She drops the printed map on the seat next to her and heads south.

The car's radio works, but she only likes to listen to the local afternoon talk show. Every Friday they feature a dog to be adopted. Most days Maggie likes hearing what's going on in the county. She bristles when the host gets too full of himself.

Despite the fact it's the middle of the morning, she tries the radio, only to hear a peculiar mix of chanting and harps, or is it broken pianos?

"Ugh," she grumbles, snapping the radio off. Instead she imagines the free dresser with a fresh coat of chalk paint and beams at her plans.

Maggie takes the lonesome exit, miles from the last one she's passed. A long stretch of road that she's not sure she's been on before reveals a few horse ranches. On the right she passes a fenced field that holds a small band of alpacas, standing about like poodles with oddly-stretched necks and clipped ears.

"Everyone knows alpacas are a scam, people," she says, broadcasting a knowing expression via her rearview mirror.

She scans the landscape. Where the h-e-double-toothpicks am I? She's not sure what the closest town is – Nipomo? Guadalupe? The woman said "out in the country off 101" as if everyone knew where that was. Well, this must be the road.

Maggie picks up the printout, rotating it to recheck her orientation. The Google Maps wants her to stay straight for another mile or two. Ahead she finds a sign for Pioneer Springs Road. She's supposed to end up at a lane that connects with it, so why not just turn here? Who makes these Google Maps anyway, she says under her breath, dropping the paper map to the seat. Some college kid who's too smart for his own good.

"And I don't mean Asian," she says out loud. "They're fine."

She turns left with a defiant spin of the steering wheel and looks to the distance for a target.

A mile down the road Maggie discovers a car pulled to the shoulder in the opposite lane. The color and size of the vehicle cause her pulse to quicken.

She checks her mirror and slows the Country Squire. When she's within twenty yards of the stopped car she spies the unmistakable beacon of her daughter's red hair.

Maggie's mouth falls open. She pulls off the road, braking opposite the parked Honda Fit – turquoise, with its identifying golf-ball sized dent in the front bumper. The young driver tilts against the steering wheel, sobbing into her hands.

Chapter Seven

WHEN HER VISION CLEARS, AND SHE comprehends that the woman hurrying across the road is her mother, Suzanne reaches for the door lock switch and presses it twice. She wipes her face and checks the rearview mirror to see if she can deny she's been crying.

Her mother raps at the window, like she's trying to rouse her daughter in the morning.

"Suzy! Suzy!"

Suzanne stares straight ahead until the insistent noise threatens to explode her skull. She presses the switch for the front window, which winds down in robotic tones. Suzanne reaches for a tissue and blows her nose. She turns to face her mother. For a moment they do no more than stare. Suzanne tries to project the most annoyed look of defiance she can recall from adolescence, but her body is too weak to fight. She settles for an expression of fatigue.

"Suzy, what is it? What's wrong? What are you doing?"

Suzanne shakes her head.

"Have you been attacked? What happened?"

"What?" Suzanne says, bewildered.

"Did somebody hurt you?"

"Mom, I just stopped the car. No. I'm fine."

"You're not fine! I see you. Why are you crying?"

"Mom, what are you doing here? Are you following me?"

"No! No! What do you mean? I'm driving this way. I'm picking up a dresser. What are you doing out here? Why are you crying? What's going on?"

Suzanne gets her breathing under control and throws together a plan to address her mother's questions. Give her the minimum, Suzanne commands herself, then leave. Do not let her control you.

"Mom, I'm fine. I was having a little cry."

"No, you were bawling! I saw you, Suzy. Why do you think I stopped?"

"Mom, I was crying because I was upset about a little boy."

Maggie scans the car like she's missed something. "What little boy? On the road?"

"Mom! Stop. Stop and listen. I did an observation – a project for school. I observed a little boy at his school."

Suzanne points to the notes on the clipboard in her passenger seat. "I watched his interactions. It was a little sad for me. He seemed alone or isolated. It got to me."

Maggie examines her daughter's eyes.

Suzanne dodges the familiar glare. Tell her you're finished and leave. "I'm fine now. That's all."

"What little boy? Whose little boy is he?"

"His name is Manny, not that it's any of your business. It's a school assignment. Please. I need to get going."

Maggie continues to stare, doubt erupting across her face.

"I know you, Suzy. I'm your mother. I know when you're upset."

"Let me live my life!" Suzanne shouts.

Maggie recoils from the open window. Suzanne takes the opportunity and pushes the switch that sends the window glass climbing, far too slowly.

"Please stay out of my life!" Suzanne says in her firmest voice. The muffled words careen around the interior of her car.

Maggie narrows her eyes as Suzanne starts up the Honda and speeds away. She turns the other direction and takes in the road leading from wherever her daughter has come.

...

All afternoon he's been aware of a thin sheen of sweat on his forehead. Dan leaves the clinic determined to go get a drink. He curses to himself, wondering why October is this hot. California needs seasons. A faint acrid smell causes him to look off toward the north. Haze paints a grayish wash over Cerro San Luis and Bishop Peak.

Why didn't he ask Suzanne to call him as soon as she left the school? At least during the day. Why did he suggest that evening? He kicks himself for not being more business-like about it.

He drives downtown where a few streets are already barricaded for Farmer's Market. Circling the block by the courthouse, Dan finds a space front and center at the lawyers' bar. A stuffy heat inside the car bothers him. Sweat collects at the back of his neck. He wants a cold drink. He can see the wall-length mirror inside, behind the bar. One or two guys sit on barstools, where he wants to be. Elevated bar tables are loaded with chips and salsa, surrounded by bodies in charcoal suits and black belted dresses. He already hears the dissonant hum of legal chatter in the bar. Dan weighs that against the allure of gin and tonic.

Before he can reach a decision, his mind skips to another impulse. He starts up the car and pulls out of the parking space. His swimsuit is rolled in a towel in the trunk. Better to go crank out some laps and soak in the mineral pool at Avila. He's got cold Negra Modelo at home. Dan punches the buttons on the car's stereo and calls up the distorted, crunchy guitar and desolate echoes of Neil Young's "Hitchhiker."

Offshore fog creeps in along the parched coastal hills. The overcooked inland air at Avila Valley rises and blocks its advance. No more than half a dozen cars sit in the parking lot at the hot springs.

He changes and walks outside, dipping a foot to check the temperature. The outdoor pool's summery water is the perfect antidote to the day's withering heat. A few people claim recliners near the mineral pool, though no one is swimming. Dan slips into the blue pool and pushes underwater, gliding as far as he can without kicking or taking a stroke.

The sensation is like being under an ice ceiling, safe from whatever conflagration rages above. He kicks, stretches forward in another glide, pulls his arms back in a stroke and marvels at the instantaneous escape. If the surface were frozen, another version of himself might be above this world, cutting a path, seeking a sudden angle. Here he's free of his everyday skin. He can feel himself swimming out of it, shedding it, some type of future human evolving, an aquatic descendant of itself. Streaming through the liquid world, he notices the dappled whiteness of his body and wonders if he could ever become a sea creature.

That thought triggers his memory of an evaluation he did at UCLA. The kid whose mother was sure he was a genius – Billy, aka Melvin. An imaginative kid whose only real problem was that his parents named him after a grandfather. He told Dan humans descended from whale-like mammals who came ashore and developed limbs. He articulated his hypothesis in a way that mostly convinced the psychologist. Dan grins at the memory. A sharp eye for the white whale, Billy! Blowing a long blast of bubbles, he surfaces to refill his chest.

At the far end of the pool Dan decides to swim nine more laps before he'll let himself check his phone. The water refreshes his mind and he considers ignoring the phone altogether. Let the world spin on its axis. Let Suzanne find her own orbit around it. That thought lasts for a few seconds. He shoves off and begins his countdown.

...

Suzanne does not look back. She's afraid what she might do if her mother is following her. Manny's charts lie safe in the passenger's seat. She grabs her water bottle to keep it from leaking on the papers. Opening it to take a deep drink, she aims for the highway toward San Luis and home.

She can shower and get everything packed before needing to be at Amsterdam for her afternoon shift. She's sure she can talk them into letting her go early. Friday and Saturday are open. She can swing back by the ranch to get Annie Fisher and they can be on the road to Big Sur while daylight holds. Though the sun may set by the time she gets there, she knows the safe places to pull off and park for the night. The Fit's seats fold flat, creating a perfect camping cocoon for her and the dog.

Remember Annie's bowls. Take your pillow. Suzanne lets herself savor a shiver of excitement at the thought of waking up to the sound of surf climbing up Big Sur's remarkable cliffs. The aftermath of the shiver sends her eyes to the rearview mirror, then the side mirror. She can't see any sign of her mother's station wagon.

At the ranch she stuffs a sweater, an extra top and shorts in her bag. She pulls out her hiking boots and the sleeping bag from the closet floor. From her bedside, a red Swiss Army knife. The refrigerator's got a couple of apples and some cheese sticks that should suffice. The pantry shelf yields a few packages of raspberry fig bars and a gallon jug of filtered water. She grabs the half-full jar of mixed nuts from the counter. Plenty of food for two days, and she can always head to Fernwood if she hikes a lot and is famished. For Annie Fisher, scoops of kibble in a baggie. Suzanne places the items in a Trader Joe's shopping bag, remembering to grab a roll of toilet paper.

Amsterdam is nearly deserted, even for a usually quiet Thursday afternoon. A handful of students click, drag and type away at solo projects. One guy sits with a guitar case, way too early for open mic. He looks up from what might be a small notebook of lyrics and scans the room, like he can't quite figure out where he'll be playing. Two regulars – gray-bearded guys retired from the university – lean back in leather chairs sipping coffee and comparing notes on how much of their pensions their wives will receive if they die first.

Suzanne's in luck – Tevy needs the extra money and is happy to cover her evening hours. Suzanne wipes down the coffee bar, makes a round scooping up empty mugs and checks with the kitchen staff to see if she can lighten Tevy's load. She checks her watch and runs down the list of last minute tasks: gas, pick up Annie Fisher, don't forget to call him. Tick, tick, tick – in no more than thirty minutes she'll be on the road north.

...

The laps leave Dan a little more winded than he'd like to admit. He steps to the deck chair where he left his stuff, buries his head in the towel, and shakes the day out of his mind. Then he squats to pull his phone out of his shoe. No calls, no texts. Dan stands and lets out a long breath. He jerks his head to shake away water tickling his ear canal.

He decides the thermal spring water might be the answer. It bubbles into a tiled pool, square and no more than a foot-and-a-half deep. A dozen or so people might be able to wiggle in together. For now it holds only a well-tanned elderly Asian man whom Dan recognizes from previous visits. He lies floating on his back with eyes closed, smiling a polite greeting.

The heat of the cloudy, sulfurous water climbs Dan's legs and confirms that this is the therapy he needs. He lowers himself in the shallow pool and stretches out so only his toes and his face break the surface. The velvety mineral water coats his skin in a way that reinforces the illusion he might be shifting form. It makes him sleek, softer, waterproof. Faster than a mere man. His muscles unlock; his spine adjusts itself.

Two young boys splash down the ramp to the mineral pool, knocking him from his reverie. "Not there!" comes a weary mother's voice. "That's not a jacuzzi, Steven. Boys! Over here!"

When the waters resettle to a gentle murmuring, Dan opens his eyes to find a blonde woman in sunglasses gliding down the ramp into the pool. Her breasts sway, contained in a red, scooped top. Her black bikini bottom is high cut and tied at the sides, showcasing bronzed legs. A sweet little hummingbird tattoo graces her left hip. She moves across the pool, testing the tiles at the bottom of the pool and keeping her arms ready for balance.

"Mmmm, so warm," she says as she slides into the water, perpendicular to him. "Ah," she adds as she leans back against the tiles.

Dan offers a neutral smile. He wonders if he can turn himself into a version of the blissful man in the corner. He makes an effort to avoid glancing at the woman's breasts, but the sun dances on the pool's milky waters and it's impossible not to appreciate their presence.

As the ripples in the pool settle, she says, "Do you know how hot they keep the water?"

Before Dan can open his mouth, the tanned man says, "One-o-four. It comes up from the spring hot enough to cook you, so they cool it." He giggles to himself, as if he's imagining their fate in the natural temperature.

"It feels so smooth," she replies. She brushes one arm, then her right cheek. "I'm already five years younger!"

Dan grins again. He splashes handfuls of water on his face and slicks back his hair. Resist, resist, he murmurs. He ducks under the heated waters for a moment and emerges in the steam.

She's Robyn, "but not like the bird." She repeats her name for the man in the corner, who keeps his secret grin and replies, "Roy." She's been through Avila before, always on business for Hewlett-Packard. She's amazed she's never been to the mineral springs.

In response, Dan says a little too much about himself. "You must come here all the time!" she replies when he mentions his work with emotionally-troubled kids.

He considers a scrambling of the evening – he turns it over. It might be fun and that would be a change of pace. Why not? But Robyn's kept her sunglasses on, leaving one mystery that can make all the difference in the world. At one point she's relating an anecdote and uses "party" as a verb. Dan senses a tremor of intimidation and decides Robyn might be slightly more than he can handle. The bubble of imaginary adventure pops.

She asks about fish chowder and Dan gives a noncommittal recommendation for one of the places near the pier in Avila. Roy jumps in with a detailed comparison of local offerings. Taking the assist, Dan pushes himself up and excuses himself, pointing toward the men's locker room. Robyn tosses a little smile, shy of a wink, and returns to the older man's menu rundown.

Relieving his bladder brings him back to earth and clears his head. He pads back to the deck where his towel and shoes wait. Still no message on the phone. He pulls on his shirt and chooses to head out, offering a pained wave on his way past the thermal pool.

Inside the car, his overheated body steams the windows and windshield. He exits the parking lot, windows cracked, and aims for his place in Cayucos. The horizon pulses in a riot of flames that climb toward darkening skies.

At home Dan pulls a Negra Modelo from the refrigerator, levers off the cap and checks his phone again. It's evening, Suzanne. He remembers she had work, but how hard would it be to take five minutes to call?

He paces toward the deck, spotting Venus over the Pacific, alarmed that the sun is disappearing. Could anything have gone wrong? How would he know? Vicky might have called if something major had cropped up. Maybe even over something minor. But she would use his office number. He should have made a plan to call the school in the afternoon – it would have been simple to ask if Suzanne completed the observation. Another mistake.

He takes a long swig of beer. He checks his body and relishes the lingering massage of the thermal waters. Relax, Danny boy, relax. Stop thinking about mistakes.

He decides to take a shower to wash away the hint of sulfur he can smell. As he tugs off his sweatpants, they brush his groin. He acknowledges his over-eager erection, shaking his head and reconsidering his impolite exit from the pool. He pictures Brynn – her raised eyebrows, her hips – and estimates how long it's been. Opening the vanity drawer, he spies the peachy-colored tube of coconut skin balm she brought over. The stuff she called "sex bomb," like a giddy adolescent. It became her code for wanting sex. Leaning in close, she'd whisper the words one at a time with a muted explosion of her lips on "bomb."

He skids on a patch of nostalgia and squeezes a drop of the cool cream, placing it as she would. Then he grasps himself and drops into fantasy. He reaches for the shower handle, turning on the water to a luxurious degree of warmth. Another more generous squirt of the balm and he's in the shower, pushing, pushing, water smacking his back.

He blinks and to his amazement Brynn vanishes. Instead he's wading into the milky thermal pool, dropping his swimsuit and kneeling before Robyn. He pulls her up and kisses her. She slips her tongue in his mouth, stirring him, then turns and drops to her hands and knees. He yanks away the bikini ties and pushes, pushes. That's it, she says. That's. It. Push. Robyn, not the bird. Red breast robin. He cups her breasts, lifting her. She presses back against him. Push, push. Red. Red ochre. Chestnut red, auburn, oxblood? Push, push, push. He groans and leans his forehead against the tiles, crashing into the unexpected, intoxicating head of dark red hair.

...

Suzanne runs back up the steps one last time, having forgotten her pillow. Her camping bags and Annie's bowls are loaded; Annie herself perches up front. Locking the front door, she turns to find Jeff smiling.

"Going camping?"

"Me? No. Just a quick road trip. To see some people."

"Awesome," Jeff says. "We should go camping some time. Joshua Tree. That place is amazing."

"Yeah, I've heard," Suzanne says, nodding and trying to step backwards. Then she reconsiders the agreeableness in her words. "Might be a little too much desert for me."

"You know Gram Parsons? He died out there. It's famous. His buddies cremated him there. Gram Parsons the singer? Grievous Angel?"

Suzanne frowns, desperate for an escape.

"It's crazy because when he died his brother or uncle or somebody wanted the body to come back to Louisiana – they had some kind of a scheme to collect his insurance or an inheritance? But his buddies knew he wanted to be cremated out in Joshua Tree. So, they get a hold of a hearse somehow and go out to LAX and talk the guards into letting them take his coffin. I don't know how they did it, but you know, fast talking.

"So, they drive him out to Joshua and dump five gallons of gas on his open casket and light him up!"

"Jeff..."

"Kaboom! The fucking thing explodes like an atom bomb! Not really, cuz it didn't even cremate him. Just burned him kind of crispy. So there's this mushroom cloud, so some campers and rangers find the body. It got sent back to Louisiana in the end. I don't what happened to all his money. Or his music, or whatever."

"Jeff, I have to get going. My dog's in the car."

"Yeah, sure. Adios! We'll go out to Joshua sometime. It's great." As she starts down the stairs, he calls, "I'll watch the place. Shoot me a text if anything comes up. You've got my number, right?"

Suzanne drives so fast she's almost past Cayucos when she thinks of Dan Tunbridge. Aiming for the exit ramp at Cayucos Drive, she decelerates and steers to the side of the road. She fishes through her purse for his card until she remembers that it only includes his office number. She never added his cell to her phone's contacts. It must be in the recent calls. Scrolling back, she locates it. For a second she debates whether to add a new contact.

Suzanne checks her eyes in the rearview mirror and is taken aback at her dilated pupils. Breathe, she reminds herself. Draw deep, hold for seven, exhale for eight. She finishes the routine and allows her body to melt into the car seat.

Then she clicks the phone to life and taps his number.

He answers a split second after the first ring. His voice croaks. She's hit by the thought he might be in bed – with someone?

"Thanks for calling. Sorry. Hold on. I'm eating toast. Long day."

She waits.

He clears his throat and says, "How are you doing?"

She sticks to her observations, describing some of the things Manny did. She adds, "I have the charts for you."

Dan's quiet for an awkward moment. "What about Emmy, Suzanne?"

"Right," she replies. "It was okay. It was…strange."

He waits again. "You don't have to tell me about it. I just wanted to know that you're okay. That it went okay."

"Yes."

Another uncomfortable silence.

"She was beautiful. I didn't expect…I mean, I didn't know what to expect. She was so happy. I felt happy for her – it made me cry. At one point she came up to me and touched my freckles. She doesn't have freckles. I think they surprised her?

"It was like meeting a stranger, except…I had this crazy fear we'd recognize each other, that each of us would be shocked to see each other? But it wasn't like that. It was so peculiar because we were strangers. I kept thinking, how can we be strangers? It was like she lived in one world and I lived in another. Like I was a time traveler. Someone from the past, or the future."

He says, "It didn't leave you upset or…"

"Angry? No. I don't feel anything like that."

She hears him standing up. A pickup drives by her car with staccato music blaring.

He says, "Are you in your car?"

"Yes." She sees her dog in profile. "Annie Fisher and I went for a drive."

She listens to him thinking. From the elevation of the off ramp she can see the jumble of homes in the beach town. How far off is his place? Can he see the ocean? If he looked inland would he see a Honda Fit at the top of the exit? What would she see? Would there be two silhouettes in the window?

"How did things end up with Vicky?"

"Good. She was…kind. We talked about Manny."

He says, "Ah."

"What will happen to Manny?" Suzanne says.

"Manny? Well, we talk each month about his progress and adjust our plans. Is that what you mean?"

"I mean when he's older. With other kids."

"We're hoping he lives a fairly normal life. It may be a little harder for him overall. He needs some skills for interacting. But he can learn those, if he gets the right kind of support."

"I cried for Manny, too. More for Manny." She's surprised to hear her own words. For a moment she fears tumbling back into that hole. She scans the violet sky for an escape.

"I should go. And let you go."

"Suzanne, if anything comes up – if anything bothers you, would you give me a call?"

She pauses, wanting to be honest that she'll be away but not wanting to tell him where. Finally, she says, "Okay."

When they've said goodbye, Suzanne pulls back on to Highway 1, pointing toward the last light of the day.

At Ragged Point she considers stopping for hot chocolate. Instead she lets Annie Fisher sniff and pee at the edge of the parking lot. Then it's back to the sheer drop-offs and the climb through winding curves. Suzanne swings into them, fearless of the falling evening. At one point she passes bikers straining up a hill. Beyond them she travels alone in early night shadows.

Nearing the pine-shrouded campground at Plaskett Creek, she considers turning into the circle of sites and taking a chance that the rangers won't be around. An impulse dissuades her. Instead she continues a few hundred feet up the road, to the pull-off on the ocean side the surfers use. You can load a surfboard of the right length into a Fit. More than one guy has assumed she surfs based on the car alone. Here you can pull in close to the other vehicles. They're friendly, she tells herself. Annie Fisher is a great ambassador. Suzanne spots a black Tundra with a camper shell festooned with band logos, a World Wildlife decal and a Neil Young "EARTH" sticker. As she considers parking next to it, a dark-haired girl in a fringe jacket pokes her head from the side of the truck and waves.

"Perfect," Suzanne tells her dog. "We've got neighbors."

The guy and girl in the truck have driven down from Humboldt, though he grew up on the coast near Montana de Oro, only a few miles from the ranch where Suzanne lives. He remembers passing the ranch and wondering who lived there. The couple offers a bowl of stew to Suzanne. She takes out her apples and cuts slices with her Swiss Army knife. The guy salutes her dexterity with the knife. He and his girlfriend are planning to hike to nearby falls in the morning and they welcome Suzanne to join them. She thanks them, saying she and Annie Fisher will probably stick to the beach. Crawling into the Honda, she unrolls her sleeping bag.

With Annie close by on her own pillow, Suzanne wiggles herself into a comfortable position on her side. She slips into leggings and a loose jersey, anticipating she might need to get up in the night. The car protects her from the marine layer that kisses the coast where she's parked. She doesn't need to zip up the bag and instead, drapes it like a tent awning. The last of the day's light evaporates, leaving her to imagine the small world around her.

For a little while images from work and the preschool skitter through her mind. Manny's face and the eyes of the curious girl. Her hair color, the fall of her curls – everything so familiar. The perfect little lips. How could she be a stranger? Would there be a moment – if they sat reading together or laughing over a game of pat-a-cake – they would both burst into tears of recognition?

Suzanne sighs, wanting those thoughts to vanish. She wills the ocean to wash them away.

The Pacific delivers its rolling, droning anthem. Not the rising and falling noise of breakers, but a low guttural roar – an ancient story song. Suzanne curls in a fetal position, hands tucked between her thighs. She hears a bright hiccup of laughter from the couple next door, snuggled in their camper shell. With a tentative movement she touches herself, circling lightly, then pressing. From the pines over her car comes a rustling whisper: Suzanne. His hushed voice. She flips away from the sound, not wanting to acknowledge it. She says no. The trees whisper again. In the balmy darkness, she dips her fingers past the waistband of her leggings, finding herself, pressing, pulling, letting everything fall away from the world. She opens her mouth to the ocean's Gregorian call and lets it flood over her. Not here, not here, I'm not here. With one last yearning pull she rises, vanishing into the endless black canopy of diamonds.

...

Maggie exits the closet, yanking her flannel nightgown into position. She steals a quick glance at her husband. Mac steps into his pajamas, trying to avoid any motion that might seem combative. They've quarreled all evening and Mac can't find an exit. He understands that when Maggie gets agitated she needs to whistle and hiss and blow steam until the boiling recedes. Even then she can't be touched until the scorched, coppery surface of her skin cools. He's never been sure whether his words are a part of the calming process or if they only fill the time. If he sits there and says nothing, she'll fire herself up for another blast of super-heated vapor.

He picks through memories to find the sweet girl who's in there somewhere. That sprite who bounded out of the redwood grove at camp in the Sierras all those years ago, daring him with a flicker of her eyes to follow. A name beyond his imagination – Marguerite. She claimed to have been raised in the woods and she wasn't kidding. She knew the scientific names of ferns and burst out laughing when he asked if she ever climbed a redwood. "Like that one?" she said, pointing to a giant.

For a shy, circumspect adolescent from the desiccated suburbs of Fresno the idea of Maggie and her family living in a camper in the woods like characters in a folk tale seemed inconceivable. She painted an entrancing, panoramic mural that made him believe in the magic of God's created world. She convinced him that God planted love in that mysterious world, waiting like huckleberries to be discovered and savored; that clothing was a stupid invention – a claim that aroused him; that God could know his heart and only God could steer him. He ached to be her Adam.

When he discovered later that she could also withdraw in fiery outrage and summon a kettle-like suit of armor, he learned to wait with patience for the spell to break.

"I can tell you don't believe me even though you say you do. It doesn't matter. Her baby is at that school. That very school. I know what it means when a mother cries tears like that. I know those tears, Andrew!"

He tries again. "Maggie, I believe everything you told me."

"Little girls, Andrew. In the play yard."

"Yes, yes. The kids were the right age. But we don't know she's there, Maggie. That's all I'm saying. How can we know?"

She climbs in bed and flips to her side, silence her retort.

Mac lifts his side of the comforter and slides into bed trying to keep the mattress steady. He lies still on his back for a moment, corpse-like. Is it his turn to speak or have they finished? Maggie wiggles her head in irritation – a sign for him to turn off his bed lamp.

Her voice rises in the dark. "If you do not go down there and see if she's there? If you brush me off or you drive your truck by that school without stopping? If you do not find out if she's there, do not come back to this house, Andrew. I will lock the door."

"I promised I would and I will," he says.

"Why doesn't God pity me?" she says to her pillow.

Her shallow breaths mutate into a soft cry – not the hot eruption of tears that requires his apology, but an act of self-soothing Mac knows not to interrupt. Still, he'd like to touch her shoulder. Would she shake off his hand? What if he placed his palm on her hip? What if he stroked her thigh the way he had every time they'd made a child? Naked, the two of them under God's warming eye in a rolling field of poppies. Maggie certain that her tender nipples and heightened sense of smell meant she was primed to conceive. Her ravenous hand groping him, inviting him. Her insistence that he enter her from behind – something about the mouth of her womb and her instinctive determination that his seed flow deep within her. Afterward, pulling his muscled forearm against her moistness, pressing and squeezing with her thighs, panting and sending herself into another convulsion of joy and fertility.

It was joy, without a doubt. They loved each other's touch. God's euphoric animals. If he touched her now, would she remember their frenzied mating? If he offered his arm, would she move against it?

Would she arch herself and welcome him? It was love and it was animated, and it was joyful. Would it reassure her that he is still that spellbound boy? Would it lift her from her agitated woe?

It was the love God had hidden for them in the world. Wasn't it love? If he touched her, wouldn't it be that love?

Chapter Eight

BEER, PINOT NOIR, AVOCADOS, CHIPS, VEGGIES, something to grill. Dan checks his mental list for Friday night's gathering. Maybe he can find that Belgian beer, Grimbergen Dubbel, that he sampled in Sweden. That would add an international touch to his effort at hosting the psych crew's barbecue.

It's been a while. They like his place at Cayucos because of the beach, but since June no one's asked if he's up for hosting. He accepts the unspoken collective acknowledgement that Brynn's gone. TJ gets how he's doing, for the most part. Word gets around from there. He wonders if he'll see Brynn's absence in their eyes – assessing the state of the kitchen and the bathroom, tracking his drinking.

But time to try again. TJ will bring her guitar. She and Deb might sing some old Everly Brothers close harmonies. A pit fire to mark October's waning days will be perfect. November and its discontented winds won't be as tolerant of them gathering. Those will be days for hunkering down and studying the horizon. Now's the time to open up the house, share some food, laugh at each other's foibles and consider the swirling ascent of embers in the night.

He finds the Grimbergen at BevMo, a fortuitous sign. The rest he catches at Spencer's on the way home. He's grabbed two cans of the salsa Brynn loved – if he's got the right box at home he'll send them off tomorrow.

Tasks completed, Dan decides to pop the top down for the rest of the ride. The sun's overhead and the wind's offshore, holding up the breakers. There's time, and it would be sweet to do a loop up the coast and back. But he's not in the mood to dematerialize and let the road pull him along, even with the right music. Instead, he's feeling sociable.

At that he pictures Robyn in the thermal pool and frowns at himself. What a strange week. Too much time in his own head. He's survived one sweat-soaked nightmare where a tsunami poured through the house, smashing his belongings, upending the Miata and tossing him to a ruined landscape. The gamble with Suzanne Verdin sits in his mind like a book with pages flipping forward or back, depending on the gusts. That no one has contacted him about her observation at the school is positive news. She sounded stable, or at least satisfied. Relieved? These are the upbeat notes that score his buoyant feeling about the barbecue. People are okay, at the heart of it, even when they've been knocked around by life. Confused, angry or twisted up some other way, but good in their hearts for the most part. Worth the time and effort. Dan grants himself a shrug of acceptance at being a psychologist. It's a decent pursuit, imperfect as it is.

He's happy with his instinct about Suzanne – that she's not damaged, that an act of kindness or faith in her might help her move down the road. So many people tether to a moment in the past, unable to believe they can be free of it. Doubting the world trusts them to make their own decisions. He pictures her manner of scanning the horizon, as if she knows her life waits to be discovered. He wanted her to see that the little girl was fine, that her decision to offer her for adoption wasn't the disaster story some might write. Pull your anchor, Suzanne, he wants to tell her. Feel proud you weren't selfish and that a child you brought into the world is thriving. He wishes there were an easy way to see Suzanne in person – to consider one of her smiles. The tone of her voice on the phone didn't quite assure him. He acknowledges the difference between what he's wishing and what may be. His gut feeling on this one has served him well. He's happy in the moment; hopeful that he's not wrong. It leaves him in a mood not for the solitary thrill of encountering an open road, but for cheery faces, whispered flirtation, laughter and who knows, dancing isn't out of the question.

Lucas wanders over in the afternoon. He's holding up a gold coin and wants to demonstrate a trick. Dan says, "Sure, buddy." He reminds himself to plan a talk with Lucas about the magic tricks. He's worried Lucas may try to impress girls with those. It should be written down somewhere for every fifteen-year old boy: Save your magic tricks for grandma. Girls do not want to see your magic tricks.

Dan plays along with the set-up as Lucas moves the coin closer to his face and flashes it about. He slips it under his right armpit and wiggles a second too long, trying to grip the coin there. Oh, Lucas, Dan groans to himself. Another flash or two of his left arm – with his right held stiffly against his body – and Lucas flips his left hand open.

"Aha," Dan says to the disappearing act, trying not to sound too encouraging. He can't help but fix on Lucas's cramped right shoulder.

At that moment Lucas raises his right arm to mirror the triumphant gesture of his left. Dan blinks in astonishment that the coin does not drop from his armpit. Before Dan can close his open mouth, Lucas dips his right fingers into his shirt pocket and produces the coin.

"You're telling me there's only one coin?" Dan says after a moment of analysis.

"One coin," Lucas replies with a grand smile.

"You got me, buddy. Not bad. I don't know what the heck you're going to do with magic. Don't try it on girls. But you've got some moves there, Lucas. Not bad."

They talk for a minute about why girls are mysterious. "I can't figure out if they're serious or just saying stuff," Lucas complains to the ground at his feet. Dan says, "I haven't figured that out either, Lucas. Best to assume they're serious."

The party goes well. Late in the evening, the host retreats to his deck from the fire at the beach. TJ and Deb put the guitar aside, letting the echoes of "All I Have to Do is Dream" hang in the air. One of the couples by the fire cuddles up. Dan's feeling a little sentimental. The beer keeps him light on his feet. When the women sang the country ballad "Together Again" their voices climbed like flowering vines, leaving no room for sadness. He sat and smiled at their contentedness.

A couple of guys and Pat, the EMT, are baiting each other over a basketball game on the TV in the living room. Dan sits alone, but the melancholy notes stay away. Kind of like the middle of a teeter totter, he thinks. Not going anywhere tonight, and happy to be here. He toasts the western stars and the ocean's gentle song and his fortune in living at the beach.

TJ climbs the stairs from the beach, taking them in exaggerated strides, one at a time, like she's playing hopscotch on a giant's court of squares. She plops down next to him at the deck's rail.

"The freewheelin' Danny T.," she sings from a happy spot shy of inebriation. "Hello."

Dan tilts his beer bottle and grins. "Hello to you."

"Not freewheeling. That was Dylan. Or James Bond. You aren't that brash. What's the word I want?"

Dan considers her question, but TJ continues on her own. "Self-confident. But, it's not that simple. Self-assured? Confidence on the outside with something else inside. Like a peanut butter cup," she giggles. "What is it?"

"A lost boy?"

"Nooo." She slaps at his thigh. "You aren't lost. It's the thinking. Like introspection, but not that. Ruminating! That's what I was looking for. Confident on the outside, and ruminating on the inside. I like that word. Ruminating. Rumination."

Dan grins again. "And you are – what's the word? Tipsy."

"No, no. I'm playing with you. Sorry. By the way, when's the mourning period over in your religion? When can you start wearing color again?"

He looks down at the black sleeves of his shirt and his black denim jeans. "I didn't realize," he says with a laugh.

"Yeah, we noticed," she answers with a forgiving smile.

"People think that?"

"Mmm-hmm. People think that."

"Wow," he says. "Huh."

"Everybody was glad to be here tonight, Dan."

"Well, I thought they were having fun. You guys sound great. It's kind of unfair how happy you two are."

TJ presses her lips together, considering things. "Early on we made a choice to be authentic – you know, take a risk and trust each other?"

Dan gives her a quick glance and says, "Trust?" He weighs his gamble with Suzanne and wonders why TJ chose that word.

She gives him an inebriated smile. "It's something you offer another person, Dan. It's a gift. You should get to know it."

"You're giving me a diagnosis of trust issues and mourning all wrapped up together, is that what you're telling me, TJ?"

They laugh together.

His mind drifts. "I think I trusted Brynn. I mean, I didn't mistrust her. Or is it distrust? I thought I handled it reasonably well considering I'm the one left behind."

"Dan, you didn't have to trust her. She was your honeybee. You were so taken with her shininess – and I liked Brynn, don't get me wrong. She's adorable. But you got lost in her glow. I don't think you had to trust her at all. You know, big trust. Not where-are-you trust. Bigger. I don't think it ever got to that."

When he doesn't reply she says, "Sorry. Am I saying too much?"

He looks at her, half-puzzled, half-amused, staying silent.

"You guys were fun," she adds. "You were great. I'm sure it was rock and roll all night long. Seriously, you had a lot of fun with her, I saw that. But you were playing tag with her, Dan. She was always going to zip away. Not from you, but away to something. You didn't do anything wrong. I know you loved her. But did it ever get beyond super happy fun love? You know – Eros? Ludus? The bubbly stuff."

"And you're saying I didn't offer her enough in the way of trust?"

"Nooo. Not really her," TJ says.

"Who?"

"All of us."

"Ok. That's useful to know." His gaze drifts to the ocean. "Wow."

"Maybe not everybody."

He says, "Maybe not?"

"How about a general skepticism?" she says with a looping gesture of her arm. "What your head might tell you is a healthy distance?"

"Oh, that."

She says, "As such, the mourning clothes."

"I hate psychologists," he tells her. "Always trying to make everything a psychological issue."

TJ smiles and takes in the sound of the ocean.

Dan says, "I tend to think of it as a second skin. Like a wetsuit. Sometimes when I'm gliding underwater I feel it lifting away – I guess that's ironic. A wetsuit for when I'm not in the water?" He shrugs. "I hadn't thought of it as mourning or grief. It's funny, because it doesn't feel like not trusting – you know, being skeptical or unsure about people. It's odd when you don't have someone you're supposed to be trusting. How can you have trust issues if you don't have someone to trust?"

He takes a sip of beer. "I do realize how empty-headed that sounds. Blame the beer. And the man in black look? That's amusing. I was looking forward to everyone coming. I did not catch that."

She pats him on the head and rises. "You'll be fine."

Dan reaches and squeezes the back of her calf. "Thanks, TJ. I can't call that award-winning, first-class therapy right there, but I'll still cover the bill."

TJ heads off to collect Deb. Voices from the beach call, asking if they should put out the fire.

"No, I'll get it," Dan waves back. He wants to sit outside a while longer.

Inside the house, howls erupt over a shot or a referee's call. Pat spins like a break dancer, letting out a brawny curse. In a few more minutes everyone's through the house and heading out the front door. Dan waves them off, thanking all for coming.

Alone in the kitchen, he reviews his clothing. Well, it's perfect for the night. Head out there and hide under the stars for a while. On the way he grabs a skinny arm of driftwood, eager to stir the embers.

•••

Suzanne and Annie Fisher hike out to the curving sand spit at Andrew Molera. A mass of driftwood has been gathered and erected to form a child's dream of a castle. To form a pyre. The whole beach lies abandoned, excepting the sandpipers who scurry at the water's edge. Suzanne walks a little farther on, thinking of faces. She comes across a few ruined feathers still attached to a cracked bone. Scavengers or insatiable waves have seized the remainder of the bird.

Suzanne begins to cry, her arms clutching her waist. The thrumming waves wash her with salty mist. She heaves great sobs, returning her grief to the comforting primordial ocean.

•••

Saturday morning gets a late start. Dan stays in sweats and flip-flops, promising himself he'll run at sunset. He gathers up laundry and gets that going. He puts on a Pat Metheny album and lets the guitarist's subtle shifts and resonating chords inspire the scrambling of eggs. After he's eaten, but before the album ends, he goes to his bedroom closet and pulls out the vintage Epiphone archtop guitar he fell for at the shop in Portland. He matches a few of Metheny's notes on a song he recognizes, then waits for the album to finish. He attempts to form some of the jazz chords he knows. But his fingers fail him, bringing frustration. Dan loves the tone of his guitar. He thinks of Deb's ease with her instrument at the campfire. Why hasn't he found someone to help him learn jazz progressions? It's been a strong wish since before he met Brynn. Take some lessons, man. Show a little discipline. You either want to play or you don't. The moment threatens to sour, so he gets up and puts the Epiphone back in its case. We are going to work this out, he promises the guitar.

He decides to take a stroll on the beach for fresh air and to loosen the knot deep in his shoulder.

In the early afternoon the phone rings. His mother greets him with a bright hello, which catches Dan off-guard. She's more likely to check in on Sundays after she watches 60 Minutes, with tips on which segments he should catch. Her voice sounds robust and he can't detect any urgency in her greeting.

"Having a good day, Mom? Everything stable with you?"

"Everything but Washington, DC. That vile, despicable man. Excuse me. That rat pack of despicable men."

They agree on politics, but Dan knows better than to offer any encouragement.

"Ugh!" she adds, when he doesn't bite.

"Reading anything you like, Mom?"

She resets and accepts the assist.

"I am, in fact. Though it boggles my mind too. About the Salem witches and the trials. Very well done. It's quite psychological, Daniel. You would like that. Hysteria and mass delusions. Children saying their mothers turned into black cats. By the way, thank you for never reporting me for something like that. Men who accused their wives of flying here and there, causing problems. And the trials. Such a perversion of justice."

"You wonder how far we've come," he says.

"Well, there's a thin line between civilization and chaos, as someone said. Human beings. I don't know." With only a brief pause, she shifts the topic. He pictures her, years ago, showing him how to reverse yourself on ice skates. "But how are you, Daniel? How was the week?"

Without much hesitation or self-questioning, he brings up Suzanne Verdin and what he arranged at the preschool. He gives a tight summary and admits he's not sure of his reasons.

"It was a sense I had about her. About her needs, but also about the way she would handle it. I don't believe she would do anything to harm her daughter. I can't say I have a solid rationale. It's not that simple."

"No," his mother agrees. "Does she have people to help her?"

Dan stumbles, chagrined he hasn't asked himself that question.

"I'm pretty sure she's close to her sister. There's a woman who's a little older who lives next door. I think she talks with her. Not close with her parents."

"They got very involved in the hearing, I remember you telling me that."

"Yes. They pressured her about the adoption. Suzanne had to draw some boundaries with them."

"I am assuming you are not her therapist."

"No. That wouldn't be right. She may have someone she sees. I can tell she's had some exposure to counseling. I'm planning on checking with her to see if she wants a referral."

"It's not something I would be happy to hear about in a case. Nothing illegal, but I would think it could stir up some difficult feelings."

"Yeah, I get that, Mom. I've wrestled with it. Not an easy ethical one for me."

"Not for anyone."

"No, but I made the choice. I'm clear about that. I mean, I made the offer. She's an adult. Very different, I think, than a few years ago. I didn't know what she would choose. I felt she deserved the offer. You know, respect for her being the birth mother? Acknowledgement that she accepted the adoption?"

"She doesn't question it?"

"I can't say for sure. She wonders if it was fair. She doesn't seem angry or convinced it was unfair. I think she wonders if it was a done deal – that the system was never going to return the baby to her."

"Yes."

"That haunts me, too. That and the fact I'd seen her daughter and knew she's doing well, but Suzanne hadn't. I felt like things were out of balance."

"This shouldn't be about you."

He pauses, accepting her point.

"It shouldn't be, but it is, Mom. Partially. I accept that I inserted myself."

"Are you experimenting with her, Daniel?"

"No! Mom, please. The world doesn't need any more stereotypes about psychologists."

"Daniel, everything we do with other people is an experiment. I don't mean a test or a manipulation. I mean that it is always an open question as to how they will respond. You know that. We have to acknowledge uncertainty when it comes to our impact on other people, our expectations about them."

Dan exhales and says, "Yes."

"Draw your own line," she says. "Make sure you know your boundary. This is something the young woman will need to work through over time. The adoptive parents too. God knows the little girl will someday. I wish there were better ways to help people through this."

"I think I have a boundary, Mom. Good point. I'm trying to treat her as a mature person – a capable person."

"Are you attracted?"

He seizes up.

"Mom – no, it's not that. I don't think she – it's not that. That would complicate everything. It's something more basic. I'm trying to believe in her – or I'm trying to convince myself that people are basically good."

"That's honorable, Daniel. In the scheme of things, that counts for a lot. To believe in people – to believe they will act in good faith – a lot of civilization is built on that proposition."

He gazes out at the ocean, forming an image of his boyhood home.

"Yeah, we'll see. I don't know about civilization. I did have people over for a barbecue last night."

"Excellent! People from work? Friends?"

"Actual friends, Mom. From the clinic, yeah."

"Nice. I like that you are being sociable."

He sighs, with a smile. "Mom, I know we've talked about it before. Tell me again why you decided to stay single? You were young. I'm sure you met men. But you weren't open to another relationship."

"No other man would do," she replies.

"Oh, come on. I don't think you made any effort. You didn't do any experimenting."

"You don't know. Look, I couldn't imagine it. Your father was the one I loved. I had you. I saw your father in you. Well, to a large degree. You didn't get his gregariousness, I guess. But I had him in you. I didn't want another man coming in and complicating things with his own tendencies or preferences. I didn't want your father to be washed out of the picture."

"He was a good guy?"

"He was, Daniel. A very good guy."

"You don't have to answer this. I'm not sure you can. And I don't want it to hurt your feelings."

"Go ahead," she directs him.

"I'm wondering what I would have noticed in him – what I would feel or think, about myself, if I met him? Would I understand something about myself more clearly, if I'd known him for a day?"

"Hmm," she says. She lets the silence between them run for a few beats of his heart. Dan thinks he can hear her rocking. He doesn't detect any disappointment or displeasure over his question.

"I expect you would see what every son sees when he looks at his father – his mother too, but even more so his father. Some form of your future. Hints, clues, puzzles, certainties. In your case, you would see a man with an extraordinary sense of will."

He smiles, trying to fend off a pang of sorrow.

"Thanks, Mom. That's gratifying."

"Daniel, call me after your next conversation with the young woman – Suzanne. As soon as you talk with her."

"Uh, I'm not sure when that will be."

"Will you call me when you do? Don't wait."

He makes the promise, and they say goodbyes. On the phone the photo of her from his contact list lingers. Dan examines her face and tries to summon the man she loved.

•••

Sunday morning, he runs the five miles along the beach toward Morro Rock. Wisps of fog blow ashore until he is a lone figure tunneling into a thick, damp cloud. Slowed by the omnipresence of the fog, and with no sign of the rock ahead, Dan decides to loop back to Cayucos. The fog is so disorienting he can't locate his own trail of footprints. He runs along the waterline until the fog clears and he nears the house.

After a shower he heads out to warm himself on the deck. A hazy red sun hangs overhead. Dan thinks over the idea of stopping by Amsterdam in the afternoon. He recalls Suzanne saying she worked Sundays. If not, it's an excuse to send a simple message saying he passed by. If she's there, well, it's an opening. He wants to hear more of what she's thinking. The run failed to erase his doubts about her state. His mother's words echo in his mind.

On the stand by his deck chair, his phone issues a single, sharp buzz. He lifts it to find a text from Suzanne: "Something about what happens when we talk."

After a puzzled minute spent considering the possible meanings, he calls and finds her at the ranch apartment.

She's embarrassed about the text. She describes sending it from Big Sur on Saturday morning without realizing she didn't have service. He startles at hearing she's been in Big Sur. She explains there was an initial text that didn't go through: "A song you might like…" She says she remembered that he and Brynn loved talking on their drives up Highway 1. She thought he'd get it. Maybe he knew the song? The delayed text must have been delivered when she got back to civilization.

"Sorry," she says. "I didn't mean to confuse you."

He laughs. He tells her his mother called and she's reading a book on witches.

"How's that for confusing, hearing your mother talk about witches?"

"Real witches?"

"Well, no. The Salem trials. The mass hysteria?"

"Yes," Suzanne says. "That must be interesting for her. She probably doesn't get many witch cases."

"I don't know," Dan says. "I bet it comes up. It's amazing how much fear and suspicion there is in the world."

Suzanne lets a moment of silence pass. She says, "I should get ready for work."

"You know, I was thinking about stopping by Amsterdam later." Before she can speak, he adds, "Do you get a dinner break?"

She gets half an hour. He offers to come by. They can get a bite to eat and chat.

"I'm trying to reassure myself you're doing okay, Suzanne."

"I understand. Sure. I'm doing okay, though."

"Good, good. So it'll just be to catch up. You know, the news from Big Sur."

•••

Dan shows up five minutes before the time she's suggested and sits at an unhidden table on the front patio. Suzanne spots him and approaches with two salads, one with chicken and black beans, the other with seared tuna. She insists that he choose, so he opts for the tuna and thanks her for her thoughtfulness.

They eat for a few minutes and then he asks if she met friends up in Big Sur. He scans her face for any clues to her reasons for the drive. She says it's a favorite place for meditation. She and Annie Fisher roamed the beach and watched the waves. She mentions the couple she parked next to. "People are friendly up there, mostly."

She punctuates her comment with a relaxed, opening motion with her hand. Her face appears much less tense than the morning at the preschool.

"You feel safe, camping in the car?"

"If you park in the right places. I can be a bit of a loner. When I go camping I always meet people and hang out more than I think I will."

He mentions his barbecue and the campfire, laughing at how his mother said she was proud of him for being social.

"She didn't see me at the end of the night, stirring the embers by myself."

Suzanne keeps eye contact but doesn't speak. Dan's cheeks start to flush, so he turns back to his salad. Before taking a bite, he says, "You're doing okay?" He questions why he doesn't ask directly about the preschool visit.

"I am. I did a lot of thinking up there. But yes, I'm okay, whatever that means. I'm still a little confused how I feel. It was shocking to see her, but good to see she was healthy. Normal. Better than normal. She was bold. Very…confident. I don't know why it surprised me. She was strong and I was happy to see that. It warmed my heart. I saw she was strong."

Suzanne picks at her salad, like an archeologist uncovering layers of history from a buried artifact.

"But it was curious too. It felt like a dream. It struck me how alien we were to each other. Not alien, but unknown to each other. I mean, that's the reality. When I was walking on the beach I kept thinking how we'd have to start from scratch if we ever met. I felt I did know her. It's so hard to describe. I feel like I knew her better when I was carrying her."

He lets her words settle. After a moment he asks if she has a therapist, trying not to drift into a professional voice. She squints and explains hers left the area. Dan says he can offer a name. He knows a woman who incorporates creative work and writing in her approach with clients.

"I think you'd like her – she's artsy."

"I'm not so artsy," Suzanne says, glancing down at the table.

Dan smiles at her mild denial.

"Well, I think there's a lot going on inside you. A lot of creative energy. A lot of feeling."

She returns a tentative nod and says she wouldn't mind having the woman's contact information. He fishes a card from his wallet and slides it to Suzanne.

"I haven't mentioned you to her, but feel free to tell her I referred you."

Two young guys with shoulder-length hair approach the coffee shop pushing an antique parlor pump organ on a furniture dolly. Dan raises his eyebrows to Suzanne, signaling curiosity about the evening's music. She shrugs.

"Are you playing?"

"Nope. Not tonight." She holds his gaze.

"The song," he says. "It's Lucinda Williams, right?"

Her glassy sea of freckles delivers an affirming smile.

"I know that album. Thanks for the reminder."

He takes out his wallet and asks if he should pay at the register.

"Nope. It's covered." She brushes her hair behind one ear.

Dan tilts his head. "Thanks, Suzanne. This was just right. For me. I…"

She nods.

He catches a microscopic flash in her eyes.

They stand simultaneously.

Facing her, Dan balances a complicated twinge of desire and hesitation. He's ready to shove off when he decides to wing it.

"Can I give you a hug?"

She smiles and leans in. Like novice partners paired at a dance lesson, they embrace lightly. Dan's cheek brushes her hair. He recognizes a clean garden scent, like his mother's freesias. The touch of Suzanne's fingers surprises him and calls her keyboard playing to mind.

"I'll talk to you soon," he says.

He considers his reservations – his anxieties about being wrong about her – then finds them swept away, like a path washed clean after rain. It's all he can do to keep himself from fist-pumping at how well their conversation has gone. Is every interaction an experiment? Maybe, he thinks. Sometimes it's more natural than that.

Suzanne says, "Yes." She smiles again.

"I wouldn't mind if you call me Dan. That's what my friends use."

She glances down, then returns his look, her cheeks illuminated. "Have a good evening…Dan."

As he turns to leave, Suzanne holds her position by the table. He heads up the sidewalk, wondering if her eyes are still on him, tamping down an urge to look back over his shoulder.

Chapter Nine

MAC DOES HIS BEST TO CULL the facts from Maggie's feverish account. That she came upon Suzy pulled over and crying? No doubt about that. How many times has she spied her parked somewhere? A mother's uncanny instinct. That Suzy had been doing some project at a school? Well, that wasn't too hard to believe. Why was Maggie skeptical about that? She must have assignments. A preschool in the south county? Not a school he knew, and yes, it was a long way from the university. The adoptive parents might live out that way – might, Maggie. We don't know that. We never did. They could be in Oregon or Nevada by now. Half of California has moved one of those places. But Mac knows he can't say that. If Maggie ever believed her biological granddaughter had been moved out of state by "the custodial parents" she would demand that they follow.

When Maggie announced she would stop in to survey the preschool, Mac knew he had to insert himself. Poor Maggie wore an urgent expression that alerted people, the way a stray cat starved for milk or touch might get their attention. Most weren't frightened by her. Their faces would shift from curiosity to concern as she talked. Concern often grew to alarm if Maggie got worked up, raising her arms like an agitated conductor. She might step in a little too close. When the kids were in junior high and the problem was Maggie prying and offering guidance about their friends' lives, they pleaded and lectured her on personal space. Maggie thought their notion of boundaries was foolish.

"This is what's wrong with the world," she told them. "Let's all hide in our own little fenced-off pastures. No one cares about anyone else! The whole world's afraid of sharing what's really going on for fear of offending or bothering someone. Or because of their boundaries." Maggie offered her opinions and worries the way she'd share an abundance of zucchini. She tried to be friendly about it. She might laugh one moment only to flash irritation in the next. "I'm too honest for most people. Believe me, I know, I know I'm too honest," she'd say, expelling the fault like a cherry pit. If others agreed with her concerns – meekly or apprehensively – she'd grow bolder. "Yes! You see?!" What was the safer response than to nod? How could they ever know the tones that would soothe or redirect her? If only the world consisted of steadfast redwoods, boulders with friendly profiles and welcoming laps, ferns gathered in merry congregations, streams of hard-working insects, and an occasional curious jay, Maggie's childhood in the coastal forests would have made her the perfect ambassador. Alas, people were a complication. The idea of her appearing at the preschool would not work. She'd spill the whole story to the first pair of ears who'd listen, convinced that if only they heard the details, they'd see the outrage in it all and sympathize with her.

It required effort, but Mac talked her to a compromise by pledging to visit the school. She agreed to let him replace her only after he promised to go inside and stay long enough to take a clear look at every little girl. "Go there and tell them you're a handyman. Ask them what you can fix." In fact, he had the same idea. The Handyman's Delight: sooner or later everything in this world breaks. Say you're a handyman and the broken things pour your way.

Mac doesn't relish making an uninvited visit to the preschool. But he's learned the offhand smile that people want to see when a stranger approaches. It isn't that hard to be genial. You keep an eye on their eyes and broadcast a little more warmth if they act at all skeptical or afraid. It doesn't hurt to have a nickname like Mac, either. No one ever gives him a sidelong look about that.

Aside from his wife. Maggie has never gotten used it. To her it was a perplexing remnant of an unimaginable upbringing in a dusty, tree-stripped suburban concentration camp. She couldn't fathom why his parents chose a nickname from a boxer. That the boxer was Mac Foster, the heavyweight from Fresno, did not impress. "I don't care if he knocked out Sonny Ray So-and-So," she told him. "Why would you want your kid named after a boxer? When that kid is as skinny as Abe Lincoln! Did they want you punching people?" Even after he showed her a photograph of the giant's expansive smile, Maggie protested. "Yes, it's a beautiful smile, Andrew, but it's not like you look alike. Did they think you were Black?" She bristles at his gentle reproach about the unimportance of skin color. "Didn't they think you'd get teased or bullied? I don't understand what was going through their heads." When he claims no one bullied him, other than friends saluting him as 'Mack Truck,' she says, "Well, they could have if they wanted to, Andrew. It's a cruel world."

Mac shakes his head and smiles to himself. Andrew, Mac. Andrew, the humble apostle, the fisher of men. Mac's never considered himself to be on that level of piety. And yet, he's never shied from offering his beliefs to anyone open to hearing them. So many people hungry for a few reassuring words. The world of man never satisfies. It's left him hungry. He understands why Andrew and his brother chose to follow Jesus. Given the opportunity he would do the same thing. That his namesake died for his beliefs gives Mac a private sense of pride. Nothing he would ever mention, but something that reinforces his own convictions. In this broken world of jammed windows, rotted steps, cracked walls, and damaged hearts you had to find a way to offer yourself. He was a mender. He pictured the Apostle Andrew that way – skilled at mending fishing nets or leaky hulls. Ready to offer his skills to those who cannot do for themselves. That he needs to charge people causes Mac some regret. To be a barefoot mender in a much simpler time? Trading his work for meals and shelter? He considers how he and Maggie might have led an uncomplicated life on the shores of Galilee. He would have followed Jesus, he knows that. She too. An apostle for women. Women had sympathy for Maggie. They recognized something in her of themselves. Yes, she could have been an apostle with him. Knowing Jesus in person – as a man to talk with – would soothe Maggie. It would end her rash arguments with a distant God. What a shame she couldn't know him as a fellow human being. They would have followed. The simple mender and his earnest wife. Mac shrugs at the Bible story he's constructed. He doesn't find it foolish, but he lives in the world of man and in a world fallen far from the days of Galilee. So many things broken, awaiting repair. Andrew and Mac. Curious how they both fit. For the fractured world of man, you couldn't beat Mac.

The drive to the school takes longer than he's expected and he's a little puzzled at how remote it is. From a distance it resembles a small ranch, which makes him nod in approval. Why not? They might have animals. Is there a chance the girl is there? As he approaches the fenced property he re-examines his plan. Walk in with a casual stride. Check the fascia boards for rot or peeling paint. Check the windows. Oversized trash that needs to be hauled to the dump. Something's been neglected. Ask for the director. They like to be called directors. She'll be busy, a little harried. All the troubles on her shoulders. Be warm and humble and straightforward. Have your card ready. People like handymen. She'll have a plumber or an electrician or a guy who painted the school a few years ago. But it'll be on her face – some dissatisfaction or worry. Handymen can solve the little problems nagging at you. They aren't expensive. All he needs to find is one little problem – one furrow on her brow. Warm smile. Be a fisher and a mender.

Beyond that, his task is murkier. He is under direct orders to "look at every single little girl" at the school. Mac knows that would be a disastrous approach. The last thing he can do is study the little girls. If he can find a job to do for the school, he can be surprised by the kids, he can smile in joy at their energy. He can compliment the teachers and joke about his own kids at that age. Anything to diffuse their skepticism. The kids will be curious about his tool belt, if he can get that far. Mac the handyman. If he can find one teacher who sees the possibilities, he can be a spontaneous moment of learning. Kids should get to touch tools. Mac the handyman's here. He's already considered the idea that they might need him to return for regular work. This doesn't have to be strange at all. What are the chances the little girl is there? It's far more likely that he might earn a new client.

To face Maggie that evening he will need to record every face that he can. "Red hair!" Maggie said in exasperation when he asked what he should be watching for. "Suzy! Look for Suzy's face. Her eyes, anything. You do remember your own daughter's face, don't you?" Mac did. At this age he counted her freckles and made her laugh with the silly numbers he made up after getting to ten. He'd threaten to kiss each one. Her hair color had been more similar to his than Maggie's. His was never as red – by adulthood those highlights had faded to rusty brown. Suzy had the warm hues of red oak stain. So many times, when he wiped and finished wood in that shade, he'd been fascinated by how Suzy's hair held the same tints, as if she'd pulled color from deep in the earth, through her bloodstream, to the roots of her follicles. So, his task comes down to this: find a young girl with any shade of hair from redwood to dark walnut or a face with any sign of freckles. "And her eyes, Andrew! For God's sake look her in the eyes. Find Suzy in her eyes."

He will ask no questions and seek no names. This he's told Maggie in his firmest voice. To her objections Mac said they would go directly to their daughter if a girl at the school fits the profile. "Oh yes, we will confront her," Maggie promised. "We will sit her down."

Mac pulls his truck to a parking spot by the fenced entrance to the preschool and sets his brake. Kids race about the yard, but he hesitates to zero in on faces. A young teacher stands near the gate, watching the kids with her arms crossed. He steels himself. He checks that his card is in his shirt pocket. He won't be able to observe the condition of the building before having to speak with her.

In the second before he opens his door he dares to say the name: "Emmy." This is his secret. Maggie doesn't know, nor does his daughter. The judge never said it. None of the paperwork contained it. She was always Baby Girl V. For a long time he and Maggie called her that, as awkward as it was to say. He liked the V, their family link. After a year or two Maggie shifted to "Baby Girl." Suzy only ever said "her" or "she," and then they stopped talking about the child. Mac's kept the secret name to himself since the day he overheard it in a hallway at the courthouse. The adoptive parents huddled with their lawyer. Mac wandered down the hall, searching for a drinking fountain. He paused nearby, back turned to them and unnoticed. A young woman – she might have been a sister – scurried toward the group. When she got to them, Mac heard it: "Who has Emmy?" Someone shushed her and that was all Mac caught. He walked outside and felt his heart racing in the bright sunlight. Then he sealed her name away, wondering if he might need it someday.

Before he is all the way around the truck the teacher calls a proactive, "Hi. Can I help you?" Mac admires her alertness and understands he's been spotted as a stranger. He smiles and takes a second step toward the yard before pausing.

"Hi there. I'm Mac, a handyman?" He stoops, in a partial bow. She uncrosses her arms and looks him up and down.

"Oh! Yes…"

"I wanted to check with the director…"

"Yes! Vicky said she'd be calling someone. She's not here right now." The young woman cranes her neck toward the preschool office, then turns back to Mac, looking a little perplexed. "She took a boy to the urgent care. For a bee sting. Or a bite? We think it was a yellow jacket. He may be allergic, I'm not sure. Sorry, it's a little crazy here."

Mac says, "Oh, that must have hurt. Those bites can be nasty."

She grimaces, revealing her own fear of bees.

"Is there a nest somewhere?"

The teacher's eyes grow wide in horror. "Oh my gosh, I don't know. I didn't look."

"Sometimes it's nearby, but it might be far off. I could look around."

The teacher studies him, the fear of bees gripping her face.

"The kids look happy." Mac nods at a trio playing near a large oak.

"Yes! Fortunately, no other disasters," she says. "Sorry. Here's the gate. It's the top hinge that's broken. Right there?"

Mac blinks at her words, checking to see that he's understanding what is happening. He assesses the gate and finds it sagging. The top hinge has pulled its screws, tugged loose by a parade of hurried entrances and exits.

"Amazing," Mac says with a shocked smile.

The teacher's eyebrows rise.

"I happen to know how to fix that," he says, in a light self-mocking tone.

"Really? Oh, good. We keep thinking it's going to fall off and knock one of the children on the head or pinch somebody."

He joins in her little laugh. "I'll get my tools."

She answers with a sing-song, "Thank you." For a second he feels like a well-behaved child, then smiles at the genuine warmth in her voice.

"It's Mac, by the way." He offers his hand to her.

"Nice to meet you. I'm Miss Kerri. Kerri," she adds with a shrug.

"Thanks, Kerri. I can check for bees afterward if you want me to."

Her brow twists and she says, "Okay. Maybe when Vicky gets back? I'm not sure what they want to do."

"Sure, sure," Mac says. He wants her to know there's no problem at all.

A squawk from the far edge of the yard causes Kerri to zero in on a boy who's climbing the tree. "Jeremiah! That's too high!" she calls.

"Sorry," she tells Mac. Pointing toward the children, she says, "I should head back there."

"I'll get right on this," Mac says, nodding to the gate. "Thanks."

Kerri flashes a smile and hurries toward the children, leaving Mac at the entrance to the preschool, sunlight pouring on his shoulders. He turns his head toward the school building, then looks again at the gate hinge, astonished at this turn of life's big wheel. Bees too? Sure enough, the roof's fascia boards need scraping and painting as well. That might be a stretch and not something he can do today. He can't help feeling the school's been waiting for him. Then Mac turns from his own thought, remembering that another handyman may be coming to do the job that's fallen into his lap. That would be awkward, but there will be a way through it too. Mac tells himself to start paying attention.

...

He's in luck on the hinge. No water rot in the old screw holes. Screws work loose over time, story of the world. In fact, the screws used were too short for the job. Mac will replace them with a size larger in diameter and an inch longer. The replacements will dig in for a snug fit. With all new screws on the top and bottom hinges, the gate will be rescued from its precarious angle. He's got an armload of tools out, including a level that he places atop the gate. He makes a show of preparation, snapping his measuring tape and double-checking everything.

Seven girls appear on the yard in the next half hour. Bright blonde hair rules out two of them. One is Asian, and three others have hair that is far too dark, Maggie's Mexican-American grandmother notwithstanding. A leggy girl, looking older than the four-year old he seeks, has frizzy brown hair. The last girl could be the right age. She has no freckles that he can see. She wears glasses that seem a little thick to Mac. Her hair is light brown and cut in what he remembers as a pixie-style. As he sets the upper hinge screws, he can't make a case for any of the girls being Suzy's daughter.

Would Suzy think that? Mac imagines his daughter at the school, working on a project. Was she reading or doing art? No, Maggie said something about a boy and charts. Observations. He wishes he could read Suzy's mind. If he could grasp how she thinks about the adoption, he could help Maggie accept it. Something about it is resolved for Suzy. He's not convinced she's made her peace with it, but she doesn't fight it. No, that's not the right word. It's not that Maggie fights it. She wants a say in it. She wants a way to participate. She has good energy in her heart. She wants to be a grandmother. Mac understands that and his heart breaks for his wife. He's come to see that Suzy was meant for another path, something other than being a mother, at least for now. They would have raised the baby together, the three of them. Once they got over the storm of the pregnancy he felt convinced that was the answer.

Time has taught him other ways of looking at the situation. Suzy values her education. He's not sure that's the smartest thing. Universities make him nervous. Too many people who think they understand the world. Too much certainty about science and facts – the "great books." Who's to say about that? Not enough openness to the mysteries of God's world. Mac remembers Thoreau and Walden Pond. Now there's an education in and of itself. Leave the world of man behind and let Nature teach you what you need to know. Discover it yourself. The idea of being guided to an education by professors strikes him as contradictory. Wouldn't they teach only what they know? How would that be the right education for you? He understands that Suzy doesn't look at it like that. Somehow Suzy convinced herself that college could be her pathway to some kind of dream. He wonders if the degree matters to her too. Something to differentiate herself from him and Maggie. A line she imagines them not crossing. But does she dream of the little girl? Wouldn't she want to know, in her heart, that her baby is doing well? Wouldn't she want the same peace that Maggie needs, that he prays she'll find someday?

Mac knows he needs to go inside the preschool to fulfill his mission. He could not face Maggie's withering cross-examination without that answer. He's ruled out asking about the bathroom. No one wants a handyman who asks to use the facilities. The director, Vicky, has not returned, but he can leave his card. Whether or not Baby Girl V. attends the school, Mac wouldn't mind doing occasional jobs for them. It hits him what a crazy, perfect solution that might be, if by some miracle he finds her there. He would see her once in a while – watch her playing – without her or the parents becoming alarmed. Maggie would hear which stories the little girl likes, what her favorite snacks were. It wouldn't be enough, of course. But it might begin to piece things back together. It might warm Suzy's heart. They'd talk again. They'd write a letter to the parents and introduce themselves. Send a photo. Maybe he'd meet the parents on a pleasant afternoon while working on a window or a sticky door. It could all be a happy accident. Mac the handyman turns out to be her biological grandfather? Mac's heart beats with a swell of excitement. God does not disappoint. Maybe it is all meant to unfold exactly this way. Isn't that what he believes? Not that God has a plan – no, that's too narrow-minded a thought and it never accounts for the suffering in the world. No – God places opportunities in the world, waiting to see if you are paying attention and have readied yourself. There is always a path that leads to great happiness, if only you see the clues and act on them.

Mac decides to enter the classroom to ask the time. He has his card ready, too. Something will catch his eye, he's sure of it. He's certain there are kids in the classroom who haven't come outside. He needs to be fast. He's only got to determine if there's a girl who might be his granddaughter. As much as he'd like to be able to tell Maggie that none of the young girls was a possibility, he knows she won't accept that. She wants one definite candidate, so she can drill Suzy and try to squeeze a confession from her. Mac grimaces at the thought of that conversation, and understands it may play out that way. All that he can do is give his wife enough information that she won't go marching into the preschool on her own. If there is a little girl here who might be Baby Girl V., and if Suzy knows that, she and her mother are going to knock heads.

The room is cooler than the yard and dimmer than he expects. Mac scans for a clock and lets his eyes adjust. He's surprised not to see any teachers. A young boy sits alone at a table, rolling clay. One of the blonde girls is in a kitchen area with a girl he has not seen before. Her dark hair is thick, like a doll's hair, and her bright blue eyes give her a Scandinavian appearance. Mac decides he is not related to her. Several boys stretch out on the carpet in the playroom, constructing a helter-skelter train layout. Beyond them Mac notices the back of a child in a wheelchair. He freezes at the sight of a helmet of dark red hair.

Miss Kerri appears from the children's bathroom, surprised to see Mac before her.

"Oh, hi," he says. "I was checking the time. And I…are you expecting the director to be back soon?"

"I think so," the teacher says. "She hasn't called." She clicks a pen rapidly. "Are you all done?"

He remembers his card and pulls it from his shirt pocket. "Almost," he says. "I have to tighten it up. But I thought I should leave my card for her."

"Oh, okay…"

"I don't need to be paid or anything. I mean, she can give me a call."

She relaxes. "Well, she should be back real soon. Do you want to wait and see if she gets here? It should be anytime."

"Sure, sure, that's good." Mac indicates he'll wait outside. "I might look around and see if there's anything else I could help with."

"Oh, there is," Kerri laughs as she heads toward the child in the wheelchair.

Mac pauses, transfixed by the head of hair across the room. His eyes begin to water, and his breathing slows. Kerri snaps a lever on the wheelchair and spins it around. The child's sleepy face emerges from the shadows, like the moon slipping from clouds. Kerri sees Mac staring. She breaks into a welcoming smile.

"This is Marcus. Marcus, can you say hi? Say hi, Marcus."

Composing himself, Mac kneels down as the wheelchair approaches.

"Hey, Marcus," he coos. "What are you up to today, Marcus?" Marcus bats the tray of his wheelchair with two flattened palms.

Mac copies his gesture and says, "There you go! High five back at ya!" He smiles to Kerri's pleased eyes.

She says, "Time for Marcus to use the potty. Ready, Marcus?"

Mac steps back and watches Kerri turn to negotiate the entrance to the bathroom. He surveys the room, feeling a little deflated, acutely aware of the conversation he faces with Maggie.

Outside he checks the swing of the gate and pronounces it fixed. One of the boys and the girl with the shiny black bangs come running to see what he's done.

"What's that?" the boy says, pointing to Mac's level.

He shows them how the tool helps him check the gate.

"My dad has one of those," the girl informs him.

In a burst of energy, the two run off toward the tall oak.

Mac decides to pack up his tools. He'll go in one last time and ask to leave a note and his card. That could lead to more work. Who knows, they might not be happy with the other guy. Maybe he asked to use the facilities.

As he stands, a girl marches across his field of vision like a cartoon soldier. She wears shorts and an animal t-shirt. Instantaneously he realizes that he has not seen her, outside or in. Soft waves of coppery hair fall to her shoulder. The sunlight catches on her hair and for a second Mac thinks he's seen a ruby hummingbird alight on her shoulders. In mid-step, her knee hanging in the air for a moment, the girl snaps her head to meet his eyes, to salute her commander-in-chief. A terrible blast of heat hits Mac in the face – a cannon of memory thundering and striking him with the image of his four-year old daughter.

In a flash she races off to the play yard's oak.

Mac falls to one knee and draws a breath. His left hand trembles enough that he has to place his drill on the ground. A cold sweat breaks out on his forehead.

His chest constricts in so tight a band he fears he might be having a heart attack. Gulping for air, he steadies himself on the ground. He blinks, trying to see with greater clarity the afterimage of the young girl's face. It's not possible. How can it be? Like a riptide, his memories pull him to the anguished days at the courthouse, to the judge's final echoing words. Maggie's protests and her droning sobs in the middle of the night. Other nights when the kids were young and cried out in terror. When he'd go to their bedsides and offer to rub their backs. Suzy's ecstatic face the Christmas morning she found the castle he'd built her. Her wrenching tears the night she confessed her pregnancy. Mac fights for another breath and worries he's overheating. Everything turns red. The red of wood stain, soaking his hands. He pants and tucks his head to his knees, begging God to stop the spinning.

When he finds his feet, music clangs in his ears. He glances around, finding himself alone at the gate. God lifts his shoulders, urging him to stand. He knows now he's not dying. The heat rises.

And then she comes into focus, standing in front of him. God calls his name once: Andrew. It's the most beautiful sound he's ever heard. A tremendous surge of joy rises, wanting to become tears, demanding to burst from his eyes. And yet, he stands locked in place, commanded into a trance by an unseen magician. She stares at him, a curious tilt to her chin, her bangs dusting the tops of her innocent eyes. The scintillating light falling on her washes away her freckles. You lost your spots, Suzy, he laughs to himself. How will I count them? Mac feels the world lifting away – everything in it drifting off to space, freed from gravity. Everything but the little girl and him. They stand in a shaft of God's incredible grace, no more than two feet from each other.

He sees her lips moving. The symphony in his ears crashes to silence, cancelled by her words.

"I was on the first branch, but I didn't go higher because the Mother Tree said be safe, don't climb too high."

Her eyes, calling like unmapped tunnels.

"You have Opa's truck."

Mac listens, trying to sort the words. He turns his head and discovers the sun illuminating his silver pickup.

"Why do you have Opa's truck?"

"Opa's truck," he says. "Yes."

"Are you picking me up today?"

Mac stands motionless, certain that God himself is addressing him, speaking through this wondrous face. He fights a tremendous fear that his Heavenly Father will descend from the firmament at this very moment in a crushing, apocalyptic blow. That does not happen. Instead the colors of the world around him surge into hyper-saturated hues, like an old home-movie. Every ounce of doubt drains from his body, replaced by a charge of electric zeal.

"Are you ready to go?" he says.

"Okay," she sings, and he hears Suzy's music, delighted at his promise of frozen yogurt or some other treat they both loved.

Mac gathers his tools, guides the girl to his rear passenger door and opens it. He darts in a slow-moving, drawn-out blur, like the strange backward turning of a wagon wheel in an old Western. Placing the tools on the floor, he boosts her to the seat.

"I'll come around the other side," he says before closing the door.

Mac turns to check the preschool yard, prepared to prostrate himself before an infuriated God. But there is nothing to see.

He climbs inside and reaches back to secure her in the middle shoulder belt. As they gaze at each other, silence reigns.

"Your name's not Suzy, you're Emmy," he whispers.

The face with the incredible frame of red hair chimes, "Yes, silly!"

Chapter Ten

DAN DRIVES HOME FROM A COSTCO run. He's got the Blues Breakers playing, with John Mayall howling about someone double-crossing someone. A quick click to the next song. The jazzy harmonica intro to "Room to Move" fills the car and Dan tacks back to a brighter mood. The passenger seat overflows with a flat of yogurt cups, a tub of mixed nuts and family-sized boxes of frozen cod filets and grass-fed beef patties. Though he likes the simplicity of Costco, Dan cringes, realizing that sooner or later he will consume everything sitting in his passenger seat. Then again, Lucas will help with the burgers. On a night his mother makes garden soup he might wander over to investigate what Dan's got to eat. Halfway up the highway to Cayucos, Dan realizes the shopping or the quantity of food or the prospect of cooking has dulled his appetite. He'll go for a run before the sun sets. A spoiled haze obscures the distant hills as the marine layer keeps the air at the beach clear.

Carrying the last box of provisions inside, he notices Margaret Becker waving from her kitchen window. He sends an acknowledgement her way, and she signals for him to come over. Dan imagines her busy at her stove and guesses she might want to share something. Actually, that'll be perfect. He takes a minute to pack the food in his freezer and heads toward her back deck, where she greets him.

"Did you see the news?" The concern on her face triggers a fear about wildfires for him.

"No. What's up?"

"A little girl was kidnapped. Taken from her school."

He slams to a stop.

Margaret says, "A school down in Guadalupe. It happened today."

"Kidnapped?" he manages to say.

"They said abduction. Not like kidnappers. Someone took her from the play yard. Right in the middle of the day."

He teeters on his feet, in danger of fainting. "Jesus, Margaret."

"I know. It's got to be a custody dispute. Do you think? I can't keep my mind from imagining awful things. Remember Polly Klaas? Or little Jonbenet? Could it be a stranger? Surely they'd be on the watch for that."

"Did they say there's a suspect?"

"No, no. Only that she was abducted."

"Down in Guadalupe? What was the name of the school?"

"Something with elves. Happy Elves? No, that's not it."

"Forest Elves," he says, as if in a trance.

"Yes! Do you know it?"

"I have a client there – a little boy we're working with."

She says, "Oh my gosh."

"And it was a little girl?"

"Yes. Four years old."

"Did they say a name?"

"No. They called her a four-year old. It was on the five o'clock news."

He remains motionless, struggling to keep his balance as the world races around him.

"That's so strange that you know the school. I mean, not really. I'm sure you know most of them. I don't know why, but when I heard it I thought about Baby Girl V. She just popped into my mind. Like maybe the biological father showed up? I always wondered who he was. Sorry. I get so upset when children are taken."

Dan locks on her eyes, terror rolling through his gut. She's a psychologist; this whole encounter could be a set-up. No. That's not reasonable. Think rationally. Shut the hell up and get back to the house.

He says, "They said she was four?"

Dan's face feels as cold as a marble bust. Margaret notes his pale color and offers him a sympathetic look. Despite the sentiment it's far from a smile.

"Sorry if I upset you, Dan. I don't know why I thought those things."

"No, I'm fine. I know the director. She'll be beside herself. I might give her a call."

She names the channel where she saw the story. He gives her a grim thanks and heads back to his house.

128

Inside Dan falls to the ottoman and buries his head in his hands. When he stands again he feels emptied of blood. He moves like an afterimage of himself, a thin strand of smoke escaped from a charred, lightning-struck tree. His phone lies on the kitchen counter. He pulls up Suzanne's info, but before he can press to dial, everything jams and his hand locks in place. He scans the ocean, trying to find an option that makes sense.

It can't be the little red-headed girl. Not her, not her. He turns on the television, finding the national news. Fifteen minutes before the local station comes back on. Dan jumps on his laptop to check their website, but finds no hint of a child's abduction. He checks the clock again.

No, no, no. She can't have taken her. He would have noticed something in her demeanor. It was no more than twenty-four hours earlier they sat chatting at Amsterdam. Nothing seemed odd at all. He recalls her habit of looking away – the daydreamer's style of escaping the tension of the moment. He sees her band of freckles. There's just no way. I'm not wrong about her. Where would she take the little girl? To her apartment at the ranch? Why? That would be nuts. She wouldn't do it. She wouldn't.

He stands, checking the time again. He has minutes to call her before the top of the news hour. What can he possibly say? Did you take Emmy? Where are you? Have you seen the news? He drops to the ottoman again and hurls a loud curse at the television screen.

At six o'clock the local newscasters appear, the man sitting high in his seat, caffeinated. His co-anchor – a woman who is pregnant – appears stricken. They begin with the bulletin from the sheriff. Dan catches it in chopped phrases. A white Ford pickup. Scrambled letters and numbers from the license plate. A Hispanic man in his forties thought to be a landscaper or maintenance man. Forest Elves School. The abduction of Emmy Robinson, age 4, in broad daylight. The suspect not a relative of the girl. Search dogs and deputies combing the area near the school. A Highway Patrol roadblock at Gaviota Pass, as the vehicle in question may be heading toward Southern California. Phone numbers for tips, for anyone seeing the pickup truck.

"We've now received a picture of the young girl who was abducted. Again, authorities say she was taken this afternoon from the play yard at Forest Elves School, near Guadalupe. This is the four-year old girl, Olivia Emily Robinson."

Dan arches in searing pain as the school portrait of Emmy R. fills the screen. "No, no," he moans. He launches another string of obscenities at the television. "Is it Emmy or Emily, damn it!" In the aftermath of his outburst he hears the dreadful echo of Margaret Becker's words: "Baby Girl V. – she just popped into my mind."

The newscasters shift to other stories after saying they will return to the alleged kidnapping shortly.

He walks to the bathroom and soaks his face with cold water. In the mirror he finds raw, reddened eyes that might have come from a night of crying. He closes his eyes and tells himself to get it together. One more splash of cold water and he dries himself off.

Before he can sort the anomalous bits of information he's heard, he thinks of Suzanne again. If she's heard the news or seen the photograph she will be panicking. There's no way she's involved. He's got to call her right away. First he has to make sense of what he's heard.

As real as the photograph is, the name is not right. It's Emma Robinson, not Olivia Emily. The parents could have changed it, but would they? Dan is certain her legal name was Emma, with no middle name. He saw the documents any number of times. He saw the final decree. He scours his mind trying to remember if he ever heard Vicky say "Emily." Her handwriting on the school portrait was definitely "Emmy." He can call up a snapped memory of the page. No, he's never heard anything but "Emmy." Did he say "Emma" at some point? Wouldn't Vicky correct him? He curses again, unable to recall anything other than "Emmy."

And the landscaper? In his visits to the school, he never saw anyone working on the grounds or the building. Dan surmises that no one witnessed the young girl being abducted. Vicky or someone at the school must have provided the information to the sheriff. Why would he take her? He shudders at the image of Emmy in a stranger's truck.

He shifts back to thinking how Suzanne will handle the news. He's dismissed the possibility that she's involved, whoever the landscaper is. She will be shocked at her daughter's abduction, of course. She will be afraid the school will identify her as the biological mother. Dan's stomach sinks at the implications of that discovery. He forces himself to concentrate on Suzanne's feelings. How would anyone process news like that?

He gathers himself and grabs his phone. He steps toward the back deck, then decides to stay inside where he won't be overheard. The sun disappears and the western sky churns with color. He doesn't think

Suzanne's at Amsterdam on Monday nights. If he catches her at home, there's a chance she'll answer. But he's prepared for the call to go to voicemail, as it does.

"Hey, Suzanne, it's Dan," he says, downshifting to a casual tone. "Just wanted to check in with you. If you could call this evening that would be great. Okay, bye."

He hangs up and stares at his phone. It's too late to call Vicky. He'll try in the morning. What to say is a problem, but it makes sense to try. Who else is there to call? TJ? Dante or Kevin back in Portland? What the heck would he say to those guys? They'd be mystified by every aspect of the situation. Their advice? Get your ass back to New England before California falls into the sea. His mother too. He owes her a call – he promised an update after meeting with Suzanne. But this? Mom, I need to consult with you on a child abduction. Dan realizes that this is precisely what he needs to do. But he can't. He can't face her questions or the heavy pauses she would take.

TJ comes to mind again. First step, always – confide in a colleague. He's sure she would agree to keep it confidential. But not tonight – that would be too alarming. First thing in the morning he'll lean in her office and test the waters with her. His post-doc supervisor at UCLA, Aletha Thompson, is another possibility. He consulted with her at the time of Baby Girl V.'s evaluation. But again, how would he ever explain these circumstances? And what in the world would he ask? He can't think of a concise question other than what the hell is my next step. Brynn? They'd met not long after the case. She knew the struggle he felt over it. She said once, "I could never make a decision like that." What would it mean to call her now? How could she not see it as a pitiable effort to tug at her heart?

Margaret Becker? Would it be preposterous to confess the whole thing to her? As strange as it sounds, Margaret, more than anyone else, is the person who's heard his thinking about Baby Girl V. She knows how important the case was to him. She's seen the complicated angles. Could he trust her now? What if she learned his actions led Suzanne to the little girl? Would the horror of her disappearance and the need to solve it overshadow his choices?

Not if Suzanne is involved in the abduction. Dan shivers at the thought. She can't be. She cannot be. Damn it, Suzanne, give me a call.

...

At Montana de Oro, Annie Fisher jumps into the Fit as a fog bank threatens an advance on the cliffs. The dog shakes herself and settles into the backseat, waiting for her companion to get in the car.

Suzanne checks her phone and sees she still has no service. Halfway down the mountain from the state park it'll reconnect to the world. She's hoping no messages from her mother will pop up, but she's pessimistic. It's been a little too long since she's heard from her.

The sunset walk along the cliffs helped settle her tangled feelings. Something about the way the upturned rock formations angle into the sea, defying the waves, rejuvenated her. The past week has been like having another path scribbled over the roadmap of school and liberation from her parents that she's followed diligently for almost four years. She can sense June's graduation within reach. She'll be able to move somewhere of her own choice, somewhere that won't include random maternal intrusions and ever-present watchfulness. Standing on the cliffs, at the broken edge of the continent, it all seemed possible – a dream within her grasp. She can't let the distressing past reach forward to trip her. The little girl is happy. She is strong. Emmy is your name now. I will leave breadcrumbs for you, Little Wing. If ever you need me, I won't be hidden. But you will have to choose to find me.

The distressing past – memories that she herself has wakened. Watching the smooth progression of the waves, Suzanne asked herself why she needed to see his face. Dan Tunbridge, the untested span over a foreboding river. Why wasn't it enough to let his name fade – to kick aside the few crumbs leading to it? And now, his piercing eyes. Brown, with flecks of moonlight. His voice wafting like the aroma of baking bread. His gangly, undernourished chairs, posed one to a page, so obvious in their loneliness. If only he didn't explore her face the way he did. She wanted the waves to wash away his interest, but the ocean only laughed and teased her with its spray. No. She will not let her roadmap be altered. He's dangerous – he's rooted here, much too close to her parents and the musty cave of memories. He still loves Brynn. Brynn in Sweden. Brynn who followed her own roadmap.

As she steers the car downhill her phone buzzes twice, indicating a voicemail. Dan Tunbridge. She takes the last turnout before the hill that winds down to civilization and parks the car. A hundred feet below lie the reedy shallows of the bay. A caravan of camel-back sand dunes stretches toward the looming rock and harbor at Morro Bay. In the distance lies Cayucos – purple shoreline against golden hills.

Suzanne zips up the offset lapel of her jacket and plays his message. Hearing him say "evening" she surveys the tinted sky and the pinpricks of light along the coast. She presses the screen to call him back. Before the first full ring ends he picks up.

She barely finishes her greeting when he asks where she is. It's the wrong question.

"Why?" is her curt answer.

She hears him pausing and resetting. "Sorry. I'm a little frazzled. I was worried about you."

"What is it?" she says.

"Suzanne, you didn't go down to Forest Elves today, to the preschool? You didn't go see Emmy again, did you?"

"No. What is it? What's going on?" She swallows a lump in her throat.

"Listen, is there any way we can meet to talk? It would help if we could talk in person."

"Tell me what happened."

"Are you in San Luis? I'll meet you wherever you are."

"Please tell me what this is. You're scaring me."

He backs off again and recounts the headlines from the news broadcast. He says "taken." Something about a man, the maintenance guy.

Suzanne tries her silent chant – not here, not now. The whole car vibrates, and she cannot escape the moment. She manages to ask, "Is she safe?"

"They're looking for her. They have a roadblock on 101 South. For some reason they think he might be taking her that way."

"Who is he?"

"The gardener. I don't know. Apparently he works there sometimes."

"Oh my god."

Dan's silent.

"It's really her?"

"Yes. It's Emmy. They're showing her photograph."

"Why?"

"They don't know. No one's saying. I mean, if they know anything, they haven't told the press."

"Did you talk to them?"

"Who?"

Suzanne says, "The school. The people there."

"No, no. I found out a little while ago. My neighbor told me it was on the news."

"They showed her picture? Oh my god."

Suzanne wants to hang up and run. But where would she and Annie Fisher go? There is nowhere. They would find her. And what would it mean that she ran? She closes her eyes, trying to clear away everything from the black surround. His voice is saying something. She wants vast empty space.

"Suzanne? We should meet. We've got to think about this."

She breathes but does not answer.

"I'm scared too. I'm sorry about this. Are you still there?"

"Yes."

"I'm in Cayucos, at home. Let me meet you."

Still she does not answer.

"We can figure it out, Suzanne."

"A man took her? I don't understand that. How is that possible? How?!" She pounds the steering wheel, causing Annie Fisher to whimper in her back seat.

"Suzanne, please. Can we meet up? We need to talk."

She glares at the landscape – not at Cayucos and whatever tiny point of light is Dan Tunbridge – but at the space between them.

"Morro Rock," she says.

"You're at the rock?"

"No."

"Meet at the rock?"

"Yes."

He says, "I can be there in ten minutes. Less."

She ends the call without saying anything more. Morro Rock's cold, fist-sized silhouette lies at the center of her field of vision. A crown of foggy ramparts rests atop it, like a child's drawing of a castle. Like a fortress cast by some wintry spell into a massive, craggy island. She hesitates before starting the car. An impulse screams at her not to go. Fly! From the back seat, Annie Fisher issues a whimpered question. Suzanne blinks and resets herself. You do not have to trust him, but you will go. Be invisible. Leave a trail. She may be looking for you. Emmy, Little Wing.

The wind and the ocean, like a chorus of two-handed drums and deep groaning strings, flow over her car. Furious voices echo in the wind, as if she's ripped open a portal to an ancient ceremony of fear and chaos. She lets the anthem lift her from the ground and carry her on her back, feet forward, arms outstretched, her face to the unfamiliar constellations. Rising with her, the music crests and cascades like a raging waterfall. She presses two hands against her belly to stop the woozy churning. In the silence, she hears her mother yelling, knocking at the window. Her mother's phantom face, veering from shock to accusation to angry defiance. Her mother.

Suzanne reaches for her phone and blasts a text at Maggie Verdin, letting her thumbs fly seconds ahead of her cart-wheeling thoughts.

"Where are you? What have you done?!"

She grips the steering wheel and checks the mirror to be sure Annie Fisher is in her place. Morro Rock. Daniel Tunbridge. Maggie Verdin. In that order. Suzanne moves the shifter into drive and descends the park's serpentine road, now lit by the last crimson rays of the day, a burning river.

...

They speed past Morro Bay, and then from Cayucos to the wilder stretches of the coast. Mac keeps his eyes ahead, concentrating on keeping the Country Squire between the painted lines on the curving road. Few cars pass from the north and no lights appear in the rearview mirror. Maggie huddles in the back, propping pillows on either side of the sleeping girl, smoothing the wool blanket across her lap.

The road rises toward Cambria. At the outskirts Mac parks beyond a convenience store. He runs back and returns with milk. When he opens his door, the overhead light illuminates, and Maggie flashes a stern face. Mac eases the door closed and stuffs the milk carton into the cooler to his right.

Through a landscape growing darker they climb into the Santa Lucia range and the precipitous cliffs along the Pacific. At Ragged Point Mac slows, noting a surprising number of people in the restaurant. The parking lot is crowded as well, with a Cal Fire truck parked off the meager two lanes of Highway 1. In another moment the enveloping darkness wipes the motel and restaurant from view.

Past Salmon Creek, Cruickshanks, and Gorda, they travel in silence. They pass the signs for Jade Cove and the Plaskett Campground. He considers a stop there for the bathrooms and slows the car. When he looks back, Maggie shakes her head.

Still they climb, passing another campground at Limekiln, followed by the turn-off for the Benedictine retreat at New Camaldoli. Mac's spirits ascend as the road switches back and rises again. He drives past hulking boulders – survivors of previous landslides – with no fear in his heart. The miles and hours blur into one streaming sensation of movement. He's not at all sure what time it is. The station wagon sways through the barren, nameless stretches of the road, as confident of its destination as Mac.

Now he counts the signs for the three creeks. Ahead there is a blinking temporary road sign. It flashes, "Fire Danger High." As Mac senses that they must be near the third creek, he spies the telltale boulders and battered mailboxes marking the steep drive to Westhauser Ridge – to Gethsemane. He slows and guides the station wagon onto the access road.

The incline's almost too steep for the vehicle. Halfway up the first climb the rear wheels spin. Mac shifts the station wagon into a lower gear and moves ahead with caution. At the first switchback he pauses, then drives with more conviction. The next climb is better, as are the following three. They rise above the coastal fog. Each turn up the mountain yields a peek of the dark gleaming Pacific at their backs. In the final ascent coastal oaks crowd the narrow road. When they reach the summit, they're welcomed by an ethereal canopy of stars. Maggie says nothing, despite his success at getting them to Gethsemane. Mac wants to pause and stand under the stars. Maybe gaze out over God's inexhaustible ocean. There might be a dense, eggy hint of the hot springs in the air. He's sure Maggie would object, so he continues creeping forward along the rutted road.

The old refurbished WPA cabins stand dark. No vehicles are parked nearby, not even the Jeep used by the stoner kid from Fernwood who keeps an eye on the place. Typically Mac's cousin has an Airbnb lodger there – Europeans, most often. Sometimes a distant relative's kids, a name or face he's seen before. He writes off the quiet to it being early in the week or late in October. And is there a fire somewhere? His eyes sting. He blinks to clear his vision, and continues past the silent redwood cabins.

The last quarter mile to the trailer poses the greatest challenge to the station wagon. Mean ruts yank the vehicle left and right. Mac battles the rebellious steering wheel. He tries slowing and edging over the ruts, but that only makes the jolt on the other side worse.

They wind their way to the last twist of the road and Mac locates the space under an oak where he can park. He heaves a sigh as he brings the car to a halt. As the headlights flick off, he remembers how dark the place can be. He'll need his flashlight to navigate the path to the trailer. A wave of exhaustion threatens to swamp him. Still, their arrival at Gethsemane and the miracle of being here with her fills him from a spring of joy. He turns to face Maggie and glances at the bundled passenger, draped in darkness. Maggie puts a finger to her lips to deter him. She doesn't notice the little girl staring in terror at his face.

...

Dan wears a loose-fitting sweatshirt. The wind is off-shore and warmish. As he turns into the parking lot at Morro Rock, he drops his windows and searches for her car in the dark. One row of parked vehicles lies at the edge of the lot closest to the beach. A few scattered trucks sit elsewhere, with no sign of Suzanne's turquoise car. He finds a location with several open spots, then decides to reverse into place so he can face any vehicles coming across the pock-marked lot. He gets out of the car and leans against the hood so her headlights will illuminate him. The imposing mountain of compressed and scarred stone looms over him. Shaped like Goliath's petrified heart, it's the only remaining evidence of the giant's spectacular collapse and his last dumbfounded roar. Dan checks his phone, but there's no message.

He's giving her ten minutes more – twenty-two total since she hung up – then he's heading straight for her apartment at the ranch, come what may. As much as he wants to believe her, he cannot shake the apprehension that Suzanne might have Emmy. Nothing in their conversation stoked his fear. He couldn't hear any sign of the girl. Nothing suggested Suzanne knew anything about the landscaper. She appeared as bewildered as he is. Still. Four days after her visit to the school the girl goes missing? He curses again at the parts that don't make sense. He's got to check some records at work first thing in the morning.

Dan steers his attention back to Suzanne. With the shock of the news wearing off, she will be upset about Emmy. He makes himself say it: her daughter. She took the visit too coolly, wearing a veil of skepticism to blunt the reality of seeing Baby Girl V. grown to a preschooler. It's her faraway style – the way her eyes carry her to a safer place. This will tear aside any veil she's been using. He's sure the threat of what might be happening to the little girl will crack her defenses. Strangers shudder tonight at the little girl's fate. How could Suzanne be any less distressed? He's got to make sure she can withstand the strain of the abduction. That there might be horror beyond the abduction is too much for him to consider.

They have to talk about the school. If Suzanne has nothing to do with Emmy's disappearance and if the little girl is found and she's unharmed...Dan swears again at the swaying line of dominoes he's considering. Her visit to the school may never come up. It's possible that no one knows Emmy is adopted, aside from her parents. He has the written observations Suzanne did of Manny. He can vouch for her work. They might not face questions. It all hinges on whether the police discover that Emmy has more than one mother. He grimaces at the thought and turns away from the wind, which is trying to push him toward the immense rock.

Her headlights appear and the small car creeps forward, jolted by potholes in the sandy lot. He holds up his hand to wave, but his gesture locks in a signal to stop. The car veers in his direction.

She leaves Annie Fisher in the backseat. Dan takes a close look and finds no sign of any other being. Suzanne approaches him, her arms crossed and close to her chest, as if the whipping wind is chilling her.

Before he can speak she says, "I don't want you stressing about my problems."

"I'm not," he lies.

One corner of her mouth twists. She turns her head toward the rock. The wind blowing through her hair obscures her face and sets her head aflame.

"Okay, I am worried, Suzanne. About her and about you. I'm sorry. I can't imagine what you must be feeling."

She shifts her feet. "Have you heard anything more?"

He shakes his head. "There might be more on the news later."

Another gust buffets them.

Dan says, "If anything happens that draws you into this, I will take full responsibility for it."

"If anything happens?" Her eyes stretch wide. "If anything happens?"

"I know. I know."

"A little girl is missing! Think what she's going through. She's only four years old!"

He keeps nodding, trying to absorb her distress. "I was trying to say that I'm not going to leave you alone in this, if people start asking questions."

She takes a forceful step toward him. "I want to be left alone. I don't want you taking responsibility for me. Did I ever ask you to get involved? Back then? Now? Ever? No! Why did you tell me about her school? Why did you dangle that in front of me? You knew I wouldn't be able to resist that. Did you think about how it would feel to me? Down here? In my gut? Or did you just want to feel better about what you'd done? You needed me to go to that school. You needed me to see her, so you could feel better about your stupid report. You wanted a happy ending to the story you tell. You used me!"

She starts to turn toward her car. He interrupts her with a shout.

"No! That is not how this happened."

They glare at each other, she posed in a quarter turn away from him.

"That is not it, Suzanne. I made a choice to tell you about Emmy. Yes. For you to have the choice to see her, as I had. I thought that was fair. That was it – for you to have a choice. That was enough for me. There was no need to tempt you or coerce you. I was ready to accept whatever you decided."

"You have no idea what it's like to give birth to a little girl! To be responsible for bringing a life into this world."

He quiets. "I don't. No."

"It's not like some simple choice, once that happens. It's not that easy. I'm her birth mother!"

Like a sailboat steadying itself, Suzanne turns to face the wind. Her hair trails away, revealing a storm of freckles. The silhouette of the great volcanic plug threatens to swallow them. Wind charges up the ragged mountain – gusts carved into shrieks by the cleaved faces of the rock.

Dan tries again, straining for calm. "I'm sorry. This is all coming out wrong. I'm anxious about Emmy. I care about her and I care about you. I wanted to see that you were okay. This isn't about me. It's about Emmy."

"You wanted to see that she wasn't in my car," Suzanne says in a deep voice.

Dan recoils from the wind, flinching at its slap. He looks back at Suzanne.

"Yes. I did want to see that. Fair point."

She says, "You don't trust anyone, do you?"

He blinks and finds no words to reply.

"I have to go." She turns toward her car. With a few steps she's at the door and inside.

Dan follows to the driver's door as she starts the car and the headlights come on. He crouches down at window height, not wanting to alarm her. He waits.

In another moment the window rolls down. She looks him in the eye.

"I'm sorry for upsetting you," he says in even tones. "We'll know more in the morning. I need to check some things at work. I'm going to call you when I get in there."

Suzanne stares ahead through her windshield. She closes her eyes, her nostrils flaring. Then an abrupt glance to his face. The angry blood drains away, displaced by an expression of fear. She says, "They won't find her with a Mexican gardener."

She reverses the car and simultaneously rolls her window shut.

Dan jolts upright, off balance from the car's sudden retreat. The gap between them opens like a fissure. Agitated wind gusts rush to fill the void, knocking him sideways.

Chapter Eleven

AT THE CLINIC DOOR HE JUGGLES a large iced coffee that threatens to ruin his entrance. He'll pay later with reflux, but after a roiled night of sleep Dan needs the caffeine. This will go down fast.

Tracie, the morning receptionist, raises her eyebrows at seeing him this early in the day. He's wearing a black crewneck jersey with a gray sport coat. She notices the missing tie and compliments his appearance. Dan thanks her and offers a toast of his drink.

"No rest for the weary," he says, without much conviction.

Tracie returns his gesture with her mug, saying "The only hope of the weary."

The morning television news has been useless – nothing beyond a rerun of the story from the evening before. A sleepy-headed anchor mentioned a sheriff's press conference at 9 a.m. Dan thinks he can stream it, but he'll have to wait over an hour.

He goes straight to the files once he's in his office. His folder on Baby Girl V. is at the back of the file cabinet, right where he's stored it. He spreads it open on his desk.

Dan's report had no identifying information, so he pushes that aside. A scan of the judge's decree shows the same. Because this is a redacted version, Baby Girl V. is the only name for her. The custodial parents' names blacked out. When did he see the original?

He flips to a contact sheet that was faxed to him before the evaluation. There he finds the name he's remembered: Emma Robinson. No middle name. DOB: 07 Mar 2013. Length and weight noted. The custodial and prospective adoptive parents: Paul and Jeanne Robinson. The address of the tight apartment where he met them. They perched on the edge of the sofa like uncertain guests or reluctant relatives. Dan assigned that to their understandable nervousness.

Now it hits him that the apartment was not theirs. It must have been a friend's place. Something their lawyer arranged? A strategy aimed at preventing him from knowing the real location of their home? He's startled to realize he never considered that.

He checks the rest of the papers, looking for any mention that would draw a line to the name the news is reporting: Olivia Emily Robinson. Would adoptive parents make a change like that? Perhaps in the first moment after a judge's custodial decree, a separate petition for name change would be granted. An amended birth certificate? Or could the name 'Emma' have been a decoy as well? No, their lawyer could not have convinced the court to use a false name. The court used "Baby Girl V." in each description of the central person of the case.

Dan yields to the mystery of the names. There are more important concerns. He's got to think through what he might say to Vicky. He's got to do some serious thinking about what to say if investigators already have his name or are searching for a college student under his supervision named Marie.

And he's got to call Suzanne. What did she mean by her comment about the landscape guy? She wore such a look of panic. Was it a dreadful premonition about her biological daughter? What would a birth mother think in these circumstances?

Why couldn't he read Suzanne better? The dreaminess made it hard, of course. When people drift like that you need more clues. A word. The sound of a word can make a difference. The movement of the eyes. A pattern. What was the mist that obscured things between them – enough that they startled each other again and again?

And what had TJ said about him at the barbecue – mistrust? No, this was something more specific to Suzanne. Something in the space between them. Did he hold some unexposed doubts about her? Was his own protective skin dulling his ability to understand her motives?

Frustrated by the questions pecking at him, Dan turns back to the computer to check whether the local channel's web page holds additional details. A banner above the story of the abduction indicates the news conference will be streamed live. Half an hour to go.

On a notepad he starts a list. He writes "Probable" at the top of one column and "Possible" at the top of another.

Before he can add more he hears a tap at his office door and TJ pokes her face in.

"Hey. Are you tracking the abduction of that little girl?"

Dan draws a deep breath, trying to meet her gaze.

She studies him for a moment. "You okay?"

He gives a tired nod and she comes in, closing the door behind her. "What's up?"

He points to the chair beyond his desk and TJ sits.

"That's one of my schools," he says. "There's a little guy there we've been evaluating."

"Forest Elves?"

"Yes."

"I thought that might be yours. Do you know the girl?"

Dan pauses. It's a span he's got to cross. Like one of those swinging, wood-slat rope bridges that always, always, always snap at the most perilous moment in a film.

"Yes, I recognize her. I'm not working with her – she's not a client. But I know her."

"Oh, man, I'm sorry," TJ says.

"Yeah, it's awful. I haven't talked to them yet, but the director will be devastated."

TJ furrows her brow. "Could someone take her like that? These days?"

"No. I don't get it. Vicky watches those kids like a mother wolf. Their play yard is huge. I don't know. I'm sure they didn't expect their landscaper to do anything like that."

"Do you know the parents?" she says.

He grinds to a halt, still gripping the unsteady ropes of the swaying bridge.

"TJ, I need a favor. I need a confidential consult on this. You okay with that?"

Her eyes widen. She draws a sharp breath.

"Sure, Dan. I can do that." She blinks.

He looks off before returning to her eyes.

"Thanks. It may not be anything. I'm not sure I know what's going on. It may be a coincidence that defies belief. I did an attachment evaluation for the court when this girl, Emmy, was an infant. When she was adopted."

"Aha," TJ says.

"I haven't had any contact with her or the adoptive parents since then. That was four years ago. I did spot her at the school when I was there to observe Manny Galvez. Something about her face jumped out at me."

"You're sure it was the same girl?"

"Yeah. Her birthday is memorable. One day after the day my father died."

"Oh, I'm sorry," TJ says. "I don't think I knew your father passed away."

"It was before I was born. So, it's not a day I remember. On the other hand, I remember it well."

TJ smiles. And waits.

"Anyway, Emmy. She was called Baby Girl V. when I did the evaluation.

"It was contested?"

"The birth mother petitioned for return of custody, but the court didn't go for it. Unwed teenage mother. Baby already attached to adoptive parents. Some technicalities on paperwork, but mainly a 'best interests of the child' case."

TJ nods.

"Yes, well – I met the birth mother a few weeks ago. When I was giving a talk to a psychology class at the university. About adoption and Baby Girl V."

"Whoa."

He gives her a look of surrender and expels a breath.

"Have you talked with her?"

"I need to call her," he says.

"She was there for your talk?"

"Yes. She approached me afterward."

"Hmm. How did that go?"

"For her? She wanted to see who I was, and she wanted me to see her. We didn't have any contact at the time of the evaluation."

"Was she angry? Does she blame you?"

"No. Nothing like that. She wasn't agitated at all. Not that I could see. She did ask whether I'd ever thought of a way it could be fair for everyone."

"Yow. Right to the heart of it. How did she seem, on the whole?"

"Stable, maybe a little distant. She's the dreamy-sounding one – on the phone?"

"Aha. I remember the voice."

"She's getting through school, you know, pulling her life together. Some individuation issues with her parents. Stable as far as I can tell."

TJ takes a long pause to think something through. Dan understands he's out on the rope bridge at this point. Not a moment to hesitate or panic. Keep your feet going and keep your eyes on that point on the far cliff.

"She didn't ask for information?"

Dan says, "No. Not a hint of that. She seemed – stoical about the adoption? I don't know the right word. I don't think she has anything to do with this, if that's what you're wondering."

TJ uncrosses her legs.

Dan says, "You'd call her?"

"I might. You know, to check in. Would she open up to you?"

"That's what I'm thinking."

"You would need to refer her to someone, of course. Or if it's a crisis…"

"Yes. I already gave her Jane Klein's card."

"Ah, so you've talked with her."

"Yes. We talked a couple of times after my presentation."

"Technically you're good."

"Yeah, I don't know. It doesn't feel settled. I have no idea how she's going to react to the abduction. And if it goes downhill?"

TJ says, "The timing is odd. But it doesn't sound like she's involved, right? You aren't worried that there's something more to it?"

"That would shock me, TJ. That's not my sense of her at all."

"So, the call is a reasonable idea. The referral to Jane is excellent. I'd try to get her in for some support while this is all happening. I hate to say it, but it could get a lot worse."

He reaches into his pocket, absently checking that his keys are there.

"And I'd take a step back too."

Dan checks her eyes.

"Thanks, TJ. Big help. This is a weird one."

"Won't be the last weird one, around here." She stands up. "Pop your head in if anything else comes up."

He gives her a thumbs up and exhales. When she's closed his office door, he shuts his eyes for a long moment, trying to see if he's made it to the last swaying slat of the rope bridge.

145

Suzanne opens her door to assess the morning light and feels her phone twitch in her pajama pocket, signaling a text. The message has been traveling for a hundred miles toward her apartment balcony, where it falls like a marathoner with a last gasp. The text is in green, not the usual blue. It means her mother is out of normal range. Stamped from the previous evening, the message has been delayed by the haphazard geometry of cell towers and transmission lines. Her mother writes: "Come to Gethsemane! She's beautiful!!! All is forgiven!"

Suzanne closes the door in acute shame, the text confirming the terrors that stampeded through her fitful hours of sleep. She stands still long enough to picture her mother at the weather-beaten trailer, the young girl on her lap, her mother brushing hair from her eyes, talking to her in exaggerated tones.

Spinning from the door, Suzanne rushes to gather her bag and Annie Fisher's leash. She hurries to her nightstand and grabs the Swiss Army knife. Snapping open the blade, she examines the knife and commands her trembling hand to hold still. The knife's stainless-steel blade mirrors a fragment of her face. A moment passes before she closes it and returns it to her nightstand.

Back in the living room, Suzanne turns toward each wall, demanding an answer on which way to go. Dan Tunbridge's apprehensive face appears – the desperate look he gave her at Morro Rock. She sighs in frustration. Then, thumbs flying, she sends him a message. Slapping her thigh twice, she calls Annie Fisher. Together they race down the stairs to her car.

•••

A quick run to the men's room and Dan's back in his office in time to call up the press conference. He wonders if Suzanne will be watching it. All night her words about the gardener tormented him. If only they've caught him and found Emmy unharmed. For a second the awful image of a man touching the little girl threatens to swamp him. He forces himself to concentrate on the computer screen.

The press conference starts with a string of men parading to the microphone, each introducing himself. Dan hears none of it. His attention fixates on the large poster propped on an easel next to the speakers. Emmy's face – an enlarged version of her school portrait – beams as if she's won a prize. Dan cringes at her expression.

Underneath the photo her printed name shouts itself, mocking him: Olivia Emily Robinson.

Then the stabbing thrust below. Date of Birth: July 3, 2013.

Dan slams against the back of his desk chair. He blinks at the perplexing numbers. July 3rd? July? He grabs the folder on his desk and tears at the papers until he sees the date: 7 March 2013.

He stands, like a boxer knocked into a stupor by a hammer-like punch. Before his eyes the school photograph with Vicky's handwriting materializes: Emmy R., 3-7-2013. The British slash. The European convention of listing day before month. The date he read as March 7. Not the day after his father's death, but the third day of the seventh month.

In the seconds it takes him to go from bewilderment to understanding, Dan falters. The room tilts forward and falls, like a ship diving into a heavy swell.

He catches himself and absorbs a shock of euphoria. It's not her! It's not Baby Girl V. Emmy R. is not Emma. One is Olivia Emily, one is Emma. Somewhere, another Emmy – Suzanne's biological daughter. But not at Forest Elves Preschool! It's not Baby Girl V. She hasn't been abducted. A watery weakness in his knees drops Dan to his chair.

Now the sheriff explains something about vehicles. A silver pickup, not a white one. The camera pulls back to reveal a ravaged couple to his left. He introduces them as Eric and Christine Robinson. Parents of the abducted girl.

Dan starts to swear but fumbles at the words. How could he have gotten it so wrong? He's never seen the man and woman on the screen. The devastated parents of Olivia Emily Robinson, born July 3, 2013.

Jesus, she's not even adopted, he thinks. She's a little redhead with the same last name and a common nickname. The abduction has nothing to do with Suzanne, with Baby Girl V. or with him. The spent, pleading faces on the screen make it impossible for him to set aside the horror of what has happened to them and their daughter.

But Dan's world has flipped and he's astonished how it feels.

He tears his eyes from the screen and springs to his feet. He's got to call Suzanne. If she's seen the press conference she may not have understood the mistake he's made on the birthdate. She would know the date is wrong, but what would she make of it? And would she recognize that the stricken parents are not the people raising her daughter? He pulls out his phone, uncertain of what he'll say, but determined to catch her.

He finds a text message from Suzanne, sent twenty minutes earlier. "Sorry about my anger. It's not you. Heading to Big Sur. My parents."

Dan curses and dials her number. He groans when it goes to voicemail. Still, he leaves a message: "Suzanne, call me right away. Big news. Good news. Please call."

The walls of his office grow closer and closer, compressing the air and making it impossible to breathe. He shudders again at the face of the young girl who is missing. The caffeine drives him to manic jitteriness. If only he could go for a run. A sudden hunger grips him and he remembers he skipped breakfast. He needs to get out of the office, get away from the computer and from his office phone. Suzanne won't call him there.

He checks the charge on his mobile phone and makes a rapid decision to head to the Depot Cafe. He can get an omelet and try to stabilize himself. He needs Suzanne to call.

On the way out, TJ catches his eye from her office. She asks if he's okay.

"Much better," he says, exhaling loudly. "Forgot breakfast this morning. I'm going to go grab something and try to start this day over."

She says, "Most important meal of the day," offering a mother's smile.

Dan gives her a thumb's up and heads out of the clinic.

There's no call by the time he gets to the cafe, no call by the time his breakfast arrives and no call as he finishes paying. The food settles him. That he hasn't heard from Suzanne disappoints him. Halfway through the omelet he decided to stop trying to influence the flow of events. The crisis is over – one crisis at least. Suzanne may not know yet. She may simply be running from the shock of it. Big Sur is her buffer zone. She'll get the news when she's ready. If not from him, some other way. He doesn't have to be the messenger. Let her address it her own way. Believe in her. She'll call if she needs to call.

He turns the Miata into the clinic lot and kills the engine. The food subdues the skittery energy of the coffee. Blood surges to his feet, his fingers and his cheeks, like the aftermath of a hard run.

Get some work done, man. Get something done. He thinks of calling Vicky to be supportive, but questions his ability to be helpful at the moment. He starts to take a deep breath but finds the air fouled. The morning light has gone orangish. A second whiff and he recognizes the distinct tang of wildfire. The office air-conditioning will be welcome.

...

Dan is returning the Baby Girl V. folder to his file cabinet when he hears a soft knock at the door. TJ's eyes appear as she tips the door open.

She says, "Want an update from Deb?"

Dan turns toward her. Of course, Deb would be getting the inside story from the sheriff's department.

"Yeah, what's up?"

"Well, it's not the landscaper. The bros pulled him over and all they have him on is driving while brown. He's totally clear – working somewhere else all afternoon."

Dan remembers the fragment from the press conference about the pickup truck. "He was the white truck?"

"Yeah, that was wrong too. Now they're looking for a silver pickup. And get this: a white guy named Mac. Think they might be able to find one of those?"

Dan goes ice cold in an instant.

TJ squints at the sight of his stricken face. She continues talking, expressing her words carefully.

"They're checking into the family."

He leans back against his desk, knocking a file tray and a small framed photo of the house in Walpole. He estimates whether he can reach out for TJ's arm, whether she can save him from the force of gravity yanking at his shoulders.

TJ steps into his office and closes his door with a soft click. She brushes a wave of fair hair behind her ear.

"Dan, you don't have to tell me anything else. I'll listen, if you want."

"Jesus, TJ."

She waits.

"This is a mind-bender. There are two Emmys. Two Emmy Robinsons. There must be."

She studies his face, her brow furrowed.

149

"I was wrong about her. I got the birthdate wrong."

He hangs his head and closes his eyes. A frightening swell of magma erupts from the earth beneath him, demanding that he react. Somehow her parents have taken the girl. They're in Big Sur. Suzanne is going to them.

"Jesus," he says again, blinking at TJ in amazement. Her expression paralyzes him, but thoughts flood into his mind. It's the wrong fucking girl. It's not their granddaughter.

"Wait a sec. I'll be right back," TJ tells him in a commanding tone.

When she returns she hands him a card.

"Call Deb. She'll be discreet, I promise. It can be on background. She won't mind. She knows you. If you need to tell her something or you need her help, call her. Okay?"

He scans the card and glances at TJ.

"Dan?"

He stands.

"Thanks, TJ. I appreciate it. But I have to go."

Dan grabs his jacket from the door hook. He looks at his colleague again, trying to decide whether he should apologize for the abrupt end to their conversation.

"Please don't tell Deb about this," he says before he can stop himself from asking such a preposterous favor.

Without a further word, he rushes down the hall toward the parking lot. Commands explode in his mind. You've got to catch her. First Suzanne. Then the little girl.

He heads to Santa Rosa Street and aims north. Passing the hospital, he checks the gas gauge and sees he has only a quarter tank. Swearing at the interruption, he turns into the last station in San Luis.

Still no call or message from Suzanne. Before pulling away, he sends a rapid text to her: "Stop! It's not her! Call me!" Then he guns the engine and flies up the road on Highway 1.

When he approaches the ranch where Suzanne's apartment building stands, he considers driving in on the remote chance that she hasn't left. Then he tosses that idea and accelerates again. He climbs over the hill before the men's prison, hitting 80 and telling himself to zip through the light at the prison's entrance even if it changes to red.

Mac and Maggie. Dan remembers hearing her father's real name from his conversations with Suzanne, but struggles to pull it up. The oversized grandparents' rights buttons. Of course. How the hell did they find the school? How would they know to look for her there?

He can't imagine that Suzanne would tell them about her visit, let alone reveal that their biological granddaughter was there. He checks his phone again, cursing the service along the coast. Did they follow her there? Something happened. They must have stumbled onto a clue.

He swallows at the other possibility, refusing to let its acrid taste rise in his throat. Suzanne would not take the girl and she would not help her parents do it. He can't accept that possibility. He'd tear up his Ph.D. and toss it in the trash if he was wrong about her. She's running to stop them. She's trying to save her biological daughter from their reach. He's got to stop her before she gets in any deeper.

What was it about Big Sur? Her mother's hippie upbringing? Could that be it? What the fuck could they be thinking? And where in Big Sur? How will he find any sign of them?

At Cayucos Dan asks himself if there is anything he should grab from the house. He's got his phone. A charging cord under the armrest. He's stuffed Deb's card in his jeans pocket. It's ridiculous to consider, but he's got a multi-tool in the glovebox with enough blades to get himself in stupid trouble if he ever used them in a threatening way. Is he willing to threaten someone? Jesus, not with a knife. He grips the steering wheel and steadies himself. In the trunk, a first-aid kit. He has two tiny packs of Mylar emergency thermal blankets. No water, no food. He tells himself to stop thinking and push on – he can grab water bottles along the way.

The car bites into the road as he presses the gas pedal and speeds toward the two-lane section of the coastal highway. The road tugs him left and right as he pushes his car to a full-throated growl. Twice he passes slower cars when he shouldn't.

The highway stretches ahead like a ribbon of black ice. He rides an exhilarated high at skating off from his teammates. He's racing as if nothing else but his frenzied breakaway matters, no other shot will ever matter, no time but these seconds remain, no other moment will count. He is speed and precision and determination – this long strip of ice either his friend or his foe, it doesn't matter which, it doesn't matter but for the goal. He's got to stop her from becoming part of a crime.

At the edge of San Simeon, Dan pulls off the road. This is where the cell signals will start to go squirrelly. He checks his phone before running into the convenience store to buy two liter-bottles of water.

Before he starts up, he checks again, finding nothing from her or anyone else.

Dan types a message to Suzanne: "Wait at Ragged Point. Wait for me. Please trust me."

In a fever, he taps send and tosses the phone to the passenger's seat. Then he hits the gas and swerves back onto the road, launching a tsunami of gravel at whatever lies in his wake.

Chapter Twelve

THE SWEEP OF UNDULATING COASTLINE PROVIDES a clear view of the uncrowded road. He presses his car toward 85, taking advantage of the long stretch before the chain of switchbacks in the hills ahead. At San Carpoforo Creek, a beach scruffy with driftwood marks the crescent bight where the ocean's breakers and freshwater streams surge together like frenzied armies. The road takes an immediate hook, thrilling the Miata. Dan leans into the climb toward Big Sur. At a hundred feet of elevation he downshifts into a switchback that leaves only inches at the edge of the road for dauntless bicyclists. At two hundred feet the Pacific reveals itself as the coast's ultramarine skirt. At three hundred feet, it transforms to the immense gleaming pate of the globe. He climbs higher, sweet-talking his car to keep its grip on the black-top.

In the final mile to Ragged Point the road snakes through ominous curves. He tries to imagine Suzanne's state. Does she have any sense of what her parents have done? She must know something to be following them. Has she seen the texts he's sent? Does she understand that Emmy is not Baby Girl V.? Dan tries forming the first sentence he'll say to Suzanne. Instead her mother and father crowd into his mind. How could their thinking be so brazenly twisted? What antisocial impulse would lead them to take a child like that? Anger? Indignation? Self-righteousness? How could Suzanne turn out so different from them? He remembers Suzanne's comment that her parents blamed him for the outcome of the adoption.

A disturbing chill slithers down Dan's spine. Could her parents know he is coming after the child? Only if Suzanne alerted them. The thought causes him to tighten his grip on the steering wheel. Has he missed something shaded in Suzanne's extended, quiet pauses? She called herself a dreamer like her father but could it be something more complicated? Her wish to disappear. Her faraway gaze. Dan forces himself to consider again whether he might be wrong in the risk he's taken – whether there is any way Suzanne might be allied with them in the abduction. The idea seems absurd, like a predictable double-cross in a half-baked TV drama. He shakes it off and holds steady to the bending road. He wants to see Suzanne's face. He needs to see if she will look him in the eyes or if her gaze drifts to the distance.

Dan pushes aside his agitated thoughts. The car speeds ahead until he reaches the flattened overlook perched four hundred-some feet above rocks and waves. The restaurant and motel sit among rugged Monterey cypresses leaning at perilous angles. Stripped and silvered from the chest down, the trees stretch muscular limbs inland, sheltering fledgling needles from unkind ocean winds.

Other than driving on and checking every turnoff for a turquoise Honda Fit, Dan has no plan if he can't find Suzanne here. His hopes rest on an oasis of cell service. He cruises past a line of vehicles near the gas station and restaurant. More cars sit by the motel rooms, though he doesn't think she'd wait there. If she would wait. If she would just wait. Then, beyond a group of picnic tables, Dan spies the back of her car. Suzanne is parked under a weathered cypress sculpted into a figure bent at the waist, grasping for – perhaps tossing off – a boat's mooring line. She stands beside the driver's door, zipped in her jet-black jacket and watching his car approach. He decides to park next to her, taking care to leave a safe distance between their vehicles. He turns off the engine and pulls the handbrake tight. Like dishes rattling in a minor earthquake, his hands and knees tingle, still under the influence of the rough road. Dan draws a full breath.

When their eyes meet, they both freeze. Dan struggles to find words. Suzanne says, "What is it? Why are you staring at me?" She locks her eyes on his.

"Nothing. I still feel like I'm moving." Dan keeps his pose. When Suzanne does not look off, he relaxes his shoulders, and continues to study her eyes. "Thanks for waiting."

He clarifies his text, blurting out that the little girl is not Baby Girl V. When she says, "What?" in alarm, a woman at the picnic tables turns toward them. Dan's description of his error and the two Emmy Robinsons confuses Suzanne. He suggests they take the path heading out to the overlook at the cliffs. She calls Annie Fisher to follow and walks with her arms clutched to her chest. Slowing his explanation, he lines up the key facts. His misreading of the birthdate. A little girl born in July who could not be her daughter. The uncanny similarity of names. His shame at the mistake. His relief that the missing girl is not her daughter, despite the horror of her abduction.

Suzanne turns away, stepping toward a knee-high stone wall that borders the cliffs at the edge of their world. Her hair flares and leaps, like a candle's animated flame. He checks his memory, noticing she's taller than he has realized. Her body more athletic than he's thought, tucked in flattering jeans. She wears scuffed hiking boots. From behind he sees no mask of freckles – no record of unanswered questions about her. A great pain seizes him over the complications he's brought into her life. It's too much to confess aloud. Dan focuses on the ocean, seeking some respite from his self-reproach.

When she turns, her eyes burn in fierce verdant tints.

"Tell me her name again."

"Olivia Emily. Olivia Emily Robinson. Emmy."

"My parents have her," she says, clarifying her own thought.

Dan says, "Are you sure? How do you know?"

"My mother saw me the day I went to the school. On the road back, I pulled over because I was crying. And she saw me. She was driving somewhere to pick up a piece of furniture. She looked at me and she knew. It's so insane, because I wasn't thinking of her. I was thinking about the little boy, Manny. I was crying for him. But it was only half a mile from the school, and she was heading that way. I'm sure she knew. She looked at my face and I saw it in her eyes. She must have driven by the school and…I have no idea what they did. She probably made my dad go there with her."

"Mac."

She nods.

"They're trying to find a Mac who drives a silver pickup."

She stares at him.

"Suzanne, how did you know they came up here? Have you talked with them? Why would they take her to Big Sur?"

"My mother sent a text. They have her. They'd take the station wagon. They always travel in that, not my dad's truck."

"She told you?"

Suzanne squints at him. "They're at the trailer up on a ridge, way back in the oaks. They go there for spiritual retreats."

"You know where it is."

"They took us there as kids. They call it their Gethsemane. There's a trail back to hot springs." She hesitates. "My dad baptized us there."

Dan stares as her words sink in. "Jesus."

Suzanne sets her jaw and does not take her eyes from him.

The fog lies well offshore, purpled and fringed in dark yellow, like an old bruise. Dan sniffs and recoils at the bitter air. "How much further to the ridge?"

She guesses they face another hour of driving. The turnoff is well before the Pfeiffer Canyon Bridge, and it's unmarked. She only remembers it by landmarks and old mailboxes.

"I have to stop her. This is my mother's idea. She's been obsessed with finding her and baptizing her. I've got to confront my mother once and for all."

"But she's not their granddaughter. She's not your daughter."

"She could be my child. Today I have to be her mother."

"Suzanne, you can't go up there. This is kidnapping."

Her stare remains unbroken.

"Look, I can get us help. We're still in San Luis County. I have a contact with the sheriff. If we go up the road another mile we're in Monterey County. That means a whole other agency, and god knows what else. Let's call the sheriff and get their help."

"You don't have to go. I do."

"Do your parents know you're coming?"

"No. But they'll assume it."

"Do they know I'm following you?"

Her face twists. "How would they know that?"

He turns toward the mountains to the north. She catches the doubt in his eyes.

"Oh my god," she sputters, shaking her head. "You are really something."

Seeing she's lost patience with him, Dan races through a mental list of reasons why she should not take another step in that direction. He's desperate enough to try and grab her car keys – anything to prevent her from this deadly spiral. But he's paralyzed.

She calls Annie Fisher. "Come on, girl. We're leaving."

Dan says, "Br – Suzanne, please don't do this. I'm trying to prevent a huge mistake. Let me call for help."

She turns to him, her face flooded in disbelief. "Did you come here with Brynn? Was it a favorite place of yours? Did you two drive up here? Walk out here?"

Dan cocks his head at the name, as if hearing an echo. He stumbles trying to retrieve an image of Brynn's face.

"Don't pretend I'm Brynn. Don't make me a replacement for her."

Dan says, "No. I –"

Suzanne says, "I don't know why you followed me. I don't know what you think is going on. And I don't really get why you care." She gestures with her phone. "You wanted me to trust you? Trust doesn't happen because you text someone and ask them to trust you. Or because you chase after them. It's not like that. You told me you made a choice and you wanted me to have a choice. Now you have to let me do this. This is something I have to face with my mother – my father, too. My old self would never do this. I have to do it. Go back – you don't need to save me."

Dan takes a long breath and considers her words. "I don't know what I'm doing. I'm sorry. I'm making this up minute by minute. I don't have any goddamn experience dealing with nutcases who abduct children. And believe it or not, I have been trying to learn how to trust you, Suzanne."

He shifts and puts his hands in his back pockets. "This is a mess and it's my fault. I caused this. I can't sit back and let you harm yourself. I'm responsible for that little girl's well-being." He gives her an affirmative nod. "I also understand that this situation comes down to your choice. I know I can't stop you."

Suzanne assesses his expression, keeping her arms crossed. Dan fears she will insist that he leave. He wants to say she's got to protect herself. But against what? A dark vision of the future roars up the fractured cliffs of the coast, threatening to wash them both to the boiling waves far below. Dan considers her question about why he cares, but he can't sort it out in the swirling moment. Whatever has drawn him here, he will not go back.

She lowers her chin. He sees nothing but her resolute eyes. She sighs and looks away.

They walk back to the parking area in silence, Suzanne and the dog a step or two ahead. When they get to her car, she opens the driver's door and sends Annie Fisher to the rear seat. She turns to him, but he interrupts before she can speak.

"I'm going to follow. You aren't doing this alone." He takes his phone and points to it. "I'm texting a friend to meet us here later. We're going to need help."

She searches his eyes.

He says, "Will you trust me on this part? Just this part."

After a moment scanning his face, she nods. Then she slips into the driver's seat and closes her door.

Dan hurries to his car and climbs in. Before he can text TJ, Suzanne begins to back out of the parking lot. He types in a fever, cursing when he has to backspace. "Meet me at Ragged Point. You and Deb. Need you both! Emmy will be here."

He drops the phone to the passenger seat and starts up the car. Reversing, he sprints to the road. Suzanne has waited. Two Cal Fire trucks idle in the berm of the road. Men in bright yellow turnout gear with reflective stripes gather by the trucks, pointing at the sky. To the north a foreboding tower of pyrocumulus clouds – white and silvery at the top, orange-gray at the base – expands above the Ventana Wilderness. Suzanne pulls onto the blacktop and speeds off. He winds the Miata to the screaming upper limit of first gear, yanks the shifter to second and chases after her.

...

Suzanne steers through the curves and switchbacks, then surges ahead on the rolling climb toward Big Sur. She's far above the ocean, zipping past wasteland stretches of old rock slides. Gorda and the campground at Andrew Molera disappear. She flies through the fortress-like rock shed tunnel and over a wide-open bridge. Another familiar bridge at Limekiln. The black sports car clings to her wake, swaying as she sways, never falling behind.

It must be midday, but she's lost track of time. Concentrate. Trust your memories. When more trees appear, she begins scrutinizing mailboxes. She passes the retreat at Esalen and senses she's getting closer. The heat of the day presses against her car. Suzanne rolls down her window and turns from a blast of over-baked air that reeks of ash. The sun turns a hazy red, casting weird light and dulling her windshield. She's tempted to roll up the window and turn on the air conditioner. But she's afraid that might detach her somehow from the turnouts and drives that lie along the road. Instead, she rolls down the passenger window too, determined to grab whatever sensory clues the land might offer. She looks back to Annie Fisher, who sniffs the hot wind and clings to her seat. "Sorry, girl," Suzanne says to her image in the rearview mirror.

When she takes the next curve to the right, her lane is blocked a hundred yards ahead. A red pickup stands beyond a wooden barricade. Suzanne slows the car. The truck carries the logo of the Big Sur

Volunteer Fire Brigade. A kid close to her age, dressed in suspenders and fire pants, a blue t-shirt and a Giants cap, waves her to a stop. He ambles to her window.

"Hi, ma'am. Are you heading north?"

"No, I'm trying to find my parents."

"We're advising everyone to turn back, ma'am."

"Is the road open?"

He hesitates. "It is now. But there's a mandatory evacuation at 3. The fire's over the ridge, back in the wilderness." He checks his watch. "Two and a half hours from now." He gives her an expression that says he knows she's not local. "Your parents live up here?"

"They're camping, kind of. Not at the state park. They have a trailer up on Westhauser Ridge."

"Westhauser Ridge?" he says with an amused smile.

"Yes."

He points down the road. "You passed it."

Suzanne looks over her shoulder. "You're kidding."

"No. Back at those mailboxes." He glances at her car and says, "It's a gnarly climb."

She lets out a small laugh. "Yes. I've been up there a few times."

"They need to get out of there, pronto. Have you talked to them?"

"No, no. There's no service up there."

He grimaces. "Well, if you go up you need to get them out of there by 3. Yourself too. The fire's coming this way. They're expecting it to be down here by tonight, the way the winds are blowing."

She looks up at the ridge.

"I'm serious. Are you sure they're still there? The smoke is bad up that high. They need to get out pronto." He studies her as if her parents might be insane.

His question catches her. The idea that they might not be there sets off a mild panic. Where would they go? The only answer she can come up with is that they would go home. Suzanne blanches, realizing she hasn't been watching the vehicles heading south on the road. Wouldn't she notice the old station wagon's boxy lines and out-of-date design? Their curious profiles, like country folk meandering into the city on a sleepy Sunday drive. Her mother always seemed so small in the station wagon. Her father too tall for it. Could she have missed such a distinctive sight? Suzanne pushes aside her doubts and thanks the firefighter. He checks the road and signals her to do a U-turn. When Dan copies her about-face, the young guy waves him into the turn, watching both vehicles head down the road.

Suzanne veers left onto the drive that immediately angles upward. The mailboxes are familiar now. She stops and sets her brake, but keeps the car running. A small cloud of dry dust rises as she steps out. She takes a moment to study the ridge and finds herself under a dark sky of falling ash.

Dan rolls down his window as she approaches. He's red-faced and wipes sweat from his forehead.

Suzanne says, "You don't have to go up. It's a steep climb."

He nods at the challenge.

"This is my problem," she insists.

He shakes his head. "I'll stay back, but I'm going up there with you."

She exhales. "There's a group of old cabins at the top. We'll have to park near them. There won't be room to drive all the way back."

"I'll be behind you," he replies. "Are you good?"

Suzanne returns an intense look. "Yes. I am."

He studies her face for a second, then sizes up the ridge.

Suzanne hurries back to her car and starts the ascent. In the first climb her wheels send up a spray of dirt clods and dust. She clenches her teeth, then relaxes as Dan drops back. When she's climbed to the next switchback, he comes up the hill with alarming speed. In the next ten minutes they loop back several times and reach the summit of the ridge. The towering fire cloud looms ahead. It rises no more than a mile inland from the collection of cabins where they park.

Suzanne steps out of her car with Annie Fisher. Dan retrieves a water bottle. As he walks toward her, he surveys the rough cabins.

"They're not here?" he says, nodding toward the buildings.

"No. The trailer's back this way." She points down a rutted, twisty lane cut by a single vehicle. Coastal oaks hang over the drive, casting gnarled shadows. Suzanne considers asking him to wait by the cars but assumes he won't. "It's not far."

Dan takes a card from his pocket and puts it in her hand. "This is Deb's card. She's a deputy. I work with her spouse – her wife. TJ. They're solid people. I trust TJ like a sister. I texted her, Suzanne. I asked them to meet us at Ragged Point. They will know what to do. If we get down there with Emmy – or without her – we are going to need their help. Promise me you'll head there and wait for them. If we get separated, whatever happens. Will you promise me that?"

Suzanne looks at the card and says, "I want her to get home."

"That's what they'll do. They'll help us. I promise."

Suzanne slips the card into her hip pocket. "Okay." She removes her jacket and tosses it into the car. She's wearing a heather gray tee tucked into her jeans. "My mother is going to put up a fight. She can be nasty. She is not going to like what I have to say. My dad may be more reasonable. If she's worked up, he won't contradict her."

Dan offers her the bottle of water. She thanks him and opens the cap to take a sip, noticing how dry her mouth feels.

He says, "What do you want me to do?"

"I'm going to walk in there and tell them it's over. I'm not listening to anything they say. I'll pick up Emmy, turn around, and leave."

"I'll stay back," he says. "Signal me if you need help."

Suzanne nods, a rush of scenarios flashing through her mind.

"She'll probably be very frightened," he adds.

"Yes. I've thought about that."

"They don't know who she is, do they?"

"No," Suzanne says. "They think they've got my daughter."

She catches a squint of fear. Her own apprehension crests.

"That's how I'm getting her out," Suzanne tells him.

She takes another mouthful of water and offers the bottle. He shakes his head, telling her he has his own. Suzanne sees a look of desperation on his face – a deep worry at what the next minutes will bring. But she can't be deterred by his feelings. She has to find the little girl.

"I'm going," she says after a moment weighing her thoughts. She turns and begins walking along the dirt road.

They say nothing. He coughs several times. Her eyes begin to sting. She blocks the thought that her parents have left the ridge. Something convinces her the station wagon will be pulled under the trees. But they may not be at the trailer. She has not mentioned the hot springs since Ragged Point. Suzanne understands that she may be hiking there in a few minutes. She checks the smoky skies.

Another fifty yards and she spies the back of the station wagon. The trailer is tucked beyond the oaks. She sees no sign of her parents.

When she gets to the back of the station wagon, Annie Fisher runs to the picnic table under a battered blue tarp. Suzanne's father rises from a crouch and turns.

"Annie?"

He looks up and steps out from the tarp.

"Suzy, you came."

"Where's Mom, Dad?" She swallows hard and says, "Where's Emmy?"

He blinks at the name. Then he offers an awkward, self-conscious grin, overly friendly, too accommodating. "She's inside. She's fine. She's beautiful, Suzy." His eyes well up.

"Suzy?" Her mother's voice calls from the shaded doorway of the trailer. Maggie's face appears. She's holding the little girl with the red hair on her hip.

"Suzy, look!" her mother says, stepping down from the trailer. "Look!" She brushes the little girl's hair away from her face. "Look who's here, Emmy. Look, look, it's Mommy Suzy!"

The little girl's mouth turns down in an expression that begs for someone to respond. Suzanne catches her father inspecting the person who stands a few feet behind, near the station wagon.

"Mother, I'm not talking about this. Give her to me right now."

Maggie steps forward, her face shifting to form a question.

"Who is your man friend, Suzy?" she says, with a knowing tone drawn from the past. Suzanne's stomach churns.

Her father steps forward, extending a hand to Dan. "I'm Mac Verdin. I'm Suzy's father."

Dan accepts his handshake and the two men keep eye contact. After a second, he says, "I'm Dan."

"Dan who?" her mother says, smiling through her teeth.

"This is Maggie, Suzy's mother," Mac says.

Suzanne turns to Dan's face. She does not tell him to be quiet. She does not tell him to hide anything. She looks him in the eye and sends a private message, an assent without words.

"Dan Tunbridge," he says. "Glad to meet you both."

Mac shrugs and smiles at Suzanne, oblivious to the name's significance. Maggie's face goes cold sober as she searches her memory. She scans Dan's clothing, dissatisfied with her own thoughts. "Tunbridge?" she says.

Dan says, "That's right."

Emmy begins to squirm in Maggie's arms. Suzanne steps forward and says, "Mother, give her to me."

Maggie angles sideways, trying to keep the young girl in her arms. Mac turns to his wife and reaches to hoist Emmy on his hip.

"Now, Suzy, wait. Hold on." Suzanne halts at her father's command. "She's fine," he continues. "Let's not scare her."

Suzanne's eyes grow wide. "Dad, do you not know there's a wildfire? Do you see the smoke?"

"We're going to hold a baptism," he says. "That's all. That's why we called you. We waited for you."

Suzanne grows furious. "No! You will not do this, Dad."

Emmy cries out at the discordant voices and wriggles free of Mac's grip. Annie Fisher issues a sharp bark. As Emmy slips to the ground, Suzanne crouches and holds out her arms.

"Emmy, remember me from school? Remember?"

Now Mac stands paralyzed, hesitating to pick up the girl. Emmy looks at Suzanne with a protruding lip and races to her arms.

In the seconds that elapse, Maggie steps toward Dan and plants herself in front of him.

"You're the psychologist? You're Tunbridge the psychologist?"

He says, "Yes, Mrs. Verdin. I'm the psychologist who evaluated Suzanne's daughter."

Maggie turns to her husband and says, "Andrew…"

Suzanne cradles Emmy. She locks in a stare with her father.

"Oh god. Oh, no. Suzy, what are you doing?" her mother cries.

"This is over. You stay away from my daughter," Suzanne commands her mother. Then she stares back at her father. She rises, pulling Emmy to her chest. The little girl wraps her arms around Suzanne's neck and clamps her waist with her legs.

"Oh…" Suzanne's mother sputters, her eyes wild and flashing. "No, no, no." She spins on her heels and rushes into the trailer.

Suzanne takes two steps backward and signals for her dog. Her mouth is too dry to whistle.

"Suzy!" her father calls.

"No, Dad." She raises her left hand, demanding that he hold still.

"Suzy, she's ours too. Please. God wants this. Don't you see? He put her right in my arms."

"No, no," she says to his face, shaking her head.

"Suzy, you weren't there. He delivered her to us. He said my name. He's here. He's watching over all of this!"

"You do not touch my daughter again!" she bellows.

"Stop it, Suzy," he says, pleading with his eyes. "Please let us baptize her. Like you. You can carry her. Please. You know this place. It's our Gethsemane. We'll walk back to the springs and after that you can go. Please. It will bring us peace. God wants this, Suzy."

Suzanne blinks away outraged tears.

With a metallic slap, the trailer's screen door flies open and Maggie rushes down the steps. She comes forward and pauses, a look of single-mindedness on her face. Suzanne sees the gun in her hand and jumps backward in horror.

"Whoa, whoa, wait a minute," comes the even voice at her side. She turns her head to see Dan taking cautious steps toward her parents. He holds his arms out, waist high, like a rancher quieting sheep.

"Let's all stay calm. Can we do that? There's a little girl here."

Suzanne backs away, bumping the station wagon.

"Can we talk about this, Mr. and Mrs. Verdin? Mac? Let's talk. There's a lot to untangle here," Dan says in subdued tones. He glances back at Suzanne.

Maggie stands in a trance, her eyes jumping between Suzanne and the psychologist. Her arms hang at her sides, open, like a doll's. The gun points at the ground.

Mac sees the gun. His look shifts to astonishment.

"Hey, hey," he says, reaching for her upper arm.

Maggie pulls free, stepping aside. She targets Dan with her eyes.

Dan twists toward Suzanne, keeping his hands outstretched and visible. "Go," he whispers, enunciating the word. "Go now." He turns back to her parents.

"Mrs. Verdin, can you put the gun down? Please? I'd like to hear what you're thinking. Please, I want to listen to you."

"You ruined our family! We're a natural family! Andrew, tell him!"

Suzanne begins to step backward. She slips at a rut and steadies herself, afraid to turn and run. Another step. Another.

"Suzy!" her father bellows. "You will not go!"

He takes two steps forward. Time zooms to a slow-motion cascade, like a dream of falling backward. Intense heat presses down from the agitated sky. Suzanne fights for a full breath. The oak trees flail their arms. Not here, a tiny voice inside cries. She shushes it. It's okay, Little Wing. We're safe. I have you.

Dan tilts toward Mac, dipping a shoulder and gathering his arms in an athletic block. Mac crashes against him, chest first, and his shocked head flies backward. Then he is tipping over, felled like a tree. Dan takes a step back, arms up, not in surrender, but signaling that their collision is over. A dull glint of sunlight flashes, drawing Suzanne's attention to her mother's hand. It rises but the gun remains angled toward the ground. A frightening shot cracks the overheated air. Her mother's face twists in pain or outrage. The gun fires a second time. The last thing Suzanne sees as she swings to race toward her car is Dan falling, reaching down, as if a serpent has struck his foot.

When she gets to her car, Suzanne opens her passenger door and places Emmy in the seat. Annie Fisher jumps in. The little girl howls, calling, "Mama! Mama!" between sobs. Suzanne wipes sweat from her own forehead, and notices that her hands, arms and neck are soaked. From the backseat Annie Fisher stretches forward, licking at the ear of the bawling girl. Incredibly, her crying pauses. Suzanne smoothes Emmy's hair. "It's okay, Little Wing, we're fine now."

She starts the car, reverses for a few feet and surges ahead, aiming for the first switchback. As they careen down the hill, Suzanne reaches into her pocket and retrieves the card he gave her. She reads Deb's name and title. She says the name, TJ, to herself. She says, Dan Tunbridge, then changes her thought to Dr. Tunbridge. Reaching Highway 1, she pauses, debating which way to turn. When her senses return, and time resumes its crawl, she drives straight to the roadblock and the young firefighter in suspenders. He sees her approaching, but this time does not call for her to stop. Instead, he stares at the young girl in the passenger's seat.

Suzanne sticks her head out as he walks to her window.

"I need you to call a paramedic!" Before she can say more, she's forced to stop. The heat and a tightness in her chest make it impossible to take more than quick breaths. The light hits her in a bright flood, and her head spins.

"What's wrong with her?" he says, leaning in to see the girl. "She should be in a car seat, ma'am."

"No. Not her. Up on the ridge. A man's been shot. He's injured."

The fireman draws back and scrutinizes Suzanne.

"Are you a paramedic? Please. Go up there. I think a man's been hurt. Call someone."

He asks about the cabins and she describes how to get to the trailer. "It's your parents?" he says. "And the guy in the convertible?"

Suzanne closes her eyes in exasperation. "Yes. Stop asking questions! If you can't go up there, call the paramedics!"

He steps back, tugging at the bill of his hat, then pivots and runs toward the fire brigade pickup. Suzanne waits until he's opened the door and climbed in. She checks her mirrors and turns south on the road. Emmy begins to fuss again.

"Hey, Little Wing. Hey, sweet girl."

Suzanne rolls up the windows and turns the air conditioner to recirculate. As the cool air fills the car, she begins to sing a lullaby from childhood. "I'll protect you from harm, and you'll wake in my arms…"

She catches her smudged eyes in the rearview mirror and yields to stinging tears of exhaustion. Far off, through a haze burned rusty-red by a dying sun, she detects a faint silhouette in the road. Is it the outline of a girl, or a teenager, or is it a young woman? The phantom vanishes in wisps of smoke. The wind calls, "Suzanne," halting her tears. She's surprised by the voice's tone. It's not her mother's voice or her sister's – no one she's met. The voice soothes, its music odd but familiar, sung from an undiscovered country. "I'm coming, Suzanne. One day. Leave a trail." She listens and blinks her burning eyes.

Squadrons of heavily-equipped trucks bearing resolute warriors roar north, lights flashing. Out of nowhere a helicopter overflies the redwood treetops, pounding the air and compressing Suzanne's eardrums. She coughs, choked by a pall of scorched oak and chaparral. A pickup loaded with surfboards and two barking dogs streaks south, followed by a rush of SUVs and ash-speckled sedans.

But for Suzanne the road curving along the lip of the coast lies unobstructed, and its companion, the immense glittering ocean, stretches to the horizon. Like a great blue heron revealing its stunning wingspan, she launches herself, carrying the young girl toward the refuge of the protected clifftop at Ragged Point.

Portland

HER AGREEABLE VOICE CHIMES LIKE A tower clock, dispassionate and certain.

"Well, someone showed some sense. No judge worth his briefs or his boxers would let a charge like that stand."

Dan gazes from his mother's porch to her rolling side yard, capturing a photograph from his childhood. He zooms in slowly on a riot of purple lilac bushes, thinking of summer heat and lemonade, the sharp kick of firecrackers, and games of Capture the Flag played into nightfall. His eyes drift further to her neighbor's white clapboard two-story with the gambrel roof and flared eaves, once a backdrop for epic snowball battles fought by kids whose nicknames and ruddy features he can still recall. For the first time in six months his chest loosens and relaxes. His breathing opens up like surf effervescing as it comes ashore. April presents itself, and New Hampshire awakens, shaking off the weight of winter. Enlivened by the heady scent of blossoms, robins and blue jays vault from tree branches to the ground, picking at morsels. Hand-blown clouds, tinged with white gold, sweep over the scene, guided east by spring wind – east toward Maine and its ever-reshaping shoreline – east to Portland.

He nods his head to the various points she's delineating but stays silent. Though his mind drifts, he's fascinated by how she assembles a legal argument like a post and beam barn. He's keeping time with the porch rocker, content to be far from the interviews, depositions, and choices of the past few months. As long as she doesn't ask him to explain more their alliance holds. Janet Tunbridge slows her rocking and pauses to assess his face.

"You look tuckered out, Daniel. You're too thin."

"I think it's all over," he says. "When I get back I'll see the lawyer again. He claims they're satisfied with her father's plea. And the rest."

When he tips his rocker rails back too far, an ice pick of pain pierces the ball of his right foot.

"Well, they should be," his mother says. "He's taken full responsibility. Three years in county prison is about right, under the circumstances. I don't hold much sympathy for his wife, but that's wrong of me, given her injuries."

Dan replays the tape in his mind. Andrew Verdin shouting at his wife, grabbing the gun and throwing it into the woods. Maggie struck motionless, staring off. The tall man crouched over him, pressing on his foot. A hot jet of pain. The panicky urge to get to his car. Standing, hopping, crashing against the station wagon. Mac lifting Dan's arm over his shoulder, helping him to retrace his path. Collapsing into the Miata. More explosions of pain and a crimson patch blooming on his foot. Navigating the road out by sheer will. Coasting downhill in neutral, left shoe pressed to the brake, hands fastened to the wheel, arms rattling. Blue and red stroboscopic lights. Deputies with drawn guns. A bullhorn barking, "Stop the car now!"

It all mixes with the segments he's constructed from news reports, TJ's comments, and his lawyer's information. The couple – thought to have perished in the evening as the wildfire came over Westhauser Ridge – located the next morning halfway down the mountain, near the wreckage of their station wagon. Two ash-covered phantoms – two broken pilgrims. The kidnapper, with a fractured shoulder, a nose crushed to one side and scorched clothing. His wife, with hair singed away, ferocious burns to her scalp and hands, her hoarse screams of "Mama! Mama!" flustering the young firefighters who found them emerging from the charred landscape.

"And they certainly shouldn't be charging Suzanne," she adds.

"I'm not sure that one detective has given up. He was convinced we were all in it together. I can't tell you how many times he asked me to explain what 'big news – good news' meant."

Janet Tunbridge grumbles and rocks a bit harder.

"I made a huge mistake, Mom. More than one. There's no other way to say it."

"Well, you got yourself shot in the foot, that's plain."

Dan turns away from her rebuke.

"No, I made a wrong choice. I didn't see the ramifications. I didn't see how it might ruin her life."

She rocks, letting him make his case.

"It may keep her from ever meeting her daughter. How's that for irony? I never saw that possibility. And the distress for little Emmy?

Sure, kids are resilient, but you never know what she might remember. The trauma for her parents? I didn't anticipate any of it. Or if I had the faintest hint of any of it going wrong, I thought I was smart enough to prevent it. I overestimated myself. I was wrong."

She waits for more. Her head shifts and she stops her rocking.

"Perhaps you were wrong. That's for someone else to say. I won't speak for her or them. But you were not wrong about the young woman. You were not wrong about the type of person she is. You know, there is room in a person's conscience for acts that can be wrong and right at the same time. Sometimes they don't sort themselves so neatly."

He stops his rocking and notes a breeze that invigorates him. Suzanne's eyes flash before him. Her last desperate expression. Her arms wrapped across the back of the small girl.

"I'd like to meet that young woman, Daniel."

He blinks and checks her face.

"Yes. I admire her grit."

"Mom, that can't happen." Dan clears his throat. "The lawyer warned me in no uncertain terms. He says there could still be charges of child endangerment. There are already cease-and-desist letters from the parents. And the adoptive parents? Baby Girl V.'s parents? No one's heard anything from them. That could all still be coming.

"Suzanne has a life. I can't risk causing her any more distress. She didn't respond to the card I sent her. I have to take that on face value."

She gives a short "hmm" and tracks a bird hopping on the lawn.

"I'm moving, Mom. That chapter is over."

"Life isn't that simple, Daniel. I thought you would have learned that by now."

"I have." He twists his head away from her.

She studies the yard. Dan takes her silence as an apology for being too sharp-tongued.

"Well, I'm simply stating my wish to meet her. I'm not giving an order from the bench. You'll make your own choice, I'm sure of that."

...

In the morning Dan drives the rental car back to Portland. His shipping pod has arrived at Dante's storage unit. Dan and he unload it, before joining their teammate for burgers at the brewery. Everything's set with Kev's cousin out on Peak's Island. Dan needs to be there by

May 15th so they can get the inn ready for the first weekend of the summer. He'll take a week to wrap things up in Cayucos and San Luis Obispo. That'll leave plenty of time for the drive to Maine. He'll take a bag of clothes, the laptop, and his guitar – the one item he couldn't trust to the pod. Dante and Kev debate which route he should take across the country. Dante argues for seeing the Crazy Horse Monument. "Largest mountain carving in the world," he says, gesturing as if the choice is obvious. "Fuckin' Crazy Horse." Kev shrugs his disagreement and says, "Grand Canyon." Either way, they push for barbecue in Kansas City and deep-dish pizza in Chicago. "Graceland – where's that?" Dante says. Kev remembers his parents taking him and his siblings to an amusement park near Pittsburgh with a twin racer wooden roller coaster. "Right next to each other. Two trains, two tracks – out and back! You gotta do that, man." Dan chuckles at his memory and promises to keep an eye out for the park. The trio orders another round of Allagash Black and makes plans for the summer.

...

On Thursday afternoon in downtown San Luis Obispo Dan walks west on Monterey, the courthouse at his back and receding. The papers for placing his psychologist license on inactive status are notarized and ready to be mailed. The DA has a copy – part of the arrangement Dan's lawyer negotiated. "None of your options for Maine are foreclosed," the lawyer told him, like he'd been spared a day in the stocks on the town square. Dan hasn't fought any of it. The county put him on administrative leave right after October's events. He wasn't out of Stanford Hospital or home to Cayucos before they acted. In the first week of January, they offered him a probationary assignment to the Older Adult Full Service Partnership. Given his lack of training with dementia or adult disorders, it was an affront to the program's clients. He resigned in a two-sentence letter to the Behavioral Health director.

He's cleared out the place in Cayucos. TJ got him on the couch at Pat Kealani's house for his last three nights. Early Sunday morning he leaves on the drive east. At breakfast – their last together for a while – TJ shook her head, ashen-faced, still stunned at everything he'd lost. He nodded, trying not to weigh the damage. "I'm looking at it as one of those crossroads where you make some kind of transformation or you don't," he said. "I hope I don't lose everything I've accomplished. I'll need to find a new way to put it to use." TJ smiled, refusing to cry. Dan said, "Forgive me for not telling you everything in real time?" She replied, "You told me more than you knew." Before they parted Dan hugged her for a long moment, keeping his eyes closed. She made him promise to her eyes that he'd return to visit.

Crossing Osos Street Dan enters the shadow of a sandstone mercantile building from the 1800s. The first level holds the bar where the lawyers congregate. He rubs his unshaved chin and looks around. A well-loved flannel shirt hangs like an old sail on his frame – he's down a few pounds. The conspicuous edifice looms like a fortress. Fuck it, he thinks, and hops up the steps.

Inside he seats himself at the long bar. Its expansive mirror reflects a stretch of the horizon, including green hills at the north end of town. I will miss those, he admits to himself. The mirror erupts in a wash of glaring red light. Dan grips the edge of the bar and focuses on the reflected scene, trying to locate the source. His heart races and, for a second, he questions whether there is a loose end he has forgotten. But it's a traffic signal, which flicks to green after half a minute. Inhaling, he locates his face in the mirror. As he swivels on his stool and positions his right foot, the bartender approaches with his drink.

"Thanks," Dan says. He picks up the glass and toasts the bartender. "*Morituri te salutamus.*"

"How's that?" the bartender says with an open expression.

Now Dan straightens up and assumes a pretended game face. "We who are about to die salute thee."

The bartender sizes up his customer, considering what he's witnessed. He reaches for a small bottle of water and tilts it toward Dan. "To the gladiator."

Overhead, menacing brass and wooden fan blades slice the air. It is not yet two o'clock, but the lawyers have begun to collect. The hum of their legal chatter adds to his dizziness atop the bar stool. Adrenalized lawyer arms and hands gesticulate. Lawyer faces contort in a circus of argumentation, bluster, incredulousness and triumph. Dan keeps his back to them. Slippery condensation on his glass makes the gin and tonic impossible to grip. From a long way off come the words to his alma mater: *And the granite of New Hampshire, in their muscles and their brains.* He allows himself one laugh of pity. He gets the glass to his mouth and stiffens as a cold slap charges into his throat and tumbles deep into his chest. He downs the drink. Closing his eyes, Dan revels at the icy fire skating unrestrained through his bloodstream.

An intimation of red off his left shoulder causes another errant beat of his heart. Dan turns sideways to find Suzanne Verdin framed in the bar's entrance. She stands erect in a slim charcoal suit over a silk scoop-neck tee. Her hair is cut in a bob, trimmed in a faultless angle at her jawline. For a second he swears this must be her older sister. But her eyes – the colors of forestland – and her entrancing lake of freckles match his memory.

She says, "Hi, Dan."

He stares for a moment longer. "Hi, Suzanne."

When she smiles in reply, he says, "How are you? Your hair – that's a great look." He shifts on his feet, self-conscious of his appearance and unable to find the boldness to offer a hug.

They move to stools and a round table off the far corner of the bar. Suzanne orders tea and it arrives in a clear glass cup and saucer. Dan shifts to ice water.

"No, no, none of that matters anymore. Not to me," he says when she asks if he's concerned about them being seen together.

"Me either. We met with the woman from the district attorney's office," she says with a gesture toward her suit. "My lawyer says we don't have to do anything more."

"So, you're all right? Everything feels settled?"

Suzanne nods her head.

He says, "TJ told me that Emmy – Olivia Emily – is doing well. I guess her parents are still struggling."

"I wrote to them," Suzanne says.

Dan pauses at her words. "I'm sorry I only sent you a card, Suzanne. There was so much to say. I'm a little annoyed that I listened to my lawyer so obediently. He kept warning me..."

"TJ called me. We went to lunch once. She was quite kind."

Suzanne glances down and asks if his foot is healing.

"Yes, pretty well. I've got a couple of wires in there – and two last little pellets. The surgeon wants to see if they'll migrate another quarter inch before she goes after them." He offers a shrug and a tight smile.

"I'm really sorry about what my mother did."

"It doesn't matter," he says. "I don't hold any negative feelings about that. How is she doing? She's at the burn center near Denver?"

"Yes. She's staying with my sister. Her scalp is healing, and she's grown some hair. Her hands still give her trouble. They've contracted?" Suzanne holds her hands upright, fingers curled. "The physical therapists seem concerned about that."

Dan nods his head. He's trying to assess Suzanne's emotional state. She's calmer, he decides. No, she's less distant.

"She's very angry with God. And my sister says she's confused or still in shock. Sometimes she asks why her mother isn't visiting her. She may mean her daughter…me? I'm not sure about that. My brother and I might go out there this summer."

"And your father?"

Suzanne lets a rueful smile escape. "He's almost philosophical about his plea. He cries about Mom, and he talks like God has put him on a mission. He wants to be a minister in there and teach the other men repair skills. To be honest, I don't know that he gets what he agreed to."

Dan says, "He begged me to tell everyone that it was his decision. He was concerned about protecting your mother and you."

Suzanne keeps a neutral expression and looks away. When she turns back she says, "I understand you're moving to Portland."

He confirms the news. "Three more days. I'm driving across and taking some time to think about the world – myself, too. Most of my stuff is already there. I flew back for the car and to say a few goodbyes."

Her minute wince stings him.

"Suzanne, I – my plan was to write you a long letter when I got back there. I was hoping the trip would help me get some things clear in my head." He sighs at the empty sound of his words. One more slip on the ice in a season that would be a clown circus, if it were entertainment.

She tilts her head and says, "What will you do there?"

He tells her about Peaks Island and his summer opportunity helping with the inn's weddings and family reunions. Tending bar the rest of the time. He mentions the ferry to and from Portland, the coves on the north side, the shore to the east. Come October, when they close up, he might find a place in the city. "Beyond that?" He answers himself with a shrug.

When he asks if she is on track for graduation and what she has planned, she says, "Well, I'm moving to Portland."

He blinks and scans her face.

"The other Portland," she says with a soft smile.

He laughs to himself, impressed once again at her ability to startle him. She explains that her brother goes to Portland State. There are schools there she wants to visit. She'll live on the third floor of the row house her brother and his partner are renovating. "Plenty of coffee shops up there," she says, offering her joke with a shy glance.

He issues a broad smile. "Yes. And they've got a great free streetcar system downtown. You hop on and hop off whenever you feel like it."

She mirrors his smile. "It's not free anymore, but it's still great."

Dan wonders at how Suzanne carries herself, how centered she appears. In one moment when he expects the faraway glance, he finds it supplanted by an equilibrium that leaves him envious.

Through a pained smile he says, "Have you ever thought of a way that it could be just for everyone?"

Suzanne's eyes open. She holds his gaze. In a voice arising from a whisper she says, "You know, you're the first person who's ever asked me that."

He takes in a breath and swallows.

Her eyes crinkle in a warm smile. "I did figure it out, though it took me quite a while. Once I saw it, it seemed so simple. For me, the fair solution is to give her the time to grow up and make her own choice."

Dan weighs her words. He offers a slow, affirming nod.

Shifting her hands, Suzanne says, "I'm very sorry about your job, Dan. I feel awful about that."

He shakes his head, as if he's anticipated her comment.

"There's a point when everything is collapsing, where you're trying to catch all the spinning plates? Where you still think you can pull it off. When it all comes down around your feet, it can be kind of liberating."

The moment commands him. "I meant what I wrote, Suzanne. I owe you a big apology. I put you in a terrible spot."

She shakes her head no, closing her lips and resisting tears.

"From the bottom of my heart, I'm sorry."

For a few minutes they accept the quiet that descends.

Dan speaks to the tabletop, blinking. "I visited a museum in Lyon once. It had a beautiful sculpture garden. Inside I came upon a painting that kind of stopped me in my tracks." He offers a simple smile.

"It was a scene from the late 1800s in France – a wedding party at a photographic studio. I don't recall the artist, but the painting stayed with me. It fascinated me, even though it depicted an ordinary moment. The young couple came to pose for a photograph. Her mother is bent and fussing at the dress. Family members off to the sides, watching. Father of the bride sitting at the back smoking a pipe. The photographer stood with his head under the box camera's hood.

Everyone lost in their own thoughts, not paying attention to much else.

"It's striking because it tricks your mind. It's a painted scene, but it looks like a photograph. A painting that might as well be a photograph, since there's a photographer present. Maybe it was a comment about photography never being able to replace painting, I don't know."

Suzanne returns his smile, her chin lifting.

"Anyway, the painting is like a window into the studio – like you're peeking in on strangers, who are oblivious to you. You don't know them at all, they don't know you. You're not in their world.

"And then you see her. Tucked to the side of the photographer, leaning against one wall, a little girl of 8 or 9 has her head turned and she's looking directly at you. She's wearing a blue-and-white checked dress; a straw hat with flowers. Those old lace-up boots? She's a mix of little old lady and grown woman and girl wanting to be grown up. The thing is, she's staring right into your eyes. She's not paying any attention to the people in the studio. She watches you, as if she's been waiting. As if she wanted to be found."

Dan touches the corner of his eye with his forefinger, stemming a tear. "I was hoping it could be like that. I still hope you'll meet her one day."

A private smile emerges on Suzanne's face, like the thin horizon of the ocean. Her chest rises and falls. Dan explores her eyes, seeking an indication that she's found a sense of peace about her daughter.

After a long moment of silence passes, Suzanne says, "I'm so sorry you never knew your father."

Her words force him to catch his breath. He stares at her, surprised and stilled. Stripped of his shield, child-like before her words, he opens his eyes, awakened to some essential explanation. Dan finds himself in Suzanne's face – a young soul in a painting, searching for a pair of eyes.

She takes a sip of tea. He swallows ice water. They sit without speaking, gazing off, glancing at the other's face, then looking at each other's hands.

Dan pushes back against a terrible wall of sorrow closing in on him from both sides. He's afraid she will stand at any moment. He's ashamed of his scruffy face, his depleted courage, and the shirt that casts him as a college sophomore who gave up on laundry weeks ago.

"I was planning – I thought I'd go out to Montana de Oro tomorrow evening, or Saturday, and say adios to California. There's a Mexican place out there I like. Any chance you'd be interested in that?"

She gives him an open smile and says, "I'd like that very much."

•••

At ten before six a car rolls up the dusty ranch drive. Suzanne brushes her hair back from her face and takes a centering breath. She's pulled out a sleeveless black midi dress decked at the hemline with a garden of wine-red camellias. Over it she wears a jeans jacket with a vibrant spray of hand-embroidered feathers across the shoulders and sleeves. She's a little self-conscious that it's funky and rescued from the Salvation Army shop, but her new self rebels against those concerns. She hurries to the door.

"Annie, you behave."

Suzanne wants to be down at the carport before the neighbors hear her visitor's arrival. But as she closes her door, Dan comes up the wooden stairs in a pressed denim shirt and a black linen jacket.

"Am I too early?" he asks when he notices her expression.

"No, no, this is fine." She fumbles with her key.

"Isn't Annie Fisher coming along?"

Suzanne turns and faces him with a quizzical look.

He says, "Would she wait in the car while we eat?"

"Yes, she would."

"Settled. You can't make her stay here all by herself."

Suzanne glances over her shoulder at the sound of Jeff shuffling on the balcony in bare feet and baggy shorts.

She turns back to Dan. "You're sure?"

He calls through the screen door. "Annie! What's up, girl?"

"Let me grab her leash," Suzanne says. She fights her irritation at Jeff's approach, looking his way again.

"Hey, you guys going out for grub?" Jeff says as he ambles toward them.

"Hey," Dan calls, raising his eyebrows in an amused greeting.

Suzanne hustles out with Annie Fisher and locks the door with a decisive snap.

"Bye, Jeff," she calls, steering Dan toward the stairs. Jeff throws a salute and calls, "Dude!"

Over generous plates of food at La Casita, Dan runs down his list of the ten things about California – people not included – that he will miss most. Montana de Oro is on the list. The restaurant too.

"Not only this one. Small places like this. It's more the feel of the place. The food's great, of course. You know what I mean?"

"Very authentic," she says.

"Yes – authentic." He considers her word. "I'll miss that."

Dan shields his further thoughts and takes a bite. Suzanne follows his eyes to the golden stucco wall above the opposite booth. A souvenir marionette of a peasant boy, with arms akimbo, hangs by three strings. He assesses the ragged character's untroubled expression and carefree pose. His lips press together, forming a tight, undecided line. Suzanne recalls his fear that he might have been used in the court case. She smiles inwardly, sending him an unspoken message. You've clipped those strings. Awake – your good heart's made you a real boy.

Dan looks back to her face and raises his eyebrows with a philosophical tilt of his head. He offers a sanguine smile and digs his fork into an overflowing tostada. Suzanne gauges his mood as wistful but decides to go ahead with her observation about his move, even if it may be awkward. She reminds herself that a grown-up girl would do it.

"Then again, Maine is a lot closer to Sweden."

Dan's mouth parts before he catches himself. "Huh," he replies. "For me, it doesn't feel a mile closer."

She cocks her head and waits.

"Brynn and I wrapped up in November. In-between my foot operations," he adds with a sprinkle of self-pity. Then he shakes it off. "I came to understand something about myself. About her appeal. I mixed up being in love with being in awe of her. Not that there's anything wrong with awe." He smiles. "It might not be enough."

Suzanne holds still as he glances down, then returns to her face.

"Anyway, it was a useful insight. And – there's a Sven."

"A Sven?"

"A Sven in Sweden. Can you imagine that? She found a Sven in Sweden."

Suzanne reaches for her beer, grinning at his quip.

He copies her and proposes a toast to Brynn and Sven. They clink their mugs and exchange looks of understanding.

She comments that his mother must be pleased he's moving to the East.

"Oh, yes. She's pleased. She won't say so, but she beams like I finally decided to stop biting my fingernails or something."

Suzanne catches a thought darting across his face.

"How old is she?"

"She's 68. I'm not sure she's ever retiring."

Again, the quick movement of his eyes.

"She's a dedicated gardener. You'd be amazed by what grows back there. Blueberry bushes chest-high. The flowers. It's so different than here."

Suzanne tilts her head, then takes another bite. He's holding something back. Not a concern, she guesses, but a minor hesitation.

He describes some of his favorite places in New England. Woodstock. Franconia. Annisquam. Ogunquit. Boothbay. Acadia. The names leave her dizzy. They sip at ridiculously large frosted mugs of Mexican beer. Her ears tingle. He raves about the crisp air and summer's last rays of sun in September. Cider, fizzy and warm. The charm of the old red barns.

"You should come visit," he says. "You should come to Portland in the fall."

"Can you get to Portland from Portland?" she says, side stepping his suggestion.

He grins. "You might have to go to Seattle to get to Portland."

An ambiguous pause lingers. Without warning, Dan leans forward and whispers, "Come in June, Suzanne – after you graduate."

A rush of cold seizes her chest, as if she's swallowed too much beer. For a moment she's irritated by the thought he might be teasing her. Then a stab of light in his eyes reminds her of pain. She offers an empathic smile, aware now of how lonely the drive across the country must feel to him.

In a defensive gesture, she lifts her heavy mug with two hands and takes a drink before answering. "You and your hockey buddies will probably be busy in June."

Dan leans back. A sigh slips out before he can stop it. She notices an expression of gratitude for letting him off the hook. He says, "Sorry. That was too forward of me."

"No, it's fine. I'd like to see it all. You make it sound alluring."

178

"I am looking forward to seeing those guys and playing hockey back there," he confesses. "But I learned some things about that too. I have a better line on my impulses. I think."

They turn to their food, neither certain what to do next.

"Tell me about your childhood," Suzanne says as she prepares to take a bite. "What were you like as a boy?"

He cocks his head and considers her question.

"I wanted to be able to levitate," he says, bewildered by his own memory. "Like a super power. Not flying, but floating – about as high as trees? I dreamed of having a suit that would let me rise up and hover or drift along. It wasn't quite flying. I don't know why not. Something about willing myself to hover and float. It was a frequent dream for me. I loved the sensation of it. Other people would be amazed that I could elevate myself by thinking it or holding out my arms."

He laughs and checks her face, blushing at his childhood wish.

"Your super power is action," she says. "Movement."

He weighs her words.

She says, "Skating, running, driving. Levitating."

"I would always return," he says, slipping into a daydream. "I never floated off." He adds, "You're right. I do like to be in motion. And then come back."

She sends a gentle smile. "Annie Fisher is like that."

Dan retrieves another memory. "My mother said she never had to call for me. The neighbors had a hand bell they'd ring for their kids to come in. They shouted, too. But my mother said I'd show up like a homing pigeon."

Suzanne studies him. "You love her very much. I can tell."

Dan makes a little sound in agreement, his lips pressed together. He avoids her eyes. She catches his chest expanding and relaxing.

He pulls out his phone and calls up a photo of his mother, offering the device to Suzanne. She grins, nods with certainty, and offers another smile to him.

When he remains quiet and still, Suzanne says, "You okay?"

He rocks his head from side to side, juggling mixed feelings. "I need to go see my neighbor's son tomorrow. Lucas. It's going to be tough. He's fifteen and, you know, trying to figure life out. We kind of bonded over a few things. He'd like to get his hands on my car someday, the little weasel." Dan draws in a breath and feigns annoyance. "One of those smart and nerdy kids. I'm kind of concerned about him getting through high school. Not the academics. His dad's out of the picture. I promised to come back for his graduation."

"You guys can stay in touch, right?"

"Yeah. Sure. He's super tech savvy. I won't be able to get away from him." Dan offers a sheepish look, not trying much to cover his feelings. "Goodbyes aren't my strong suit."

Though their plates still hold food, the meal is ending. Their mugs remain half-full. Suzanne stops herself from reacting to his comment about goodbyes by concentrating on placing her fork on her plate. After a few seconds, she says "Let's go say hi to Annie Fisher." Dan agrees.

At the car Suzanne rewards her dog with a strand of chicken saved from her enchilada.

He says, "Would you still like to go up to Montana de Oro?"

"Yes," she says, adding a pretended note of indignation.

"It's okay if we put the top down?"

Suzanne brightens. Dan flicks the latches and folds the top back carefully. Something in the way he smooths the canvas feels drawn-out and formal to her. His hands linger on the car, then he pulls them away, as if he's aware of her catching him in a private moment. Suzanne checks Dan's face, but he keeps his head down as he reaches to open her door. His silence – or is it distance – unsettles her. Her door clicks closed; in another moment his makes the same concluding sound.

When the car starts up, Dionne Warwick's aching voice flows from the stereo. On the drive over, he let his head rock sweetly to "Anyone Who Had a Heart." She wanted to sing. How unfair to see him move like that and to have to say goodbye this way. Now "Walk on By" comes on. Suzanne imagines a far-off evening of jubilant, crazy dancing – twirling in a creamy dress, bare-footed, her head adorned with a garland of white rosebuds. But she doesn't want to know who the man in the vest and loosened tie is, so she spins away from his face. She wants to say the word, goodbye. Say it, Suzanne. It's a grown-up word. Goodbye.

An amiable wind moves with them; the sky forms a dome reflecting the blue of his shirt, the pastel petals of her dress. As the convertible climbs the hill toward the state park, Dan turns to her.

"I'm trying to think of your super power and I'm getting two."

"Oh?"

He nods.

"And what would those be?"

"One, invisibility. And two, surprise."

"Surprise? Really? I don't think I'm surprising."

"Oh, yes," he answers.

Suzanne says, "I get invisibility. I told you I dreamed of vanishing."

"Why do you think?"

"When you said your mother never had to call for you? Mine never let me out of her sight. She didn't have to call either."

"You had to vanish."

"My dad too. It wasn't all her. They wanted us all to be so close. She could be harsh, too. She was always a domineering presence. You had to make yourself disappear. I did. After the birth too."

"I think that's changed for you," he says. "Since October."

She agrees. "When life won't let you disappear, vanishing's not much of a super power."

Dan says, "Surprise is indispensable. Don't lose that."

As they slow and pull to a spot near the cliffs, Suzanne takes in the expanse of sky and tries to imagine a road trip through the southwest and across the midsection of America into New England. She opens her hands to the unlimited landscape surrounding the convertible.

"What a great car for the trip. For seeing the country. As long as you don't hit storms, I guess."

Dan blinks, then shifts to a tight smile. "It would be."

Suzanne returns a puzzled look.

"I'm going to be enjoying the scenery in a Chevrolet Cruze – or comparable vehicle."

"A rental? You aren't driving this?"

Dan shakes his head. "Nope."

"Why not?"

His hands drop from the steering wheel to his lap. "I'm thinking I'll ask Lucas to keep an eye on it for me."

She pulls back, tripped up by his words. She flashes to his lingering touch of the convertible roof. A final touch. Her cheeks begin to flush. "Wow. That's really…"

"Kind of dumb," he says.

"No."

"Well, his mother's a little annoyed with me."

Suzanne wants to laugh, but hesitates. Her lips remain parted, the surprise of his decision still in the air.

Dan offers a composed smile. Then he raises his eyebrows. "To the cliffs?"

As they climb out of the car, Suzanne frets that Annie Fisher might run ahead. April is the season for rattlesnake broods. She links the dog to her leash. Annie Fisher tugs them down the path to the sea.

At a point that narrows like the prow of a ship, they pause. Waves heave against defiant rock formations, survivors of ancient upheavals. Dan points out a line of pelicans in flight. He's amazed how they glide effortlessly, inches from the water's surface. Suzanne tracks the sun inflating to a heavy red globe as it falls home to the sea.

She says, "Do you think you'll be happy back there?"

Dan turns his back to the ocean and settles against a wooden fence rail. He looks off to hills that recede toward the east. "It's strange to think there's a whole continent between here and there. Literally, I'm going from one coast to the other. It's kind of a journey to the past, but I'm trying to look at it differently." He squints as he catches her eyes. "I think I might like teaching at a college or university. I'm not sure I could do it. But in a couple years, if I were teaching a few courses somewhere, I think I'd be content. Happy?" He pauses. "Maybe more than that."

Suzanne smiles warmly, but keeps private her amusement at his conditional thought, his self-doubt. Of course, she signals with a slight tilt of her head. Of course, you could. I've seen you do it.

Before she can say something out loud, he quizzes her. She takes in his words, but steadies herself against a playful, probing light in his eyes. "What about you? Where's your happiness? Will it still be genetics?"

She nods and asks if he's read about genome editing and the incredible promise of snipping out segments of problematic DNA. How it might cure people of genetic diseases. How it's likely to be used in utero to prevent birth defects. She gestures with both hands, surprised by her enthusiasm, and excited to tell him. She dreams of working in a hospital as part of a team. Changing people's lives. She tells him how incredible it would feel to know that she's made a difference that way. It might be as a genetic counselor. Or a nurse. A researcher. It doesn't matter as long as she can be a part of helping people. Babies, children, families struggling with disease, the elderly.

She stops to catch a breath, telling him how remarkable the science is to her.

In that instant she discovers her companion's eyes drawn open like windows in a summer cottage. His searching eyes, lost in her words, her music, her face. She gasps, light-headed from the near-ecstatic state she's aroused in herself. His face transforms, growing older before her eyes. And then she sees it. She sees a panoramic future, she sees it all, and she sees that he sees it. A shockwave rolls through her body, thrilling her. This is the moment, this is the man – her future conjured right before her. She's frightened, thrilled again, astounded to see her life cleaving – childhood and adolescence falling away like massive ice shelves offered to the sea. His eyes afire, clear and certain. Their bond ignited in the atom of the present, rocketing off into the decades; her heart pounding and threatening to escape her chest; his eyes pulling her, reflecting it all back to her, telling her I see it too, every detail of it.

The waves continue their drumming, but Suzanne lets her heart slow to a tenable rate. Neither speaks. They hold each other's gaze for one breaking wave, then another. She looks away to the first stars of the night, her eyes glistening. When she glances back, he's smiling and recording each shifting aspect of her face. He blushes at being caught staring, but stands before her unashamed, naked in his own dreams of what might be. She sees it all.

Annie Fisher circles around Suzanne, testing the limits of her tether. She knocks against Dan's leg. He bends to her, to rub her cheeks and ears. Without hesitating she licks twice at his cheek and locks on his eyes.

"Oh, you've got kisses for me? You've got kisses?"

Dan looks up to Suzanne's face. She holds his gaze, as if their eyes have been tracking each other from their earliest moments of consciousness, from the first day each saw another human face. As if somewhere far from this cliff, in a house, on a bedside table, a story preserved in a journal – with a photograph tucked in to mark the page – calls them to discover it.

•••

Returning from the bluffs, they slip into the seats of the convertible and click their shoulder belts. A fair breeze touches their heads and dances across the surrounding field of poppies, their petals tucked and bowed for the night. Overhead the gems of the Milky Way spill across the moonless night. Venus, Jupiter, Saturn, Mercury – from an extraordinary distance each planet tugs at the couple, advising them. Further out – no more than a thousand days away – a meteoroid tumbles toward their sky, dreaming of finding the right place to sacrifice itself in an incandescent arc of fortune and love. At their backs, the ruby echoes of a sunset and the tidal rush of long waves assure that a full moon will return.

The car starts up, humming, keen to move. Each of them looks down the road winding away from Montana de Oro.

"Long way or short way?" Dan says, offering an auspicious glance.

Suzanne Verdin appraises the cut and fit of his question, her lips sealed. She tilts once toward his face, then toward the road.

"I was going to say the long way. Now I'm thinking the short way?" Without looking at him, she adds, "You decide."

Daniel Tunbridge holds his focus to a point far down the road. Gripping the top of the steering wheel with both hands, his face grows bright as sunrise. He reaches to touch the shifter, then turns to Suzanne, lifting his hand to caress her neck, to find her lips.

www.ingramcontent.com/pod-product-compliance
Lightning Source LLC
Chambersburg PA
CBHW070304120726
47910CB00007B/2366